THE LONG LOVE

THE LONG
LOVE

Katharine Gordon

This first world edition published in Great Britain 2001 by
SEVERN HOUSE PUBLISHERS LTD of
9–15 High Street, Sutton, Surrey SM1 1DF.
This first world edition published in the USA 2001 by
SEVERN HOUSE PUBLISHERS INC. of
595 Madison Avenue, New York, NY 10022.

British Library Cataloguing in Publication Data

Gordon, Katharine
  The long love
  1. Love stories
  I. Title
  823.9'14 [F]

ISBN 0–7278–5601–4

Typeset by Palimpsest Book Production Limited,
Polmont, Stirlingshire, Scotland.
Printed and bound in Great Britain by
MPG Books Ltd, Bodmin, Cornwall.

For
Ron E. Hornsby
and
Jack, his grandson,
with love

One

It seemed that the story had finished. Silence had fallen in the room, only the fire crackled and then flared up suddenly as if to mark the end of the narrative. The light of the flames illuminated the old lady who had been speaking, her head bent, leaning on one slender hand. The rings on her long fingers sent sparkles up to gleam on the gold border of the sari that had slipped back from her head. Zeena's face had a dreaming, lost look in that moment of light, but then the flames flickered down and Arina could no longer see her grandmother's expression.

"Oh, Grandmother! Don't stop, you can't leave the story there!"

"But of course I can! In any case, my heart of gold, there is nothing more to tell you. My story ends there."

"No it doesn't – what about the journey, and your marriage, and – and—?"

"And – and – and what? So many 'and's, Arina! my story ends in that garden. The rest is not my story."

Arina sprang to her feet, smoothing down the silk shirt and full Punjabi trousers she wore. She knew that she was going to be told to go to bed, and was clinging to the moments of time left before she would be sent off.

"But if it is not your story, then whose story is it?"

Zeena rose to her feet, and Arina knew that the evening was over. She would have to go to bed. Like a baby, she thought rebelliously.

1

"Grandmother! If not your story, then whose?" she dared to repeat.

"Go to bed, child of my heart. Sleep well – tomorrow is another day, and who knows what excitement there will be. Perhaps you will hear the beginning of your own story."

Oh, no, thought Arina, with a sinking heart, not boarding school! Surely she was not being sent away to school!

"I don't want to hear any stories about me. I want to hear a romantic story, with sun and hot weather and flowers – like the rose that was the signal that you gave Grandfather. I want to hear your story. All of it. There is nothing in my story that I want to hear – please Grandmother. Don't send me away to school! I am too old—"

Zeena sighed. "Arina, how old are you?"

"Too old for school – I am seventeen! You know that, Grandmother. It is my birthday tomorrow, and you promised you had something to tell me—"

"Too old for school . . ." Zeena said slowly, reflectively. "But all the other girls in your class are going to St Kilda's – don't you want to stay with your friends?"

"No. I hate the thought of leaving you, and leaving Glen Laraig. Don't send me away, *please!*"

"Arina, don't upset yourself about this. Go to bed now, let us see what happens tomorrow. I can promise you this – I will never make you do anything that you don't want to do. My dear child, having heard my story, do you think I would force you into anything? Now go. Sweet dreams."

There was a finality in Zeena's voice – and she was speaking English, which always signified the end of an evening. Arina did not argue any more. She took her grandmother's hand, kissed it and raised it to her forehead as she had been taught. As her grandmother said, tomorrow was another day, and something interesting was going to happen. She knew it.

Zeena stood up and put her arms round the slender figure, and kissed her granddaughter with warmth. "There's my good girl. Go and dream of flowers and sunlight, my heart of gold."

"I shall dream of Chikor, and Pakodi, and gardens full of flowers."

"Tell me of your dreams tomorrow. Just go now, you have kept Sushi waiting long enough."

Sushi had lived in Glen Laraig, having come from India fourteen years earlier to look after Arina – and nothing either Arina or her grandmother did would ever upset her, she would willingly die for either of them.

Left alone in the firelight, Zeena was still haunted by the past, the days of her youth. Telling the story to Arina had brought those days very close again. Looking into the heart of the fire she saw visions of her former life, the places, the people. A garden where she would never walk again, the palace where she was born.

Regrets – do I have regrets? She denied this to herself at once. No regrets. But deep in her heart she knew that when she said the word "home", she still did not think of this house, this country as home. Home was far away, across miles of land, and terrible seas – perhaps if Alan had not been killed, if they could have lived together longer, Glen Laraig might have become a home.

All those years ago, he had worried that she would be homesick. He had done everything that he could think of to make her happy and at home, constantly asking, "Dear heart, are you happy – are you really content?"

Her reply had never changed. "How could I be otherwise, when you are with me, lord of my heart?"

Now, in the firelight, she saw herself a girl, riding away from the old Pakodi palace without a backward glance because Alan was beside her. The journey from Madore to Faridkote had been blissful. The roads she knew so well, were leading them to the mountains, a rumour against the sky at first – then every day those great snow-covered ramparts seemed to come closer. Until on the last day of the journey, there they were, magnificent, unbelievably high, towering above the blue slopes of the lesser ranges.

"The lords of the hills," Alan had said, gazing up at the high peaks.

She had laughed. "That is what they call the hill rulers – all except my uncle, Atlar Khan. He is called the 'heaven born' because the mountains around Pakodi are so high, and his palace is built above the high pass of Manamahaish. It is a fort really, so old that it seems part of the mountains. I will show you my favourite places in the fort, where I had my room, the peacock room, there is a window on every wall, you can see for miles. I promise you, in the early mornings, I have looked down on eagles."

She had, for that moment, forgotten that they were not continuing their journey to the hill states. It was hard then, to say goodbye to Gulrukh, who was bathed in tears, and to see the red *palanquin* start up the first slope of the way to Panchghar. She had watched until the *palanquin* had reached the turn of the road and then Alan had covered her eyes, saying, "Do not watch her out of sight, beloved, it brings bad luck."

They had ridden on, into the town of Faridkote, its railway station, and had embarked upon the journey to Karachi where they would find the ship that was to take them across the seas. It was then that Zeena began to feel the aching longing, the desperate, lost feeling that would never really leave her, not in all the long years that were to follow. Homesickness – the disease for which there is no cure.

Now Zeena closed her eyes against the pictures she saw in the fire, but she could not shut her ears to whispers from the past, and the voices called back the memories. She saw Alan's face, alight with love, and felt his lips on hers – those burning kisses. These were memories she would never lose. She accepted the pain and smiled through it.

Thinking of the little ruined pavilion where she had first

learned what love and passion were, first burned with that sweet fire. That was when Arina's story began, though she did not know if she could – or should tell the girl that. Could she tell her in words how it had been? Say "that was when I conceived your father"? No. Those moments were her own, not even Arina could be party to those precious memories.

All too soon, though, the other memories came, the memories of that horrible voyage. She was fortunate to have carried the child safely during the journey. The seas that her people called "the black waters". Oh how well named those seas had been. She had prayed for death frequently on that ghastly journey, she had almost hated Alan because he did not suffer from seasickness – his shining air of happiness and health did not help her, lying felled by nausea.

She was so weak when they arrived in Plymouth that she remembered very little of setting foot on British soil or travelling from the sea-town up to Scotland, except that it had seemed to take forever. She was conscious that Alan was anxious, that he wanted her to be able to enjoy her arrival in his country. She saw how he looked out of the train windows with excitement, constantly asking her to look at various places known and loved by him, and she did her best to oblige him, to feign interest – but she was so cold! She shivered her way through the journey, wondering if she would ever be warm again. The warm robes that she had been used to wearing in the Chikor winters did nothing for her here. This country's chill entered her bones, and she lay curled up into a foetal position, and shuddered through the days and nights.

When they reached Edinburgh, Alan spent three days buying everything he could think of to keep her warm. She stayed in the hotel bedroom, staring out across Princes' Street, terrified at the crowds and the traffic. Where had all these people come from? She found the sight of the castle on its black rock intimidating, and when Alan came back with rugs and fur wraps and heavy woollen skirts in bright colours, she barely looked at his purchases. She looked at him apprehensively and asked, pointing to Castle Rock, "Is your palace like that – is your palace also a fort?"

Alan had laughed tenderly, "My sweet love, I have no palace to give you. My house is not the house of a king, though kings have taken shelter there in the past. You will like our place – wait until you see it on a sunny day, when the loch gleams blue and the hills behind are green. Peacock colours for you, my love. We leave here tomorrow, we will be home in two days, and you will be warm and comfortable. How have you been today? Were you sick again? You will get your land legs soon, once we stop 'stravaging about', as Jessie would say."

"Stravaging? Jessie? Who is Jessie?"

"Jessie is our housekeeper. She runs the house and everything to do with it. You will not have to lift a finger once we get home."

Home! Zeena lay back on her pillows and looked across at the castle on its black rocks and closed her eyes, to see the white walls of the Chikor Mahal. Home.

It was growing dark when, two days later, their carriage drew up outside the house at the top of the glen. It was raining, and a chill wind fretted the waters of the loch. The doors of Laraig House were wide, and Jessie was on the steps to welcome them. There were other servants behind her, but it was Jessie who put an arm round Zeena when she stumbled on frozen feet. It was Jessie who helped her to bed, with two hot "pigs" – stone hot water bottles wrapped in flannel beside her. It was Jessie who told Alan – and Zeena – why she had not yet got her land legs. "Bless you both! Mistress is carrying your child, Captain Alan, what else. She'll be fine. That sickness will stop soon."

Alan was overcome with delight and admiration for Zeena. But she just felt miserably sick and wished herself away, back to where she belonged, where the air was clear and sparkling. The mountain air of Chikor.

The nausea did not go away. Zeena suffered it, but it was

the cold pain of homesickness she found hardest to bear. The great old house, full of stairs and passages and small, dark rooms, was, to Zeena, what she had always imagined a prison to be like. Certainly, from the outside it was not inviting, grey and sprawling, some of it over four hundred years old, every generation of Alan's family had built wings and towers and passages leading to more little rooms, and even steeper stairways. The bedroom where she and Alan slept was his parents' room. It was the only big bedroom, with wide windows overlooking a view of the hills and the loch. It was, in spite of a big fire, bitterly cold, always. There was no dressing-room – and a very small bedroom had been converted into a bathroom, with an enormous bath on claw feet that crouched threateningly in the middle of the room. The water closet was the smallest room in the house, it smelt terrible and was freezing cold because the tiny window was permanently propped open.

Alan had taken the condition of the house for granted. He had been born there, had grown up in this harsh environment and thought nothing of it. Zeena's obvious horror made him look at the house with different eyes. He promised great changes for the future. "When the winter is over – nothing can be done until then."

The grey clouds of winter closed down over the loch, the hills were hidden in wreathing mists. There was nothing that Zeena could relate to, even Alan seemed to have become totally foreign. He was so busy! Streams of men came and went, affairs of the estate and the crofts and farms beyond the glen filled his days, and when he was in the house he was closeted in his study with kilted men. The only time Zeena saw him was at night, when he would come to their room once she had gone to bed, climb in beside her and take her cold shuddering little body into his arms and, kissing her, fall asleep at once.

She continued to feel either nauseated or she would be sick in the early mornings, and he would try to help her, and bring her cups of tea with milk which made her feel even more unwell. Tenderly he would whisper to her that this would soon be over: "Doctor Graham says it never lasts more than three months." He felt proud that she was carrying his son, and yet guilty at the same time. His conviction that the child was a son amused her when she was not feeling sick. "You are a Moslem at heart, Alan – or is it just that all men want a son?"

"Oh? I thought it was all *women* who wanted sons. You would like a son, my love, wouldn't you?"

But Zeena could not answer. All she wanted was to stop feeling sick. And not to feel cold – oh to be warm again.

Alan had not thought that she would feel the cold so bitterly. At his wit's end he suggested that perhaps her blood needed stirring. "Exercise," he said. "That's the thing. Riding. When you are dressed, I will take you to the stables, and show you my horses." Alan had reason to be proud of them. They were splendid animals, Zeena caught her breath and for a moment she forgot her discomfort and longed to ride.

"Oh, Alan, how beautiful your horses are. Which one is for me?"

"The most beautiful of all, a queen among horses for you, my love. See, there – that is Shiraz. What do you think?"

The little mare was perfect, a light chestnut beauty. Zeena was delighted with her. "I will be proud to be mounted on such a mare. Alan, your animals are in such good condition and you have been away from them for so long. Who cares for them when you are with your regiment?"

"That is something we will not have to worry about, but in any case I have an excellent man in charge of my stables, and he will stay on, even though I will not be returning to my regiment. I am here for good now."

The pleasure had gone from his face, she saw the sorrow in his eyes and wished she had not mentioned his regiment. Did he too feel a loss in his life, just as she did? She would have said something to him about it, but he had thrown off his sorrow, and was calling the boy holding Shiraz to come forward.

"You must try her, just take her round, see how she feels to you – I promise you, she is as gentle as she is spirited. It will be wonderful to see you on her – I will never forget my first sight of you, riding across the old polo field. I thought you were a boy – do you remember, my heart's dearest?"

Did she remember – how could she forget those days? At that moment all she remembered was the early morning sun, and Chunia, and Sakhi Mohammed and Raza. She managed to smile and put her hand on Shiraz's soft nose, and say, "Alan, I cannot mount in furs and scarves and this skirt."

"Oh no, of course you cannot, how stupid I am. We will have a habit tailored for you as soon as possible. In the mean time there may be something suitable among my mother's things in the boxes in the attic. Let us go in and see Jessie, she will know. My darling, this wind has made your pretty eyes fill with tears." He put his arm round her and hurried her in to Jessie.

Within half an hour Jessie came to talk with Alan and told him that there was no question of the mistress indulging in riding. "This is a first pregnancy, and the first three months need to be watched."

"But exercise is good for her. Old Doctor Graham said so."

"Well, whatever he said, he was not thinking of her romping about on horseback. A wee walk along the shore is all she'll be needing for a bit. And only on a fine day, mind!"

Fine days were rare in mid-winter in the north of Scotland. Zeena spent most of her time in her bedroom, or in the kitchen, where the big black range was kept alive day and night, so that the kitchen was the warmest room in the house. The cook, Mrs Carter, tempted Zeena's appetite with every delicate dish she could think of, and to please her Zeena struggled to eat, was sick, and tried again. To Zeena Alan's staff were like her kind and loving servants in Chikor – she would do anything to please them.

She felt more at home in the kitchen than in any other part of the house. It was easy for her to relate to the friendly Scots servants. They were, like the servants of her home far away, members of the family.

Alan was delighted to see her becoming more at home, and prayed that this horrible disability, the constant nausea, would leave her soon. His prayer was answered. One morning Zeena woke and discovered, not really believing it, that she was ravenously hungry. Even a cup of milky tea was welcome. Life changed, and the doctor coming for a three-month check nodded and smiled over her. But still no riding. So Alan and Zeena went for long, wind-swept, rain-soaked walks, and she enjoyed them. She still felt the cold, but not so badly, and she began to take an interest in her surroundings. Alan found the companionship he had dreamed about, and half afraid, but with her loving encouragement, passion came back to make their nights enchanted.

Alan was sporadically very busy. With a newly found seeing eye, Zeena was sure that he was trying to fill some empty spaces that she could not fill. She could only hope that as, in her case, time would help him. She still felt a yearning for her own country, but it was bearable, and when she was with him, the pain left her.

When Alan was busy, Jessie would wrap herself in her thick old tweed cape, pull a plaid over her head, and with Zeena similarly shrouded in furs and a thick hood lent to her by Mrs Carter, the two would go for long walks along the shore, or up on the wind-battered moors. Of the two walks, Zeena, living all her life amongst mountains, preferred the walk on the shores of the loch. The movement of the waters under the onslaught of the winds, fascinated her and the little scuttling water birds, moorhens and coots, were sources of pleasure – a change from the green parakeets, shrieking among the mango trees. It seemed a long time ago.

One day, when the heavy mists had lifted a little from the waters of the loch, Zeena saw the white walls of a house on the far shore and asked who lived there. "I did not know that there was a house anywhere near us."

"That's the house of our nearest neighbours. When we have a clear fine day you can take a boat over and pay a call on Mrs Maclaren – she would like to see a fresh face, puir old body. Come to think of it, her son is a doctor out in your part of the world. A doctor in the army, I think. Did you come across him at all?"

Zeena was amazed. "I think I may have done, Jessie, but the man I am thinking of was not young – quite an old man."

"And you are how old, hinny? Eighteen is it? To you fifty seems old – his mother's in her nineties, but she's still as spry as a chicken. She'll be glad to get news of her boy – we'll go over when the good weather comes."

Suddenly, at the beginning of April, there was a fine day. The loch glittered, the hills were still grey, but it seemed there was a green mist over them. Alan was out of the glen on business. Jessie agreed with Zeena – it was a good day for a trip over the loch to see Mrs Maclaren.

Zeena, catching sight of herself in one of the old fogged mirrors was not so sure. "Jessie I am very big. Will she want to see me? I am a she elephant."

"Get along with you! She'll not be fashed at the sight of your belly. She'll be interested – if she even notices. After all, she's seen enough pregnant lassies in her time, and carried a child herself. It's news of Robbie she'll be wanting."

"Robbie? Is that his name?"

"Aye. Colonel Robert Maclaren. I thought you said that you knew him?"

"Not really very well. My life was difficult and strange at that time." She wondered briefly what Jessie would say if she were to describe her life in India. No questions were ever asked, she had been kindly accepted with no curiosity. She wanted to tell Jessie everything, but by this time they were down near the boathouse and Hal, the boat man, was waiting to help her into the rowing boat which looked very much like an eggshell – and the loch looked very deep. She was helped in and seated herself, full of apprehension. Jessie sat opposite and seeing Zeena's frightened face said, "Are you nervous, Mistress? Dinna worry – it's a short, calm trip. Have you not been in a boat before? How did you get about? Are there no waters where you live?"

"There are lakes and rivers – if we had to cross a river we would do it on two or three goat skins blown up with wooden planks tied across them."

"Goat skins," said Jessie, "Blown up, did you say? With planks? Dearie me. Well, you're a deal safer in this boat with me at the oars, I'll tell you. Goat skins. Well, well. Just settle down now, and enjoy your trip."

Jessie handled the oars as if she had done nothing else all her life. The air was cold, but fresh and sweet. There were gulls wheeling and crying about them, and the sun made diamonds on the water. After a very short time Zeena began to enjoy herself, and forgot to be afraid.

"There's the old lady herself come down to meet us – she's there on the shore," Jessie said.

"But how did she know we were coming?"

"Och, she would know. She has the power."

"The power? What does that mean?"

"She has the sight. She can see things."

"Is she a witch?"

"Some might say she is, but she does no harm. Here we are now – you just sit there, and I'll help you out in a minute."

But it was Mrs Maclaren who put out a steady hand and helped Zeena dry shod out of the boat.

Mrs Maclaren was tall and slim and did not look a day over

sixty, and she was delighted to see them. She started asking questions about her son before they had walked up the path from the shore and into her garden, and all the time Zeena was conscious of her eyes – bright blue, alert and sparkling. Every time Zeena met her bright enquiring eyes she felt that all her most private thoughts and feelings were being laid bare to Mrs Maclaren.

Seated beside the fire in the drawing-room, sipping a cup of tea, Zeena answered as fully as she could the questions about the health and whereabouts of Colonel Maclaren. His mother seemed satisfied finally, but her eyes were still studying Zeena. "My son always liked a good-looking girl," she said suddenly. "How is it he let you slip through the net?"

"I was already affianced to Captain Lyall and, in any case, we met at a very strange time – he was treating my companion, Chunia." Just saying the name was hard for Zeena.

The old lady looked at her in silence for a few minutes, and Zeena, under that steady stare, suddenly closed her eyes, as if she was shutting out an intruder from her thoughts.

"Ah – am I distressing you with my staring? You'll have to excuse me, I see so few folk these days – and not one of them as interesting as you. And you brought me news of Robbie – I am glad he helped you when you needed him. I expect he'll be home for the funeral," said Mrs Maclaren. "He's a great one for doing the correct thing, and attending his mother's funeral is something he'll feel he ought to do. Now, tell me, how is that young man of yours doing? Young Alan, I mean, not the one you are carrying. Next time you come, you must bring him with you – and don't be too long about it. I get lonely and bored stuck here on the side of these black waters, with no one to speak with except the sheep and the gulls."

It seemed that they were expected for luncheon. There was a great spread of food laid in the dining-room, and no lack of talk. Mrs Maclaren, when she was not studying Zeena, had great charm. Zeena found herself telling the old lady things about life in India that no one else had wanted to know, and was enjoying herself, and Jessie was listening to her mistress with her eyes on stalks. Later, when it was time to go, Zeena begged Mrs Maclaren to come and visit her.

"Oh, I'll come over – I'll come at the end of June to welcome the young master."

The end of June? "But the baby is not due until the middle of July . . ." For a moment Zeena felt herself transported back to the little pavilion, and blushed at her memories. Mrs Maclaren laughed, excited like a young girl.

"Aha, you know when the seed was planted, but the fruit comes to ripeness when it chooses, not when you choose. I will see you at the end of June." She paused and looked deeply into Zeena's eyes and put her hand gently on her cheek. "Ah, lassie, you have a long road to travel, but you are strong of heart. Remember, love endures."

The words had an echo – another seemed to be speaking behind the tones of Mrs Maclaren.

The wind coming off the loch blew cold across their faces as they walked down to the boat, and Zeena shuddered and pulled her hood down. Their farewells were said and Jessie took up the oars. The tall figure of Mrs Maclaren stood like a sentry watching them go. Zeena looked back as they turned for the other shore, and saw her still there, until the mists of the evening veiled her.

Zeena sat quietly in the stern of the boat, thinking over the day. It had left a cloud on her, and she was glad to see Alan waiting on the shore as they came in and grounded on the sand. It had been a long day away from him, and suddenly it was important that they should be together. She ran into his arms, and he enfolded her, saying, "Where have you been – over to the Maclaren house? Come, let me get you home – I have so much to tell you. I've had a letter – with such news! I can't believe it. Come in and let me tell you . . ."

His eyes were shining, he could hardly wait until she had

removed her outdoor clothes. He took her into his library, then took out a letter and tried to read it to her, but it was an official letter and he saw that she did not understand it. Her English had always been good, and had improved but these words were unfamiliar, and she had to interrupt him, saying, "Alan, do you tell me the sense of this, please."

"I do beg your pardon. Of course you would not understand 'officialese'. What it means, my dearest is this. I can return to my regiment at the end of my leave. I do not have to resign my commission! Can you believe it? In simple words, Colonel Bates says that he does not understand why I wish to leave the army, and he will not accept my resignation."

Alan flung his arms round Zeena. "Dearest heart, do you understand now? I can go back and once our baby has been born, and you are ready, you can come and join me! The regiment will be in Delhi, you will enjoy that, and in the hot weather you can go up to Dalhousie, or perhaps you would like to go to Panchghar and stay with Gulrukh – what do you say, my love?"

Zeena could say nothing, she looked at the happiness in Alan's eyes and knew that what she was going to have to say would destroy it. He waited, looking down at her, and she searched for how to answer him and finally said, "My dear Alan, I see this has given you great happiness and I am happy that this is so," she spoke in her own language.

"And it makes you happy too, to think that you can go home. My heart, I have seen how bravely you have struggled against homesickness. Do not think I did not know how you felt! I understood because I felt it too. My darling, do you not realise how close we are to each other? I am always homesick for India, I was brought up there, and the country has always had a hold on my heart – doubly so, since I found you. We will go back, and it will be our country for ever."

He kissed her again, sat down and pulled her on to his lap, and told her when he planned to leave, and detailed

15

arrangements he would make for her to follow with the baby as soon as she felt well enough. She listened to him, and said nothing – and he was too excited to notice her silence. Finally she asked him when he would go. "As soon as possible – my leave ends on the first of June, so I shall leave here on the twentieth of May if I can get a passage. I'll need to go to Edinburgh to see the shipping offices. How do you fancy a trip to Edinburgh? We can do some shopping, get you some lighter clothes to take back with you – only for the voyage of course. Once we return, you'll be wearing your own dress again – ah, how I shall enjoy seeing you in your beautiful floating silks and muslins, but no veils, my dearest! I have abolished purdah for you – it is a sin to cover your face!" His words were full of joy.

She did not go to Edinburgh with him. She said that she would feel embarrassed and, as for buying dresses for the voyage . . . "I would prefer to do that after the birth."

He went alone, and hurried back to begin packing and to arrange for the shipping of one of his horses.

"I shall take Raja with me, I want to breed from him."

The following days were taken up with his arrangements for Zeena – her passage could not be booked, but he had told her that he had made a tentative booking for the third week in August. "That will give you enough time my darling, won't it? The baby will be born on the twenty-third of July, so that gives you a month. Is that long enough?"

She agreed that this would allow her enough time, though Jessie did not agree at all. Jessie was going out with Zeena and the baby. "The lying-in period should be six weeks and no less. It cannot be shorter, it gives the mother a chance to recover from the labour, and the baby a chance to become used to the new world." Jessie folded her lips into a straight line, and Alan sighed.

"For a very young woman, Jessie Macdonald, you seem to know a great deal about child birth – among other things. Very

16

well, six weeks from the twenty-third of July. That takes us to the first weeks of October."

The passage for the family was booked on the Royal Mail steamer *City of Baroda*.

Zeena took very little part in all these arrangements. She spent her time following Alan about.

"It's as if she's afraid she's never going to see him again," said Mrs Carter to Jessie.

"Aye, or as if she thought she wasn't going to come through her labour," Jessie responded. "But I know she will come through – I'll see that she does." And Mrs Carter, chopping meat into collops, reckoned that if Jessie set her will to it, even labour pains would obey her.

Zeena slept badly through these last weeks. Alan would fall asleep holding her in his arms, and she would lie, staring into the dark all through the long night, trying to think of how she could tell Alan that she could not return to India. How would she be able to explain the shame that she would bring to her family if she reappeared in her homeland after that false funeral – her father shown to be a liar, and that evil man Tariq Khan able to bring a case against the Chikor family! The scandal that would hurt every member of the family! Shame would fall on Gulrukh and the Panchghar rulers – and she herself would be outcast, if she were not quietly removed. Perhaps the empty grave would be filled. Zeena shuddered, and knew that she could not go.

But how could she make Alan understand. She did not think he ever would. He loved India, true, but he loved it without knowing anything about the rules and customs that were part of Indian life. He would be horrified by conventions that were par for the course to her. All his ideas about India and Indians would be thrown into disorder – just as she felt about some of the customs of *his* country.

In the end, she said nothing. The days slipped by, with Alan full of happy expectations. It was three days before he was due to leave when he realised that he was going away from his beloved, leaving her alone to face the ordeal of giving birth – and that he was not going to see her again for months.

"Zeena beloved – how can I do this? Not only losing your presence for so long, but once more – oh God, once more leaving you alone when you need me. I should have asked for extra leave, I should have told them that I had to be here for the birth of my son! I was so happy that there was still a place for me in my regiment, that we were going to be able to return and live in your own country, live the life we knew. I am a selfish fool, I did not think—"

Zeena put her hand to his mouth. "Hush, beloved. You thought of everything. I understand how you saw your heart's desire being given to you – to delay would have been foolish. The time will go quickly – you will be busy, and so will I. And your child will be born in Glen Laraig – does that not please you?"

"*You* are my heart's desire, and I am leaving you, so nothing pleases me."

"I shall be here, my lord – and you . . ." She had been going to say, "and you will return," when she found that she could not speak. A darkness had fallen on her, she gasped and put her hand out to him, and when he took her hand, asking what was wrong, her sight cleared and she could breathe again. What had she been about to say? Then she remembered that she was supposed to be going out to join him. She almost told him the truth then, but knew that in his present mood he was capable of throwing everything into disorder by refusing to leave her. If he did that, and refused his commission, he would regret it, and come to feel imprisoned by her, and hatred might grow in his heart. His regiment was his life. Lara had been right. She thought of all the different occupations that he had engaged himself in when they had first returned to Glen Laraig. She was sure that these were, partly, to fill the empty space that his departure from the army had left. She smiled into his watching, anxious eyes and said, "I will be here, too busy to miss you, and the days will soon pass," and she leaned to kiss him.

The fire was dying into red embers, the room was dark. Zeena stood up and walked to the window and looked out into the darkness. The words "and you will return" had not been spoken. He had never returned. She could not allow herself to recall those days of long ago. It was time to forget, cover her thoughts, silence the voice that said, "You let him go – and you never saw him again."

The night was very dark. She pulled the curtains across the glass that reflected nothing but her own figure standing alone, and the dying fire. It was time to think of the next day, and Arina, and what she had to tell her.

A shuffling of slippers sounded on the other side of the door, there was a knock and when Zeena said, "Come – is it you, Jessie?" Jessie, white haired and bent, came in.

"Aye, it is. Are you not coming to your bed, Mistress? Sushi is falling asleep on the floor outside your door, waiting to get you undressed. Brr, this room is cold. Come away now, tomorrow is another day and it will be on us if you stay any longer – it is close on midnight."

"Oh, is Sushi still up? You should have sent her to bed."

"Oh aye? And when does Sushi take orders from any of us? She wouldn't go to bed. Said she was waiting for you, you would need her when you had been walking about in the past for so long. Come now, and sleep."

As she followed Jessie out, Zeena looked back into the room. Walking about in the past – when she should have been thinking of Arina and the future. But, oh, the early years of the past had been so sweet. Now she had little future, like the fire she was burning down. Her eyes looked past the fire, slowly burning away among the ashes, and for a moment, a breath, she saw the other figure she looked for, the one part of the past that had never left her . . . Her eyes blurred, and she turned away and followed Jessie, closing the door behind her.

Two

While Zeena had been sitting alone, dreaming of the past, Arina, against her will, was being helped to bed. Both of her grandmother's personal maids – old Jessie, who was also the housekeeper, and the slightly younger Indian maid, Sushi – were in attendance.

Arina protested, and not for the first time. "You know, at school I put myself to bed – and I make my own bed, and do my own hair."

"Do you now," said Jessie. "That's fine, but you are not at school now, and we are here to look after you."

"Well, tomorrow I will not retire so early. In fact, I might stay up all night, if I feel like it. After all, tomorrow I shall be grown up."

"Oh indeed?" said Jessie. "As I see it you will be seventeen tomorrow. Is that supposed to be grown up?"

Arina tilted her chin haughtily. "Of course it is Jessie. In *my* country, I would be married with a baby probably, wouldn't I, Sushi?"

Sushi shook her head. "Nay, piyari, I think you would be considered to be of marriageable age, of course. But married – no."

"Well, I shall be betrothed, I expect. I will meet many princes to choose from – after all, tomorrow I shall be a Begum, not a Choti Begum any longer."

"Dear dear! What a hurry you are in. You may be grown up in India, but in Scotland seventeen is very young, so into bed

21

with you. Go to sleep – let tomorrow come in its own time. Be wise, stay a little girl while you can, dearie." She leaned down to kiss Arina, turned down the lamp, and once Sushi had said her goodnights, both women left the room, laughing a little at her rebellious face, sad thoughts behind their laughter.

Outside the door Jessie said, "She knows where she is going, and what she is going to, does she, Sushi?"

Sushi bowed her head. "She has been told, my sister, from the time she was eight years old. But I think she has not accepted it as a fact. She thinks of it as being a story, not as her own future. I think tomorrow she will be told again, and will be made to believe it."

"Puir lamb. It must be hard being woman in your country."

"*Hai mai*, that is true of all countries, my sister," said Sushi, and Jessie sighed and agreed.

Arina lay in her bed convinced that she would be unable to sleep – she was so excited. Tomorrow – the magic figure of seventeen – she knew there would be a great surpise waiting for her. A journey – in her mind, journeys were connected with romance . . . the white rose that had meant a breathtaking journey for her grandmother. If she found a white rose beside her bed in the morning, what would it mean? A journey, of course – what else? A lover? That was more difficult to believe. She hadn't met any young men – except of course the gardener, the stable boys, and the doctor who came across from the white house on the other side of the lake. No one who she could imagine as a lover. No, any rose she found would mean a journey. She and her grandmother would go off together – and there was only one place for them to visit. The country of her dreams – the land of her grandmother's heart. She would find her lover there – she knew it. She thought about being in love until she fell into a deep, dreamless asleep.

She felt cheated when she woke to Sushi's gentle voice, a cup of tea, and no sign of a rose. "Where is the rose?" she asked.

The Long Love

"The rose?" Sushi repeated. "Here is no rose, piyari. It is too early for roses. Do you ride today?"

"Well, of course I ride. My grandmother—"

"Your honoured grandmother does not ride today. She is writing letters. Shall I send Jock back to the stables? He is waiting outside with your horse, Bara."

Writing letters? Why was her grandmother writing letters on this day of all days? This was the day they were going to ride along the shore to the old ruined boathouse. She was not allowed to ride there alone – and it was her favourite ride. And today was her seventeenth birthday! She *would* have her ride, and she'd go alone. "No, of course don't send him away. I shall ride alone."

She heard Sushi's indrawn breath, but paid no attention. She was allowed to ride alone as long as she first asked permission and, second, said exactly where she was going, and for how long. These were her grandmother's orders. Disobedience meant no early morning rides for a week. She was not going to have that any longer. Not now. She was seventeen and would have an adult choice – she would be free to choose. At last. Choose where she would go, what she would wear, what she would eat – free!

She met Sushi's eyes.

"I shall be in trouble if you go out alone without saying where you are going," said Sushi.

Arina stopped on her way to the door. Oh, it wasn't *fair*! She wasn't free at all, she couldn't let Sushi be scolded because she had gone out without asking permission. No ride on her birthday morning. No one could disturb her grandmother if she was writing letters. It was no good.

"Tell Jock to take Bara back," she said, and tore off her clothes and went into the bathroom to bathe and hide her disappointed tears.

Her grandmother was seated behind the coffee pot when bathed and dressed she went down to breakfast. Zeena held

23

out her hand to Arina, who kissed it and raised it to her
forehead, and was startled to feel the slight tremor in a hand
that was always rock steady.

"Grandmother – are you well?"

"Of course I am well! What should be wrong with me? Eat
your breakfast and come and join me in the library – I want
to talk to you." She stood up, and as she walked away Arina
saw that she was carrying an envelope – a big white envelope.
An invitation? Or perhaps the steamship tickets for a journey?
Arina lost her appetite. She gulped her coffee and hurried to
join her grandmother in the library.

Zeena was sitting on the wide window-seat that overlooked
the loch. "Come and sit beside me, piyari – I have had a letter
from Gulrukh Begum, my cousin-sister."

Arina saw that her grandmother's hands were trembling as
she took the folded paper from the envelope. The letter was
written in a beautiful curving Urdu script that looked like
lace on the thick white paper. She wondered aloud if her
grandmother could still read that script.

"Of course I can! Why not? It is my own language, after all.
You should be able to read it too. I spent long enough trying
to teach you. Thanks be to God that you speak it beautifully.
I did not fail in that. Now let me read it to you."

Zeena read every word in her clear voice, the Urdu rolled off
her tongue like the verses of a poem. She read slowly, but with
no hesitation. When she had finished, she sat without speaking
for a few minutes and when she looked up, Arina saw that her
eyes were full of tears. Arina took her hand and held it tightly.
"Do not weep, Grandmother – there is nothing to make me sad
in that letter."

"No, indeed. Nothing. It is a letter I have expected. I have
no surprise. Gulrukh Begum has called in my promise. Did
you understand what I read?"

"Yes – it is from my aunt in Panchghar. She has invited me
to a wedding."

Zeena smiled through her tears. She is calling you home –
and there will be two weddings. The Choti Begum of Pakodi
is to marry on the same day. You used to play with her
when you were children. You don't remember? Her name
is Gulshan. Two family weddings on the same day! It will
be a great *tamasha*. Any tears you see in my eyes are from
pleasure."

"Who else is to be married, Grandmother?" asked Arina,
who had begun to feel a strange sensation of alarm. Something
she knew, but had never believed was hovering on the edge of
her mind.

Zeena gave her granddaughter a sharp look. There were no
tears in her eyes now. "I hope you are not trying to be difficult,
piyari. You know perfectly well that the other wedding – the
most important wedding – is yours."

Arina felt her heart fall like a stone into her stomach. "So
it is true," she said.

"Of course if is true," Zeena snapped. "Do you think I have
been telling you old stories all these years? How many times
have we spoken together about your wedding? Even choosing
the colours of new saris, of heavy silk for *salwar khemise* and
measuring you only last month? Don't make me angry, Arina."

Arina shook her head. "I do not mean to make you angry,
Grandmother. But I did not think this was real – I thought we
played a game of weddings. Please don't be angry, but who
will I marry?"

"You may not want to make me angry, but you are coming
close to it. It is the man to whom you were betrothed before
they sent you here to me. He is Sher Ali, the Nawab Zaida
Sahib of Chikor. He is nine years older than you, he is your
cousin, the grandson of Gulrukh Begum."

Sher Ali – yes, that had always been the name of the
bridegroom in what Arina had thought were her grandmother's
entertaining fantasies. Betrothed to him and living in a great
house in Bombay . . .

Oh yes, thought Arina, I was told all this, and I enjoyed it. I went to bed at night, and added to the story – I even found a picture in an old book, a picture of a Prince of the Northern Hills. I showed it to Grandmother and asked if Sher Ali would look like that, and she had laughed at me and said, "I can't tell you that – I have never seen him, but that is a very typical-looking young prince." I have that picture in my room, thought Arina, so why am I making a fuss now? Why do I feel so scared?

Zeena was watching her, and saw that she was in fact shocked. She put her arm round her granddaughter and said, "I am sorry, Arina. I had no idea that you did not understand that I was telling you about your own future. Come, piyari, do not look frightened. You are going to India, your true home. You will be among your own family – and I promise you, you will have no reason to be unhappy. They are all longing to see you."

"I am sorry to be stupid. Of course I have always wanted to go back to India. I will not be married at once, though, will I? I will have time to get to know Sher Ali?"

Zeena felt the touch of a cruel memory as she looked into Arina's eyes. Time to get to know the man you are going to spend the rest of your life with! She had seen the longing for independence so many times in this girl she loved so deeply. Somewhere a voice said, "Oh, I will choose someone wonderful . . ." She wondered if Gulrukh remembered her saying that – and now, so many years later, beautiful Arina was longing for the right to choose, and still there was no right. But at least this girl was not being made to marry a monster. She said, "Of course you will have time, but you do not need that time! You *know* your bridegroom already. Have you forgotten?"

Arina looked blank. "Do you mean the picture of the 'Prince of the Northern Hills'?" Surely her grandmother could not think that looking at an old picture was the same as knowing the real man?

Zeena laughed. "Of course I do not mean that! Arina, when you were three you adored Sher Ali, you followed him about, and you always asked him for a ride on his horse. He was a boy of twelve, and he was embarrassed by your devotion – he thought people would laugh at him. Gulrukh Begum told me in one of her letters. You cannot have forgotten Sher Ali, his grey horse and his hawk with the red hood? You cried for them almost as much as you cried for Chunia – don't tell me you have forgotten Chunia?"

Arina stared, wide-eyed. "No of course I have not forgotten Chunia! How could I? Chunia was my second mother, the centre of my life. And the horse – yes, I remember that big beautiful animal! He was called Sorab, and the bird with the red hood, she had bells on her feet – little silver bells. Oh yes, I remember the horse and the bird."

"And the boy?"

"The boy . . ." said Arina, frowning, "I think the boy was unkind – and I cannot remember any more than that."

"He will be kind now, you will find. Now that you are no longer a little girl, but a grown woman. Boys seldom care to be followed about by little girls. But now he, too, is grown. You will find everything has changed."

"Yes – it is fourteen years since I was there, and there has been a war. You will see more changes than I will, Grandmother. It has been much longer since you were there."

"I will see no changes, piyari." Her grandmother had turned away to look out across the loch. "I shall see no changes . . . because I am not going back."

"Grandmother! Of course you are coming back with me!"

Zeena turned back from gazing out across the water. Very quietly, she said, "Arina, please do not make me tell you that part of my story again. You know I can never go back, and you know why."

"But Grandmother," said Arina, so shocked that she spoke Urdu, as if she felt that her grandmother might not understand

27

her English. "You are my father's mother, and these people are all waiting for you – how can I marry without you there? Why do you say that you cannot come?"

"Daughter of my son, child of my heart, you know why. Do not ask foolish questions."

"Ammah-ji, I will not go without you."

"My child you will do as you are told. It is a matter of honour."

"Where is the honour? Is it that old matter, the question of the broken contract? There have been two world wars, blood has been spilt – you are the only real family that I have. I refuse to go without you."

"You will go, because I swore on my life and on your life that I would send you back when the time came – when you were of a marriageable age. Gulrukh Begum is holding me to my promise. And for you the contract has been signed."

"How old was I?"

"You were three years of age." Arina was silent for a few minutes, then she asked, "If you had been there, would you have prevented this?"

Zeena leaned forward, her fingers held close to Arina's face, to catch the tears that were now rolling down her grand-child's cheeks.

"After all that I have told you of my life, you think, piyari, that I might have stopped your betrothal? I must tell you, knowing all that I know of our customs and habits, I would have let it go. Sher Ali is of our blood. Do not weep so, child of my heart. All will be well for you."

"Oh, Grandmother – I wanted the choice. That is all. I might have chosen him, and been happy."

Zeena put her arms round a tearful Arina. "You must go there, to keep my promise. But if you find no happiness there, you will return to Scotland." She pulled out one of her delicately scented handkerchiefs and began to mop Arina's eyes and cheeks, the tears still flowing.

The Long Love

"Jasmine – every time I smell that flower, I will think of you. Oh, Grandmother, won't you come with me? I can bear anything if you are there . . ."

Zeena only shook her head, saying with quiet firmness, "I cannot come. Ask me no more, Arina. No more tears now – come with me, and let me give you your presents. Have you forgotten that today your birthday?"

To Arina, it did not feel like her birthday. Her desire to be treated as an adult seemed to have left her, too. "I wish it was last year," she said, and almost burst into tears again.

"Well, if it was last year you would be returning to school – and you certainly would not be looking at the presents that I have for you – or the gift sent by your family in Chikor and Pakodi! Doctor Maclaren brought it back when he came on leave last year."

Last year! The present had been meant for her sixteenth birthday, and Zeena had not given it to her. It seemed obvious to Arina why it had been kept. Gulrukh Begum must have wanted her to return to India when she was sixteen – but her grandmother had refused, and had kept her for another year. "Grandmother – they asked for me last year, didn't they?"

Her grandmother was busy unwrapping a bulky package. She said, without looking up, "I have to send you back now that you are of a suitable age. Sixteen was, for you, too young. You are young for your age. It is my fault. I should have sent you to boarding school when you were eight, instead of keeping you until your twelfth year. Girls grow up more quickly when they are away from home." She had finished unwrapping the package. Arina saw that it was a box, very old and battered looking. The leather that covered it was scuffed and scratched. Zeena handed it to her carefully.

"Open it, Arina. It comes from your family." A jewel box. This is a bribe, of course, thought Arina. I wish that I had the right to refuse it, but how can I wound Grandmother, who

29

is looking so expectant. Arina raised the lid of the box, and gasped.

Pearls and turquoises and corals lay coiled on the frayed silk lining. She lifted out the necklace and found the matching earrings and bracelets, the stones set in delicate gold filigree.

"A betrothal gift," said her grandmother softly, "They were given to me, but of course I never wore them and they went back into the Pakodi strong room. You may wear the earrings whenever you like, but the bracelets and the neck chain are for important occasions. These, my child, are only a tenth of your personal jewellery, the rest of which will be given to you when you reach Chikor."

Arina, holding the necklace in reluctant hands, felt she was holding a chain that would pull her back to Chikor, that fabulous place high in the northern hills. The sight of the jewels made the return to India and an unknown bridegroom a fact, not the lighthearted fictional amusement she had enjoyed so long – stories told by her grandmother to while away winter evenings.

Arina sat in silence, thinking of everything her grandmother had said and finding it hard to accept what would be an enormous change in her life. She was distressed, and yet, deep in her heart, excitement began to stir and grow. India!

Three

Zeena watched her granddaughter's face, and in it saw the beginnings of interest and, perhaps, excitement. Persuading Arina to return to India, convincing her that she would find happiness there, was going to be easier than she had feared.

"When must I leave?" Arina asked.

"The ship sails from Southampton two months from today. I will of course come down to Southampton with you and Sushi, to see you safely on board the *Star of Islam*.

"How long will the journey take?"

"I think, these days, it takes two weeks. It took longer when I came – or perhaps it just felt longer." The memory of that challenging, painful voyage had never faded for Zeena. It had been a time of misery for her. But she did not tell Arina this. Instead, she began to talk about all the things that she felt her granddaughter should know and would be interested to hear.

Arina would be met at Karachi and escorted to Madore, where she would stay for a few days before starting the two-week trek to Azadpur.

"Azadpur?" questioned Arina.

"Yes. The two states, Chikor and Pakodi, were combined and named Azadpur shortly after my father died and Atlar Khan, his brother, inherited the kingdom. That was in 1920. Then, when Atlar Khan felt the time was right, he abdicated and gave the throne to his son Mohammed. This is a custom among many of the hill rulers – when they feel age is heavy on them, they hand on the throne. In due time, Mohammed gave the throne to his son, who is named Azad Khan. Azad Khan is the present ruler. His heir is Sher Ali Azad Khan."

"Sher Ali?" asked Arina.

"Yes. The man you will marry. Consider yourself fortunate, Arina. He is young, handsome, and speaks fluent English. He was sent to Britain to be educated in the same way that you were sent to me here. Eventually he went to Sandhurst, and now he is in your father's regiment."

The faint feeling of excitement in Arina's heart began to grow stronger. The two months that stood between her and the departure date was something she felt she could do without – it was like the interminable wait for a late train. If she had to go, then the sooner the better, reflected Arina, before the excitement wore off and she began to feel afraid and lost again.

The two months flashed by and afterwards Arina could only remember one incident that happened during that time.

Once, late into the night, she woke to find brilliant moonlight flooding her room, moving across her bed. There was music somewhere, the sound of a flute and a woman singing. The words were clear and Arina would never forget them. "Come soon, beloved," sang the voice, "come soon. Tomorrow will not wait, tomorrow is too far—"

Soft and sad, the voice faded but it didn't cease, carrying on into Arina's sleep, her dreams peopled by princes and peacocks, and the face of a young man who would not smile at her.

That night, the music was the only memorable aspect of her preparations to leave for India.

The two months slipped by unmarked, until suddenly the waiting time was over and she was walking up the gangway on to the ship, and her grandmother was watching her from the quay. Zeena waved once, and walked away with Jessie, with no backward glance. So Arina did not see the sorrow on her face.

Zeena, almost overcome with loss, was telling herself that this was all turning out for the best. Now Arina would marry and have children of her father's blood, who would take the throne of Azadpur. Surely this would pacify her father's restless spirit that had always haunted her sleep. With these thoughts, Zeena tried to comfort herself, trying not to dwell on the loneliness that awaited her.

Arina, watching her grandmother go, had nothing to give her comfort. All excitement had died, now there was only grief and homesickness. She went down into the cabin she was to share with Sushi and wept in her maidservant's arms. Sushi said nothing, just held Arina close until the weeping ceased and the ship began to move away from the quay.

Acute seasickness was a merciful visitation and overshadowed every other feeling Arina had been experiencing. This eventually passed and, to her own surprise, Arina began to enjoy the sea, and the strange life on the ship. She made friends, she played extraordinary deck games and enjoyed the long, warm days, and yet all the time, at the back of her mind was the question, "Who will meet me at Karachi, what will this new life be like?"

Four

They came in on the noon tide, and had docked by four o'clock on a hot, windy afternoon.

Veiled in blown sand, Karachi seemed colourless, a place of barely perceptible low-lying buildings, a desert place.

The docks were crowded, the quay swarming with shouting men. The noise was augmented by a rattling crane, dipping over the open hold of the ship like a great mechanical bird. In the background were buildings that seemed to have fallen into ruins before they had been properly built. Open doors gaped on darkness, secret, sinister. Bodies lay against the wall in what shade could be found, heads covered, sleeping away the hours until they could board *The Star of Islam* once the present passengers had disembarked.

Arina leaned on one of the ship's rails and looked at the chaos below. In that crowd might be someone who had come to meet her – if her grandmother and Gulrukh's arrangements had been confirmed despite uncertain postal arrangements, long gaps of time between letters, and, what she had not known, constant changes of plan due to the troubles. From fellow passengers, Arina had learned all that her grandmother had not told her. She was entering a country rent by riots and massacres, and a change of Government.

"The British have left, gone as if they had never been," one lady had told her, "and now we are an independent state. Our country is now called Pakistan. You must remember that we are no longer called Indians, we are Pakistani now," said the lady, who was the Begum Zara Ali Khan. And despite her title, she was not a relative of any of the northern princes.

"I myself come from Delhi – a beautiful city," the lady continued, "but I can never go back there now. The Hindus and Sikhs would murder me."

There were very few British people on board. "I miss my British friends," said the old Begum. "Who is meeting you, my child?" she asked, her concern a motherly one.

"My aunt has made arrangements for someone to meet me." Arina found questions trying. She had no idea who was meeting her, and did not wish to show how anxious she was.

"Well, if there is any mischance, which these days there could be," said the old Begum, "do not be worried. I myself will take you to a hotel and wait with you until someone comes."

Sushi, Arina's shadow, as always, heard this and was relieved, but Arina felt restive. She did not wish to be taken to a hotel. She wanted to be alone to face whatever happened.

Now she stared down from the ship, wondering how she would ever know who was supposed to meet her – and how they would recognise her. There would be no recognition. She had left India when she was only three years of age.

All through the long days of the voyage, she had been longing for this landfall, but now India – how could she remember to call it Pakistan? – no longer seemed interesting. Where were the gold Mhor trees, the temples, the mosques, the peacocks, the palaces of white marble, the lakes and the lotus flowers? India, the country of dreams and memories, now Pakistan, almost another country, a different time. Her heart felt a stab of disappointment, but she tried to forget it. All these things are waiting for me, she told herself, I shall see them all.

The chaos was growing worse. A gangway had been lowered down the side of the ship and was swaying dangerously under the weight of bodies forcing their way up, against the flow of disembarking passengers who were trying to get down. There was a wide strip of dark oily water between the side of the ship and the quay. The descent looked hazardous.

Sushi had packed early that morning and had locked their suitcases. The luggage that hadn't been wanted on the voyage had been brought up from the hold, and their travel documents franked by the immigration officers who had come on board. They could go ashore whenever they wished, but the thought of joining the heaving throng on the gangway did not appeal to Arina. Besides, if they did manage to get down safely on to that crowded quay, she felt sure that they would miss whoever was coming to meet them. Better to stay quietly on deck and wait. Sushi, standing beside her, agreed.

Arina had just made this decision when the Begum Zara Ali Khan came up to join them, and Sushi politely moved back to allow the lady to stand beside Arina.

"Have you seen anyone you know?" asked Zara Begum.

In this chaos? thought Arina, did not answer. She just shook her head.

"I am not surprised!" The lady continued. "How can you pick anyone out in this crowd? Always the same in Karachi. Where are the ship's officers? They should be controlling this mob. One would think that they would at least control the deck passengers. I shall tell my husband to complain to the shipping company – I think *The Star of Islam* is a Smith Mackenzie vessel, but, my goodness, who knows who is running what now, with all the British gone. There is no law and order any more. How am I going to get down? My luggage has already gone, and who is guarding it? These thieves and vagabonds will be into my cases like rats into grain. My God, I have never travelled like this!"

Arina did not know how to reply, so she said nothing.

Begum Zara Ali was quiet for a few minutes, giving Arina the chance to scan the crowds below, then the Begum continued. "Also, I am worried about you, my child. You see, when my husband comes, I shall have to go *'jut put'*, if you understand me. He is not a man to wait about. Then, if you have seen no one you know, what will become of you? I cannot leave you alone in this muddle. Better that you come with me, we go to the Palace Hotel, that is where we always stay – if, of course, it is still standing! My husband can pay a man to look out for the people trying to find you and tell them that you have had to go with us. I cannot recall who you said was meeting you, tell me again."

"I did not say, because I have only been told that some-one my aunt knows will come to meet me – they will know who I am, but I will not know them. I must wait here, I cannot come with you. Please, Begum Sahiba, you must go when your husband comes. I shall be quite safe, I have my maid with me, and I will stay until my name is called."

But the Begum was not listening. "There," she said, "I knew this would happen. There is my husband. Oh, my God, what shall I do? I cannot leave you, my child."

"Of course you must go – see, the crowd is clearing and I think there are some people who have come for me just over there," said Arina, pointing vaguely.

"Are you sure? Where are they, I can see no one, but I must go, my husband is waving at me to come down. He will make red eyes at me if I keep him waiting."

"I am perfectly sure," said Arina, untruthfully, she could see no one, but was determined to stay on board the ship until someone came.

"Then, if you are sure, I will go. Do not forget that we are in the Palace Hotel. If anything goes wrong, come straight away and ask for me."

Arina promised that she would do this, and the Begum Zara Ali Khan staggered, in high heels, down the gangway, her sari fluttering in the hot wind. She looked so unsteady that Arina could not bear to watch her, but it would have been impossible to reach her and help. So Arina looked away, searching the quay, and in the drifting, dwindling crowd, she saw a man standing a little distance from the people at the foot of the gangway. She looked down at him, and could not believe what she saw.

Five

D own on the dirty, sand-blown quay, looking up at her . . .
Had he stepped out of her dreams and become real? She
closed her eyes, opened them, and he was still there. A replica
of the young man in her picture. Of course he was not wearing
a brocade *achkan* and all his jewels – in fact he was dressed
in a silk shirt and well-worn cord trousers. He could have
been mistaken for an Englishman, but for the arrogance of
this hard-faced young man. The arrogance of coming from
a ruling family. Not an Englishman. Who was he? Could he
be . . . ?

"Sushi – look down there. Do you see that man?"

"I see him, piyari. *Bapari bap*! Gulrukh Begum has sent her
grandson, Sher Ali, to take you back to Chikor!"

"How can you be sure? You have not seen him for fourteen
years. It cannot be Sher Ali."

"Arina piyari, it is he. That man beside him, in uniform,
that is the prince's guard, Sakhi Mohammed. See, they are
coming to the steps. Pull your veil over your head, prepare
to greet him."

So this was her future husband. This was what the slender
boy of her youth – the boy she had adored – had grown into.

Sushi was right, he was certainly going to come up the
gangway, his man went in front of him, and she saw how
people made way before him. He would be with her in a
few minutes, and she was not ready to meet him. She was
glad of her veil, and closed it over her face, leaving only her

39

eyes uncovered. He had stopped at the foot of the gangway and was looking up at her.

Sher Ali was not very happy. He was just about to go on his carefully planned leave, when he received a peremptory summons from his grandmother, Gulrukh Begum, in Panchghar. The journey to Panchghar took three days – three days of his leave wasted. When he arrived, he was told that he had to go at once to Karachi to meet his bride-to-be.

"It is essential," said Gulrukh. "And also, at such a time it is perfectly correct for you to meet her and travel with her to ensure her safety. No one thinks any the worse of this. You may take Chunia with you."

"Chunia!" protested Sher Ali. Chunia was part of his life, she had been greatly loved by three generations of the family, but she was very old. It seemed to him that Chunia was older than anything, clinging to life like a dried leaf to a tree – delicate and friable. "The journey will kill her, Grandmother. How can you suggest sending her?"

"Do not be stupid, please, my dear. Chunia is old and all the stronger for it. We are not made of paper, she and I. Arina will expect to see her."

Without much hope, Sher Ali looked for help. "What does my grandfather think of this? Has he agreed that I should go to meet Arina alone, except for a servant?"

"Your grandfather agrees that someone must meet her, and you are the most suitable. It will fit in very well with your leave. Stop arguing, Sher Ali. Do you want that girl to be murdered on the train? Are you so keen a bridegroom that you cannot spend a few days of your leave guarding the woman who will bear your sons?"

"It will cause talk," said Sher Ali despairingly.

"Wah! When did our family worry about the chatter of people of no importance? None of our *jat* will talk! They will expect you to go and meet her and bring her back to me. Did

Afsar not go and collect Gulshan and bring her to Chikor last year, in safety?"

"Grandmother, Afsar is Gulshan's brother, as I am. I could take her anywhere alone and there would be no scandal. To be alone with Arina Begum, who is a young unmarried girl – that is a different matter."

"I see," said his grandmother. "Well, if you are of such a bad reputation that all our friends will think that you will deflower your bride before you marry her, then indeed I agree, you are right to refuse to go. I will send for Yacoup Ismail, he will bring her to me."

And rape her on the way, thought Sher Ali. Colonel Yacoup Ismail was a notorious womaniser.

"If that is your idea of a safe guardian, Grandmother, I will go and meet her. But you know, it is quite unnecessary. The country is quiet now. There haven't been any killings on the trains for months, and the mail train to Madore is heavily guarded. All that Begum Arina has to do is drive from the station and—"

His grandmother interrupted immediately. "Yes. All she has to do then is buy tickets for herself and old Sushi, and arrange for a purdah compartment for them, and make sure all her luggage is on the train – you are happy to think of her struggling with all this? She is seventeen, Sher Ali, she has never been out of that cold country for fourteen years – how can she do all that? Be ashamed, Sher Ali, you are not the man I thought you were. The blood has grown weaker in the fourth generation. So Go back to your regiment and enjoy your leave. I am ashamed of you."

"I have said, I will go."

Gulrukh Begum gave him a cold look. "I hope you mean it. You will take her and her maid Sushi first to the house of the Dinshaws. You know them?"

"Of course. Fram and Manika."

"Good. They are old friends of mine. They cannot come to

the marriage ceremonies, and the festivities afterwards because of the disturbances. You think everything is over, when people like the Dinshaws are afraid to travel? No, my boy, be not so hopeful. The country is still seething. We are fortunate up in the far hills and, as for you, stationed in Dera, what do you know of the state of things? You will find that I am right to be worried. You will need to leave this week for Karachi. Arina arrives in Karachi on the nineteenth. Please be sure to be there early, I do not want her to hang about on the docks alone, looking for you."

So there went all his plans for a shooting trip, followed by a couple of weeks in Lahore to see what independence had left of the fleshpots. Well it couldn't be helped. His grandmother, Gulrukh Begum of Panchghar, was a woman to be obeyed, he would as soon have argued with a hunting tiger.

He looked up at this unknown girl who was to be his wife. Not altogether unknown. He remembered her as a child – a very small child – in Chikor, before she was sent away to Scotland to that grandmother whose name no one could utter. The supposedly dead woman who was buried in the gardens of the Pila Ghar in Madore.

The child had been tiresome, he remembered, but endearing in her way. She had followed him about almost as soon as she could walk, clamouring to be given a ride on his horse. He stared up the high side of the ship, trying to see what England – no, Scotland – had made of her, what he had got saddled with. Difficult to judge from this distance. She was wearing Punjabi dress, *salwar* and *khemise*, and her head and face were veiled. That was good. He had been afraid that she would wear British dress, and be disastrously westernised. So far so good. Well, no good hanging about. Better go up and collect her. He began to climb the gangway, followed by Sakhi Mohammed.

She was still standing by the rail when he came up, so he walked over to speak to her. She was very small. She was wearing green and had pulled her veil up, not very successfully, he could see a strand of dark, shining hair. Her eyes were blue, and appeared to be considering him as he was considering her. He forgot to give her any greeting, forgot what he had meant to say and asked where her baggage was. Her eyes were enormous.

"The baggage is just over there, Sushi is guarding it. We have cleared immigration," she answered abruptly.

Was she suggesting that he was late? He was, of course, but traffic on the road out to the docks had been impossible and in any case it was not her place to criticise. Typical of a girl brought up in Britain. No charm. How she stared!

"There was no need for you to do anything about immigration," he said stiffly. "We would have done it all for you. I hope you had no trouble." He sounded, she thought, as if he did not care if she had had trouble or not.

"I had no trouble, thank you. They were very civil and very efficient."

It could have been his grandmother speaking. She was very cool indeed.

"Good. Well, if you are ready, we might as well go. No point in staying here any longer. My people will see about your baggage." Without another word, he walked away towards the gangway.

Well! thought Arina, what awful manners! She looked at Sushi, and asked, low voiced, "Sushi, is that really Sher Ali?"

Sushi looked nervous. "Piyari, of course it is."

To Arina's ear, Sushi sounded uncertain. I am not sure either, she thought, I am accepting him because he reminds me of my picture. Ridiculous. My grandmother once told me of something that happened to a bride. I might be like that, I might be being kidnapped!

She only half believed what she was thinking, but she stood firmly where she was, and gestured to Sushi to stay with her.

After waiting at the gangway for a few minutes, Arina became increasingly concerned. Was this man an imposter?

"Are you not ready?" he asked walking towards her, a look of irritation in his eyes.

She had moved to face him, her veil was caught by the wind and slipped back. Her hair was black and shining, and her face . . . She was beautiful! She looked half angry, half frightened, as she pulled her veil down quickly. She sounded as if she was speaking through clenched teeth. "I have no idea who you are. I don't even know your name. Can you identify yourself?"

"Good God." For a second, he looked as if were going to laugh. "I am sorry. Did no one tell you we were going to meet here? I imagined you would be expecting one of the family, at least. I am Sher Ali, at your service. My grandmother Gulrukh Begum sent me to meet you. I have a letter here." He pulled a crumpled letter from his pocket and handed it to her, "I'm afraid it is written in Urdu script. My grandmother does not write in English."

He smiled then, and his whole face changed. The hard line of his mouth softened, his smile made him a different person, a young man of compelling charm. "If it comes to that, I have no proof that you are the girl I am supposed to meet. I haven't even asked to see your passport. What foolishness my dear grandmother and yours managed between them! You *are* Arina Begum, I presume?"

He put out his hand as he spoke, and gently he moved her veil aside. She could not help smiling back, even as she snatched at the veil. He saw a beautiful girl, a very young woman, with a soft mouth that curved sweetly. Such eyes! What colour? But she had the veil in place again and he could not see.

"You are not supposed to do that," she said.

"Arina, no one has a better right. Two rights, in fact. For one thing, I am a family member, I am your cousin, and the second right is that we are affianced." He looked at her with the kind

44

of admiring look she had imagined and wished for, and said, "Come, Arina Begum, let us forget this confused beginning. Forgive me, I was very late."

"I had no idea who was coming, or what time they would come."

He shook his head at his grandmother's carelessness. "Poor Arina. What an arrival. Well, let us go now that we have sorted this out."

He still walked ahead of her, but this time she followed him down the gangway, with Sushi coming sure-footed after her, and behind her the uniformed guardian of princes. At the bottom of the rickety gangway, she stepped down at last on to the soil of this country she had dreamed of so many times. Now she would discover the reality.

"India at last?" she said, sighing, and saw him swing round, a frown on his face.

"No. No longer India, one undivided land. Pakistan is a word you must learn. India has been carved up, to suit the politicians. There are now two countries, and only Allah the Compassionate, the all seeing, knows what may lie ahead, and all of us without his knowledge must fear it. In any case, Karachi is not the true country, any more than London is the true Britain. This Karachi is a hybrid place, full of riff-raff playing at being cosmopolitan – a city that has lost its head."

He looked both stormy and sad, and sounded bitter. She thought he was addressing her as if he was instructing a stupid child. He was so arrogant! She lifted her chin and said coldly. "I do not think of Karachi as India. It is a city in India, and I think of it as the gateway to the country that I have heard about all my life, the hill country where I was born. I think of the northern states – of Panchghar and Lumbugh, Pakodi and Chikor – as the true India."

"Do you indeed? That is not going to get you anywhere, unless you learn to call them Pakistan." He glared at her, then suddenly smiled again. "But I think you will learn. At least your heart turns to the right places."

How he changed, from one minute to the next! His strange moods caused her to feel very uncertain of him. Sher Ali – the tiger. Perhaps he was well named. She had read about the nature of the tiger, of all the animals, this was the most dangerous and untrustworthy in temperament. Now the tiger was smiling at her with warmth. What next, though, she wondered.

"Do you feel that those high valleys are where you will be content and happy?"

That depends on the tiger, she thought, but did not feel she could say that yet. Instead she told him of how she dreamed of India, how she had listened to her grandmother's stories. She said, watching his face as she spoke, "I have dreamed of those valleys for so long, always thinking that they were my true home. I wish they had not changed the name of this beautiful land, but I expect I shall get used to it. Which of the three states do you come from – is it Pakodi?"

"Yes. Our branch of the family all have blood ties with Pakodi. Your bloodline is through your grandmother, Yasmin Begum. Her mother was a connection of the Lambagh state princes, on her father's side and Jungdah on her mother's side." Better leave it at that, he thought, as this girl has mixed blood. But it did not seem to embarrass her.

"In Scotland where my grandmother now lives, bloodlines are very important. We have clans there, not states. Jessie, my grandmother's old maid traced my grandfather's family back to at least two Scottish kings."

Her grandfather, thought Sher Ali. That would be the man Alan, who had caused all the trouble all these year ago. She would have to learn to avoid speaking so freely of *him* – and as for the grandmother, living in Scotland? And at the same time lying dead in the garden of the Pila Ghar in Madore? He wondered if the girl knew the whole story of her background.

The Long Love

"I am sorry that you do not like the new name given to the three adjoining states. That is a pity, because when my father either dies, Allah forfend, or abdicates in my favour, you will become the Begum of Azadpur. What do you think of that?" To his astonishment, she sighed, and said rather sadly, "I would prefer to be known as the Begum of Chikor, as my grandmother Zeena was." And then put a hand up to her mouth and turned wide, alarmed eyes to him.

He heard the harsh indrawn breath of Sushi, the maid, walking behind her mistress. So Arina *had* been warned to avoid making mention of her grandmother? But how could be admonish her, looking into those big, sad eyes? As he gazed into them, she lowered her amazing lashes, and said in a low voice, "I am sorry. I should not have said that."

He could not scold her. He would have time to teach her everything soon. Before he had felt that he was not ready for this marriage. Now it seemed that two months was too long to wait.

Six

S her Ali said nothing, but walked ahead, so that Arina had to run a few steps to catch up with his long stride. She tried to speak, hoping that she had not annoyed him by talking so openly about her grandmother.

"You are from Pakodi, you said. That is where I lived as a child. I think I remember it, but I cannot be sure that my memories are not clouded by stories I have been told. But I do long to go back there, for then I will know whose images of the past I have been living with . . ."

Sher Ali felt a stab of compassion. He sensed her confusion and anxiety in her voice. He began to walk more slowly so that she could walk beside him as he asked, "What do you think you remember?"

"Oh, that the valleys were beautiful, that the fort was a symbol of total safety – and I was always happy there."

"Ah, you have honey on your tongue! Even as a very little girl you could always talk yourself out of trouble and win people's hearts. I am sorry if I looked angry just now, it has little to do with you, and I apologise. How can you possibly know, having left as a child? I will teach you slowly – I have patience, I assure you. Perhaps I have not shown it, but I have a great many problems ahead of me, as does my father, and I am sure that the coming changes are not going to be as easy as the politicians – curse them – tell us. Were you not warned in Britain of the changes that are taking place here?"

Arina wondered how she could possibly answer such '

question without using her grandmother's name. In the end, she said, "No, I was told nothing about Pakistan in Scotland."

"Too unimportant to matter, I suppose?"

There, she thought, I have said something wrong again. It is hopeless, I *am* locked in with a tiger. She would have to use the word "grandmother" to explain, whether he liked it or not. Firmly, she said, "No, that is not the reason I didn't hear about Pakistan. My grandmother lives in the past. She never mentions changes. The only reason I have any idea is because I met a kind woman on the ship who told me a great deal, but she said the mountains were safe. Her name is Begum Zara Ali Khan, she lives in the Palace Hotel."

"That old gossip-monger," he laughed suddenly, "and I am sure she told you that everything was in ruins, and nothing was going to work because the British had left. Don't worry about what she said, the things she worries about are not important. From her, you may have learnt all the wrong things about the new Pakistan. I will teach you. Your knowledge will come to you as the new country struggles from birth to life." He smiled at her as he spoke, paused and said quietly, "Believe me, that is the best way to learn about Pakistan. That is how every one of us is learning, so you will be in good company. There will be plenty of time for you to un-learn old things, and learn all the things in our lives that will be new for you. Plenty of time for this, once you are over the passes and among our mountains."

Over the passes, among the mountains and locked safely away with the tiger, she thought, and wondered what the "old" things were that she had to forget. She longed to ask him, but decided not to.

They reached a line of cars and horse drawn carriages: all the vehicles seemed to be in the last stages of decrepitude, and the horses were in very poor shape. He saw her eyeing the animals, and smiled.

"I am not hiring one of those poor creatures. It would take us hours to reach Sagar House."

"Those poor horses – they are in a terrible state."

He looked cursorily at them and said "yes" without much interest. "Yes, these hired nags are always like that. My cars are here – look."

She looked the direction that he was pointing in, and saw two cars which had draw up a little way away. There was a large coffee-coloured car, which she recognised to be a Rolls, and a small dark green two-seater with its hood folded down. There was a silver animal on the bonnet.

"This is my own car," he said, his voice full of pride.

But Arina thought the car looked very small and rather like a bullet. "Is that a tiger you have on the front?"

"No! That is a jaguar. The car is a Jaguar 120, the best car in the world. Do you have any objection to driving in an open car?"

"Oh no," said Arina, who had never driven in one.

"Good," said Sher Ali. "Now let us see what has happened with your baggage. Good God! Is that two cabin trunks, four cases, and two bedding rolls? Is that all?"

"It is all we have with us," said Arina. "I believe there is more following by cargo boat, but that will take some weeks."

"Well," said Sher Ali, "We can be grateful for that. I think we can get all this in. Sakhi Mohammed, I will take the Begum Sahiba, you will come with the baggage and the ayah, Sushi."

Sakhi Mohammed was now carrying a gun slung over his shoulder, as a man might carry a golf bag. He looked worried.

"Highness, better I come with you, I can sit on the small shelf behind the Begum Sahiba – there is a hartal in Sandal Street, and talk of riots, and the police are armed and out in force."

"I," said Sher Ali, "will take the other road, the longer way, and avoid all that. There is no need for you to come with us. In any case, there is no room." He nodded, and turned away as Sakhi Mohammed saluted smartly, looking grave.

"As you wish, Highness, but have a care. We will follow you as best we can. That is a very bad road that you choose," Sakhi Mohammed warned.

The silver animal on the bonnet of the little car looked remarkably like a tiger now. As Arina lowered herself into the two-seater, she began to wish she had said she preferred the large car. Sher Ali settled himself in the close quarters of the little car beside her.

"Do you drive?" he asked.

"No, I ride."

"Ah. Yes, of course. Horses. I remember. So no driving at all?"

"Well, yes, of course I went about in a car. Robbie used to take me out. He was disappointed when my grandmother gave me a horse instead of driving lessons. But I was very happy to have my own horse, even though Robbie said a car was of more use. He said that I was a natural driver – he gave me one or two lessons."

Sher Ali did not care for the sound of this at all. He hoped her grandmother had looked after Arina properly. In his opinion, English parents gave their girls more freedom than was good for them. Modern behaviour was not wanted in a girl of the Chikor family.

Repressively, he said, "Well, you will not be doing much driving from now on. For one thing, there are no cars in Madore, and up in the mountain valleys there are no suitable roads. So that is that. Who is this man Robbie? Where did he take you?"

"Robbie is Colonel Robert Maclaren – he is the son of the old Colonel Maclaren of the Indian Medical Service in Madore. Robbie is in the IMS, too – he is a friend of my grandmother's. Why?"

51

Sher Ali looked down at her. "I asked because I need to know. That is all. I know Colonel Maclaren the second. He has the reputation of being an excellent doctor and is popular among the British, in spite of his background. I wonder if he will leave now – though there are reasons why he may prefer to stay on."

Arina longed to ask what was wrong with Robbie's background, and why he might go, or stay. But before she could speak, Sher Ali had started the car, and they were off with a roar, scattering pedestrians with a warning blast of a very penetrating horn.

There was a small steel bar, like a handle, screwed to the dashboard in front of her. Arina grabbed it and hung on. If this man was trying to frighten her, he was succeeding, but he was never going to be allowed to know it. She turned her head for a last look at the ship, but it was already out of sight. Her veil fell from her head, and the wind snatched at her hair, sending it streaming out behind her like a long silk scarf. She clung fiercely to the bar, and closed her eyes. Even with them open, she could not see anything at this speed, so it was better to keep them closed against the wind. Her face stinging with blown sand, Arina heard Sher Ali shout above the noise of the engine, which was roaring like an animal.

"Are you all right?"

Deafened, shaken, shattered, she opened her eyes, said "yes" looked at the landscape reeling past and shut her eyes again. Still shouting, Sher Ali spent a few minutes telling her about the car, its petrol consumption, and the speed that he could get out of it.

"It is a splendid little car," he said. "Next best thing to flying."

As well as being arrogant and rude, she thought bitterly, he is a great *bore*. Is this what marriage with him is going to be like? Listening to him talking about cars, and driving everywhere in this bullet?

The next time Sher Ali shouted, he spoke Punjabi. "Do you want to die, you fool?"

"What—?" Arina, shaken by his tone, opened her eyes to look at him.

His shouting, this time, appeared to be directed at a man on a donkey and a small boy who ran behind him. They paid no attention to Sher Ali's shout. As there was a cart drawn by a camel coming towards them on the other side of the road, Sher Ali was forced to slacken speed. He then drove with one hand while manoeuvring a cigar out of a case in his pocket. "I hope you do not smoke," he said, "but if you do, there is a packet of cigarettes in the pocket in the door beside you." He paused, looking at her, then said, "Arina Begum, you do not look very happy, or comfortable. Have I frightened you? I am afraid I have. Do not be worried by my driving, I am known as a fast driver, but a very good one." He noted her clenched hands on the bar and, looking at her with more interest, saw the total disarray of the girl beside him. He was stricken with remorse.

"I am so sorry! Look, I will pull off the road, and light my cigar, and that will give you time to catch your breath."

The car stopped, the wind died, and blazing heat took its place. Arina unclenched her hands, wondering if he had been driving so fast on purpose to frighten her. A good driver! If this was how he always drove, she was amazed that he was still alive. She glared at him out of bloodshot eyes, and he suddenly leaned over and took her hands and began to rub them gently.

Looking into her face, he said, "I am truly sorry. Why did you not say something? I drive alone so often that I forgot I had a passenger. If you feel in that pocket, you will find a flask of coffee. We could have a drink if you do not mind sharing a cup with me. Pass me the flask – it is very stiff to open." The strong black coffee smelled delicious as he poured it into the top of the thermos.

"You first," said, and sat watching Arina as she sipped the hot coffee, which he knew was laced with brandy. That would do her good. Her hands had been shaking when he held them. He was ashamed, he had been driving like the devil, showing off in front of her like a boy out on his first date. Fool! and worse than fool. It was cruel to have frightened her. And where on earth was her veil? Blown away, he supposed. What amazing eyes she had! Pale eyes – blue? Or were they grey, the true northern grey, like the Pathan girls. No way of finding out while she looked away from him, her hands now clenched on the cup as if she could not let go. Was she still afraid of him, or was it only his driving?

"I made you afraid. I am ashamed. Please look at me and say you forgive me?"

She turned to look at him, found him leaning towards her, very close, and drew herself back as much as she could into her corner of the car. "No. I wasn't afraid. Of course I wasn't afraid. It was the wind and the dust – this car is very near the ground, that is what makes it seem to be going so fast. What kind of a car is it?"

Behind his remorse, he felt a faint stirring of annoyance. "It is a Jaguar XK120. They are racing cars. We were in fact doing over a hundred."

"Over a hundred what? What does that mean?"

"Over a hundred miles an hour. I love speed. I do not have much opportunity to drive this car, and as I am nearly always alone in it I lose my head and drive too fast. Am I forgiven?"

"Yes, of course," Arina said, but no smile accompanied the words. She had finished her coffee.

"More?" Sher Ali asked. When she shook her head, he drank it himself and, still looking at her with what she found an embarrassing stare, he said, "You look like a little cat. You have eyes like a cat – very strange, but very beautiful eyes, do you know that?"

"Certainly no one has ever said anything about my eyes –
my grandmother said nothing."

"I do not think that grandmothers are given to that sort of
compliment. I was thinking of some man?"

"I know no man in Scotland who would make personal
remarks – and was that supposed to be a compliment?"

So, he thought, no man. He had to believe her for his own
peace of mind. No one knew how she had been brought up, so
far away from the family, and in the hands of a grandmother
who had caused so much disorder and dismay. He *had* to
believe her. He was sure there was no guile in those eyes.

"Of course it is a compliment. I have never forgotten your
eyes, Arina."

She felt for her veil, that frail protection against the invasion
of another's eyes. But of course it had blown away on the
road, and she had not even noticed it. She put her hand up
to her hair and found it tangled, rough with sand. He was still
watching her. Defensively, she said, "I do not know how you
can remember me or my eyes. I do not remember you at all.
Did we meet when I was young?"

He laughed. "When you were young? And now you are
middle-aged, and have forgotten me! How can you say that,
Arina, you who used to follow me everywhere, demanding
to be taken up on my horse. I am afraid that you are fickle.
I thought you would remember me. You looked as if you
remembered me when you first saw me this morning?"

"Well, I did not." The picture of the young man with the
horse was going to be her secret. Then, afraid that she had
been too abrupt, she said, "I remember the horse. I could never
forget that horse."

"The horse, but not the man."

Had she been too rude, wondered Arina, not feeling much
sorrow if she had but, remembering who he was and that he
would be her permanent companion, she decided to turn the
conversation.

"You speak English very well. If I were to shut my eyes and listen to you, I would think you were an Englishman."

"Oh? Is *that* supposed to be a compliment? I should speak it well. I was at school there for four years. I went to a very famous school, Harrow. They all speak good English there."

He was laughing at her, she knew it. She met his eyes, and lowered her own quickly. He had such a searching stare.

"If you knew me when I was little, it must have been before you went to school – you would have been a schoolboy, not a man. I was three when I was sent away – fourteen years ago. How old were you when you went away?"

"I went when I was twelve, and returned when I was sixteen – you had already gone. I stayed here for two years, and then went back to England to Sandhurst. I was only there a year then."

"A whole year – I was up in Scotland, and you did not come to see me."

"No."

There was something about the tone of that brief answer that warned her to say no more, but she had another question that she had to ask, could not hold it back.

"Sher Ali, I was betrothed to you when I was three – does that not seem a strange age to have been betrothed?"

He moved, and leaned a little away from her. "It is a custom of our people – you must know that. You were leaving the country for some years – my mother wanted to be sure that no errors were made, that my future wife was kept safe. Mixed marriages. They are not approved. You are a rich woman in lands and heritage. Someone might have coveted you for your possessions – you might have been too young to understand."

"I see," said Arina slowly, "but my grandmother was there, she would not have allowed any covetous man to take me. In any case, the British do not indulge in child marriage!"

So, he thought, those lovely eyes can flash – and the little cat could strike.

"I think you are angry with me. I meant no insult. It would not only be for your wealth that you would be taken. You faced, unknowing, many dangers. Shall we speak of other things?"

But she had not finished her question, and said so. "I must know this. I was not told a great many things, I would be grateful if you would tell me. When I was betrothed to you, did you not feel you would have preferred to choose your own bride?"

He was becoming embarrassed by the trend of the conversation. He said, speaking brusquely, "I was not there."

Her eyes were wide with astonishment. "But how can that be, Sher Ali, how can I be betrothed to a man who was not there?"

Now he began to sound really irritated. "Oh for God's sake, it was only a matter of signing papers! I had a proxy who signed for me."

"And I? I signed?"

"Arina, you made a thumb mark – and my mother added her signature."

"I made my thumb mark – did I cut a vein and make it in my blood?"

He said stiffly. "That is not necessary, it was legally done. You are my affianced bride. May we talk of other things now?"

"I do not think I want to talk at all at present."

"Very well." He threw his cigar away, screwed the top back on the thermos flask full of coffee, and started the car. But this time he drove at a more moderate rate. They were on tarmac now and driving between crowded pavements. Garish posters advertising films loomed above them, the traffic increased and he drove very slowly indeed. Arina forgot her hurt feelings, and was fascinated by the strange conglomerate that was Karachi.

Seven

A rina was grateful that Sher Ali was forced to drive so slowly. This city of Karachi was not to be dismissed lightly, she discovered. There were some beautiful buildings, but not the kind she had imagined she would see. This was, it seemed, a very British Victorian city. The traffic was of course more exotic: camel carts and bullock carts struggled for passage with large rich-looking cars, horse-drawn Victorias, bicycles, rickshaws, and everywhere the pedestrian crowds swirled and turned and dodged. There was always a donkey and an old man, heedless of speed and danger, there were women who appeared more like walking tents, wrapped from head to heel in garments that fitted close to the head, had a square of filigree cotton over the eyes, and fell in folds to hide everything else. There were others, graceful and free, striding careless as the donkeys and the old men. These women had large pots balanced on their heads, or laden baskets, and a child either running beside them, or a baby balanced on a hip.

"How you stare, Arina! You are fascinated by this place?"

"Oh yes – such things to see! Look, there are some Chinese people, *real* Chinese, and I saw a magnificent-looking family of Africans."

"Yes. There is almost every race under the sun here. I have not seen any Eskimos, but I feel sure that there must be some. I told you – this is not Pakistan. It is a hybrid city."

"Yes, but it looks interesting."

He shook his head. "You think so? I hate cities. Troubles

58

always begin in the cities. There is trouble here *now*, but I have chosen a route which ensures that we will not run into a riot. I didn't want to risk it with you in the car."

"Yes – the prince's guard warned you, didn't he?"

"Oh ho! You know his title – and you understood what he said. You speak Urdu?"

"Well, of course I do. I speak Punjabi, too. I did not have to be taught my own language – I am a girl of the hills. How could I forget my own tongue?"

Sher Ali smiled, and, as he looked, at her, his expression was warm and friendly again. The smile of the tiger, thought Arina, but she could not stop herself smiling back.

"You speak the language very sweetly," Sher Ali remarked. "As you say, you sound like a girl of the hills. Life will be easier for you with the family. I am afraid the older people do not speak English – or if they do, it is very little. All the younger members do, of course – most of the men of our family were sent abroad to school, but none of the girls. They went to Queen Mary College in Lahore, if they went to school at all. Most of them had governesses."

"I see," said Arina. "But I do not understand why you say it will be easier for me because I speak our language? I am not expecting life to be difficult. I am going to the home of my own family, to my aunt whom I remember as a loving, warm-hearted woman. I am going to a place I remember in my dreams. Why should there be difficulties?"

He turned to look at her, and now he was frowning again. "Arina. Listen to me. You are going to a different world. No matter how much you have dreamed, the realities will be quite different from what you remember. You have grown to womanhood in a different place, knowing a different way of life. There is a great deal that you will have to learn to accept. I can see that. You must be ready to find things difficult at first."

How straight her gaze is, a wide unblinking stare as she listens to me, thinking. She is a strange girl, a puzzle of a girl. "What are you thinking?" he asked suddenly, and saw her blush scarlet.

Arina had been considering Sher Ali's arrogance, yet despite his rudeness, he was strangely fascinating and she was beginning to like him. That tigerish change, though, made her wary and uncertain again. How long would it take her to get used to him, never mind all the other difficulties he seemed to think she would encounter? How much would she see of him before she found herself married to him? But these thoughts could not be exposed to Sher Ali.

"I am thinking about how hot it is, and wishing that I had my veil. Men stare very hard here, don't they?"

He turned and noticed a group of youths who were staring at Arina from the other side of the street, but who looked away quickly when they realised Sher Ali had a look of anger in his eyes.

"Do not think of them – they do not matter. In this country where women go veiled in public, an unveiled woman is fair game to some unmannerly men. But here in the city, where women are beginning to come out of purdah, men are used to seeing bare-faced women. Those boys were staring at you for other reasons."

"What reasons?"

"Your hair, your eyes – and possibly they were just looking at the car."

He laughed at her disappointed face.

"Don't fish for flattery. You won't get it from me. I will always tell you the truth."

Always. The word rang suddenly, echoing in her head with a deep significance. She glanced up at him, but he was watching the road. "Always" seemed a long time, a word like eternity. She sat thinking of this as the car moved on, the traffic thinned and they were away from the congested streets. The word "always" had startled her. Always was a very long time. It meant "for ever".

They were off the tarmac, the road was dusty again, and Sher Ali was beginning to drive fast. To her surprise, he apologised for the speed. "I shall have to get on," he said. "They will be wondering what has happened to us."

Arina knew that her grandmother had told her that she was going to spend a night in Karachi, but Karachi was behind them now. Where were they going? Was this the beginning of the journey to the hills?

"Where are we going?"

"I am taking you to Sagar House. You are going to spend the night there with Fram and Manika. Their family and ours have a very long friendship. It goes back almost a century. In fact they are almost family. They knew your father and mother – and possibly . . ."

"My grandmother?" Arina asked.

He said nothing to that, merely asked, "Were you not told where you were going?"

"Yes, yes, of course I was, but I forgot. There have been so many new things to think about and see." And you to meet, she thought, and half said under her breath, "One does not meet a tiger every day."

"What did you say?" he asked.

"Nothing, I was thinking aloud."

He looked down at her, frowning a little, but Arina succeeded in changing the subject. "Are these people from Chikor and Pakodi? I mean, are they from Azadpur?"

"No. Fram and Manika are Parsee. They are Zoroastrians. Do you know what that means?"

"Yes of course I know. They worship fire, and they have towers where they expose their dead to the hawks and crows and vultures."

He was amused. "Is that all you were told? These people, the Parsees, are more than that. They are a brilliantly clever and intelligent race, and most of them are extremely wealthy – old wealth. Charming, gentle people. Fram and Manika Dinshaw

61

are good examples. Actually, you spent the last few weeks before you left India in their house. They are kind and amusing. You will like them very much."

Arina had stopped listening to him. She was abruptly very conscious of being covered with dust, her clothes were wrinkled and sweat stained. Horrors! What sort of image was she going to present to these old friends of the family? Her hair – it felt like coir matting. She groaned and Sher Ali took his eyes from the road for long enough to say, "Are you all right? What's the matter?"

"I wish I had not lost my veil."

"Oh don't worry about that. Manika does not keep purdah. I told you, she is a Parsi – a very elegant woman."

"Thank you! That makes me feel even worse. I wanted the veil to hide behind. I am so dusty and untidy."

He looked at her again. "Yes, you are a bit rumpled and blown about. My fault, but they won't expect you to arrive looking like a fashion plate. I tell you this – they will be so delighted, as I was, to see that you wore *salwar* and *khemise*. We were all afraid that you would arrive in a fancy English copy of the way they think we dress, all nose rings and diamonds, or worse still, smothered in make-up and dressed in a tight sweater and a short skirt – oof, how awful that would have been. Have you always worn *salwar* and *khemise*?"

"Yes, except at school. Then I had to wear a uniform – a gym slip, or a costume if we went to the cinema." She laughed suddenly, a charming giggle more than a laugh.

"My grandmother – she was Lady Lyle all day, in public – and Zeena Begum at night. She wore the most beautiful saris and lots of jewellery. Even when she went out to dinner with friends, she was Zeena Begum at night. She looked very beautiful."

She suddenly realised that he was driving very fast, and not so smoothly, and that he looked furious. She had done it again, broken the law that said she must not talk about her beloved grandmother. At that moment, she almost hated him. But she would not show that she had noticed his displeasure.

"She would be shocked to see how I am looking, going to meet her old friends. I wish I could have washed and changed, or at least combed my hair."

"Well you cannot. We are almost there."

They were driving through traffic, camel carts, bullock carts, cattle and goats, and he was so enraged that he was behaving as if they were on an empty road. The speed was terrible. Arina closed her eyes gripped the rail in front of her and waited for the crash that was bound to come.

"It is all right, you may open your eyes now. In a minute you will see the sea, though I suppose you have had enough of that. But shortly you will see Sagar House."

The air seemed fresher, there was silence round them. She opened her eyes and saw a rugged terrain, dotted with clumps of sparsely leafed thorn trees. She could hear the sea. They turned off the main road down a narrow lane and in minutes they were running alongside the sea. She forgot to think of her appearance and began to enjoy the drive. Sher Ali, too, seemed to have become friendly again and was pointing out things of interest.

"See, this is where there used to be many wrecks. The currents here are dangerous and there are hidden rocks. Fram's family have lived here for generations. See, there are the gates."

Men were running to open the gates, men in uniform, each one with a small crest on his turban. The drive up to the house was long, with lawns on each side and well-kept hedges half hiding high walls. Arina began to feel afraid. Meeting strangers had always been difficult for her. She could go through the social paces, behave coolly and correctly, she had been well taught. But it was always an effort, even with her grandmother's poised and dignified presence to support her.

Now, dusty, crumpled and tired, alone and confused by all

the strangeness of the day, she looked at what appeared to be a slightly smaller version of Buckingham Palace, and was terrified that she would be sick, or faint, or that she would panic and run away, thus disgracing herself and the whole family, and most importantly the tiger.

Turning to speak to her as he switched off the engine, Sher Ali saw the stark panic on her face. She looked desperate, he was sure that if she could, she would get out of the car and flee. What kind of life had she lived with that terrible never-to-be-spoken-of grandmother that she should be so easily frightened now? She had been afraid when they met, he had seen the fear in her eyes, and yet she had stood up to him. She was not a coward, this little cat of his.

"Arina, light of my soul – do not be afraid of our friends! There is nothing here to fear. Come, Arina, these people are like your family, you will be made so welcome. They have been waiting with impatience to see you. Do not think of how you look – neither dust nor fatigue have dimmed your light. Come, let us go in together."

The tone of his voice reached her heart. A wave of soft colour swept over her face, her mouth curved into a smile as she looked up at him. He met her look, and was bewildered by his sudden reaction to her. Dusty, with her hair in a tangle, she did not look beautiful, but she was lit from within with a warmth of feeling that shone in her eyes and touched him deeply with no warning. He could not look away from her as they walked up the steps together to the open door.

They had been observed.

Manika Dinshaw was waiting at the door to welcome them. She saw the expression on Sher Ali's face, and recognised it for what it was. A man in love – or certainly deeply attracted. She saw, smiled to herself and went forward to welcome Arina warmly, her face expressing nothing but pleasure.

"My dear girl! At last – I am so delighted to see you back with us. It has been a long absence, but now, here you are, grown up." Grown up into a heart-breaker it seems, she thought, and turned to Sher Ali.

"Welcome back, Tiger. We were worried – Sakhi Mohammed brought stories of riots in the Clifton District, and said that the police were out. Did you run into the troubles?"

"No, I took the other road, so we saw nothing of it. I had to drive slowly, because I had Arina and she is not a speed fiend."

Manika swallowed her astonishment at the thought of Sher Ali driving slowly, and said, "Well, you had better go and see Fram, he is in the library waiting for you. Arina, come with me, you must be exhausted after the journey in that vehicle of Sher Ali's. We had hoped that you would be firm and insist on driving in the big car. We knew he would drive that little monster of his, but what possessed him to bring you in it?"

Was there a criticism in the soft voice? Perhaps she had done wrong, driving alone with Sher Ali? She looked anxiously at Manika, but saw no trace of anything but kindness and pleasure in her face.

"That is not a woman's car at all," Manika said. "What a terrible journey you must have had. Well, your luggage arrived in comfort, anyway. Come now, let us go into your rooms, where someone is waiting to see you. She has waited so long!"

Manika led her down a passage and opened a door. The room she took Arina into was enormous, and contained nothing but a four-poster bed draped with mosquito netting. There was a wide shuttered window, with a deep window seat, covered with cushions. A door led into another room, walled in mirrors, where an old woman with an armful of silks turned to see them come in.

"Piyari – my heart of gold, let me see you. Here is a promise fulfilled, I knew you would be sent. She has never broken a promise, I had no doubts. Have you forgotten me, in all these long years?"

Chunia, the legend. How could Chunia be forgotten? This old woman had been the beginning and the ending of every day, the one permanent loving guardian.

Chunia had saved Arina from death in the earthquake that had killed Arina's mother and father. As the house was falling around them, Chunia had pulled a tin bath over the baby and herself, and while hundreds died in that disaster, the baby and the old woman had survived.

It was Chunia Arina had cried for when, a terrified child of three, she had been taken away from everything she knew and was sent with Sushi to Scotland to live with her grandmother. The years had slipped away, the unknown had become loved and familiar, and gradually Chunia had faded in the memories of the child, and had become a legend, loved and honoured. Now, here she was, her single eye sparkling with tears as she looked for the child in the girl who stood before her.

"Do you remember me?" she asked again, and Arina went into that warm embrace, saying, "Oh, Chunia, my mother – how could I forget you?" And Manika had tears in her eyes as she watched the reunion.

But Chunia did not waste time in sentiment. Her child had returned to her, looking, as the old woman said, "like a beggar off the road – first a glass of tea, then we will get you a bath."

Sushi was sent running to bring the tea, another woman was unpacking cases that Arina did not recognise. Someone else's luggage? Had there been a mistake? Manika reassured her. "No, these boxes came down from Azadpur, Gulrukh Begum had sent everything she thought you would need – enough for a small army of pretty girls, just wait until you see."

Arina's pleased surprise was mixed with dismay. "Oh, dear," she said.

Manika asked at once, "What is it?" Don't you want to see these saris and the jewels that go with them? Are you too tired, perhaps you would like to rest first?"

"Oh no, it is not that. It is that Sher Ali seemed to be alarmed by the amount of baggage I already have."

"Oh, fiddle!" said Manika. "What nonsense! What does it have to do with him? Is his bride not to have her trousseau? He should see what some brides have! Don't let Tiger bully you."

"Is that what he is called?" asked Arina.

"Of course – what else? Don't tell me you have been being respectful and calling him Sher Ali all the time. You will find Tiger a very suitable name for that young man – and in any case he likes his nickname. Tell me now, piyari, how is Zeena?"

"I am not supposed to talk about her. Sher – I mean, Tiger – gets angry."

"He does? Oh, that is his grandmother, Gulrukh Begum, still obsessed by the family scandal, silly old woman."

"No – even my grandmother made me promise not to mention her name in front of the family."

"Poor Zeena – it is time that that old scandal was forgotten. Well, perhaps you had better not talk about her in front of the family up in Azadpur – up there, ringed round by those mountains, the people of the family still live in the past. Good in some respects, bad in others. But certainly, to your own husband there should be nothing you cannot say, or discuss. For heaven's sake, do not let Gulrukh Begum interfere with your marriage. She is a silly old woman, trying to be like her horrible mother, but she cannot achieve her desire, she is too kind-hearted and honest to be like that old witch Zurah Begum. You will just have to be firm with her. Now tell me how Zeena Begum is. I was only a child when she left, but I have never forgotten her. We all – the little ones – thought her story was so romantic! Is she well, has she been happy?"

Arina could almost hear her grandmother's voice saying, "remember your promise". She felt she had already broken it too often, and was determined not to break it again. She was

67

trying to think of a polite way of refusing Manika's request, when she was saved by a commotion outside the door of the room, and a woman servant coming in to say that visitors had come who wished to see Lady Dinshaw. Manika rose with a sigh.

"I shall have to go – in any case, you must be longing to have a rest. I will come for you this evening – we usually gather on the *chibutra* to have a drink and watch the sun fall into the sea, so I shall look forward to seeing you then." She kissed Arina and smiled her way out of the room.

Five minutes later, Arina was drinking tea, pale amber tea with a jasmine flower floating in it. A special glass, with a silver holder. "Chunia! You have kept my glass all these years – indeed, now I know I have come home at last."

"Of course I have kept it. What was I to do with it, throw it away? I knew Zeena Begum would keep her word and send you back. Finish your tea now, and come and bathe."

Eight

The bath was as Arina remembered it. A marble square in the floor with a drain leading from it, and a jar big enough to hold a man, from which Chunia and Sushi ladled water all over her.

"Tell me, child, is this true – Sushi says that in Glen Laraig you sit in the water, and wash your body, and you do not change the water, or rinse in clean water? Chee, how can you get clean in that way? This way the dirt from your body is washed away, and you come out pure and clean," said Chunia as she poured a constant stream of water all over Arina, from her head to her feet.

"Chunia – enough," Arina said, gasping. "How will I ever get my hair dry?"

"I will comb it dry. You had all the sands of the desert in it – did you want to keep it like that? Soon it will be like silk again, and it will not take long. You will see."

Arina longed to be done with what was beginning to look like a long ritual of dressing, she wanted to get out and see the house, and sit with them on the *chibutra*. But Chunia did things in her own time, and was not to be hurried. Sushi remembered Arina's scrambled dressing in the mornings in Scotland, and smiled to herself. Her young mistress was going to find more than one change in her life. Sitting in the window while Chunia drew the comb through her wet hair, Arina looked out at the blazing sky, scarlet and gold with sunset. She was not going to see the sun fall into the sea this evening, that was becoming

69

obvious. But she could not hurry Chunia. After all it had been a long day, and the steady draw of the comb through her hair was soporific. When Chunia had finished, though, Arina woke up and was once again impatient to see the house.

"Sit, my child," said Chunia. "There is plenty of time. See, it is almost sunset, the hour of prayer for the household. Of course, Fram Sahib and the Manika Sahiba are not believers, but all the others pray. You will be dressed and ready when the Lady Sahib comes for you. Sit, and be at peace, my golden heart."

Arina sighed and resigned herself. Looking into the garden she saw several men standing and kneeling and rising in the beautiful ritual movements of Moslem worship. Faintly she could hear the *muezzin* calling from a mosque. It was only the whisper of a call, it might have been a voice from the past, calling from another mosque far up in the mountains, a call to prayer from a forgotten sunset long ago.

Her eyes fixed on the figure of one of the men at prayer, and she recognised Sher Ali, tall and bareheaded in the golden light, praying with the other men. She wondered if these prayers were just a matter of form for him, or if he prayed with meaning. So much to find out, so much to learn about a man who had, until this morning, been only a painted figure in an old portrait.

Sher Ali, sent off so firmly by Manika to find Fram in the library, went very reluctantly. He wanted to stay with the women, listen to them talking, study this girl, Arina, who was a puzzle to him. How she could change! One moment a frightened-looking little bedraggled cat of a girl, the next, a lightning change into a beauty who touched his heart with a smile that seemed to promise everything he had ever wanted a woman to be. But was that what she was promising? What was she thinking behind that seductive smile, those strange beautiful eyes? She was a mystery, one that he wanted to unravel.

It was exciting to think that she belonged to him. He thought
of all that was hidden from him, all that was his to discover,
he was an explorer ready to discover a whole new country
of womanhood, wrapped up in one girl – untouched, unseen,
except by him. He was smiling at these thoughts as he walked
into the library where Fram rose with words of welcome. But
his smile faded when he saw that they were not alone. There
was another man there, and Sher Ali recognised him without
pleasure.

Elegant, as always, handsome and very much at his ease,
Yusuf Dyal lifted a hand in casual greeting.

Sher Ali embraced Fram and apologised for his late arrival,
turning a look at Yusuf Dyal that nicely combined curiosity
with offence. "Yusuf?" he enquired.

Yusuf smiled but, before he could speak, Fram said, "Yes,
your friend has had a long and tiring journey to bring you a
message from Gulrukh Begum. It brings us disappointment,
but perhaps you will find some of it pleasing. I will leave
Yusuf to tell you himself. I have ordered food and drinks for
you both – just snacks, as there will be a full-scale banquet
tonight. Yusuf, you will of course spend the night here with
us, before resuming your journey?"

Yusuf accepted the offer with thanks, and Fram left the two
young men alone. Sher Ali was disturbed. A message from his
grandmother, what can have possessed her to send a message
by hand. Couldn't she have used the telephone?

Yusuf settled down in his chair again and made no effort
to give Sher Ali the message.

The tiger, still standing, held out his hand. "My grandmother's letter?"

"Oh, no letter, dear boy. The old lady was in too much of a
hurry, and rather overwrought – she could not have written.
It is a verbal message, I'm afraid. She tried to telephone, but
could not get through, all the lines up that way are down.
I do not know what your plans are, but you may have to

71

change them. Your grandmother wants you back in Madore as soon as it is possible. There has been serious rioting in Faridkote. It is under martial law, and as the road to Azadpur leads through Faridkote, she feels it is impossible to hold your marriage festivities there. She expects to have the ceremony and the festivities in Madore instead. She is right, of course. This is a difficult time to get a large group of people together, particularly when most of them are ruling princes – don't you agree, dear boy?"

"Yes, of course I agree," said Sher Ali, gritting his teeth at having to agree with anything Yusuf said and loathing the patronising tone of his "dear boy".

Sher Ali's dislike of Yusuf Dyal went back a long way. He could not explain his antagonism to himself or to anyone else, for that matter. He only knew that he disliked everything about Yusuf Dyal: his looks, his voice, his maddening ability to be Sher Ali's equal in everything. They had been rivals since their school days, rivals at Sandhurst. Whatever success one achieved the other would quickly match. Yusuf seemed to treat this rivalry as a friendly competition, and in fact made it his business to appear to be a close friend of Sher Ali. But the tiger's aversion to Yusuf seemed to grow with every year. Now, to have Yusuf bringing messages of importance about his own marriage was almost more than he could bear, and he was suddenly convinced that Yusuf knew this, and took great pleasure in it.

When the servant brought in the "small eats" and the iced beer Fram had promised, Manika herself also came into the room. Sher Ali adored Manika and would normally have taken her hands and kissed them, but he found it impossible to be natural in front of Yusuf. Both men stood up when she came in and, after smiling at Sher Ali, she greeted Yusuf saying, "I am glad you are able to stay tonight. Have you brought a man, or would you like one of my servants to unpack for you?"

"Oh, no thank you, Lady Dinshaw. My chap will deal with

it, if someone will show him where to take my baggage. It is very good of you to put me up at short notice – and on such an important family occasion. I am honoured."

Sher Ali was seething inwardly. Why did Yusuf have to stay? He could perfectly well have gone to a hotel. It was effrontery for him to take advantage of Manika and Fram, when it should have been obvious to him that this was an occasion when they should have been alone with their guests. But all he could do was to keep quiet.

Manika merely smiled and nodded, and told the waiting *khitmagar* to show the Nawab Sahib's servant where to take his master's baggage. She turned to Sher Ali. "Dear Tiger, it is lovely to have you here. Such a happy time in our lives. You will be glad to know that Arina is resting, and will join us on the *chibutra* at sunset. When do you plan to leave? I understand your plans have changed."

"Yes," said Sher Ali, "I was hoping that we could stay for two or three days, but it seems that I – no, *we* – will have to leave tomorrow.

Manika sighed, her expression very sad. "We hoped to see more of you both, especially as we will not be able to attend your wedding."

Sher Ali could not believe what he heard. These were close friends, and he had been looking forward to entertaining them again up in his own home.

"But I do not understand. Why are you not coming? You must be there."

Sadly, Manika said, "Of course we would come if it were left to us. But Fram says it would be dangerous for both your family, and us. Isn't it ridiculous? Everything has changed. Did Fram tell you that we will be leaving here?"

Sher Ali stared at her, aghast. "Leaving Sagar House? What is this? What has happened? You can not leave here, it is your home, you have always been here."

"There does not seem to be any use for the word 'always' – everything is uncertain now," said Manika.

Sher Ali had forgotten Yusuf's presence, he went to Manika and put his arm round her, saying, "You are my second mother, Fram is my second father – how can you say these things to me without telling me what is wrong? What has happened?"

"Come on, old boy," Yusuf said quietly, "you know what has happened. Two things – first, independence, then, worst of all, partition. We are Pakistan now, and Fram and Manika are not believers."

Sher Ali turned on him like the animal he was named for. "What do you mean? How dare you say such things! What kind of a believer are you? Your grandfather, as I recall, was Hindu. Fram and Manika are Parsi, no one could be more welcome – there is no place in the world where they could not live peaceably, and you know it. Be quiet, who asked you to give your stupid opinion?" His shock, and the rage that filled him, blazed in his eyes, and Yusuf, who had sat down, stood up quickly as if he felt he would need to defend himself.

Manika was alarmed, too. "Sher Ali – stop! You are angry for no reason! Yusuf Dyal is right. We are not believers, and there are fanatics here, who do not want us. Fram has received threatening letters – very unpleasant threats, warning him to get out. My old amah was stoned last week when she went to the market."

"I find this so hard to believe." Sher Ali's rage had subsided as he listened to Manika, and he spoke quietly, but Yusuf had not relaxed, or returned to his chair. Sher Ali had never before shown his loathing for his rival – more, his hatred – so plainly, and Yusuf now stood watching him carefully, as he listened to Manika speaking to Sher Ali.

Manika took her hand from Sher Ali's arm, seeing that he was calmer, and said, "You find it hard to believe? So do I, but it is true, my amah is in hospital, and Fram does not care to risk anything worse happening to any of our servants, or indeed to us. I must tell you that things have been happening here that perhaps you have not heard about. Armenian friends of ours have had their house burned over their heads. The Partap Singhs have left for Bombay because of threatening letters, and the Warria family have sent their children to stay with Cuckoo's mother in Delhi while they pack their house up preparatory to leaving for Delhi themselves – they, too, will go for good. Believe me, Tiger, we must go. It is time."

"But this is ridiculous. You are letting a handful of fanatical *goondas* drive you from your ancestral lands, your family home! I cannot believe this. Listen Manika, come up to Madore, and stay there with us until this business has quietened down, which it will do. The people who are causing this trouble are nothing to do with our government! As long as the Army move in to sort them out, everything will be as it was once."

Manika shook her head. "Oh, my dear Tiger, do your really believe what you are saying? I am afraid you are wrong. Nothing will ever be the same again. I am tired of living like this, with armed guards on the gates and patrolling the gardens, waking up at night wondering if I can smell smoke, or hear strange voices? I am tired of being afraid. I would give anything to come with you and stay up in Madore in peace, but I cannot do that. For one thing, we might bring trouble to your family – I mean real trouble, danger. I cannot risk that. Also, Fram wants to reach Delhi as soon as possible. We have not lived in our old house there since Fram's father died, and it needs a great deal done to it."

Yusuf had listened to Sher Ali and Manika in silence, now he broke in to ask when Manika had decided to leave. "It is no longer so easy to cross into India, Lady Dinshaw. You will have to go by sea, I think, and go up to Delhi by the old route – not simple if you are taking all your belongings with you "

He paused and then added, "No, not at all simple. It is not known here if the mail train from Bombay is running. You will very likely have to get to Delhi by road, with a train of bullock carts laden with all your possessions – a form of transport not known in the days of the Raj. To me, it is as if civilisation has taken a backward step. Terrible, is it not?"

Listening to him, Sher Ali felt furiously angry again. It was unkind, he thought, to speak of all the difficulties of crossing into India from Pakistan when Manika was already worried and distressed. Why did this oaf Yusuf have to express his opinions and make suggestions anyway, he was not a close friend of the Dinshaws, and why was he asking Manika when she was leaving? He could do nothing to help, so why ask? On top of the hatred he felt for Yusuf, he now felt a strong feeling of distrust.

Before Manika could answer Yusuf, Sher Ali said quickly, "I don't suppose that you have had time to think of dates yet, Manika, that will be for Fram to decide when he has thought it all over."

As Yusuf was speaking, Fram came in. At once, he said, looking at Sher Ali's disturbed expression, "I see Manika has told you of our plans. I am very sad to think that we will not be present at your marriage, Tiger, and now, instead of having you here for two or three days, you will have to leave tomorrow. I have sent Moti Lal down to the main station to ask about the mail train timings. They change from day to day – indeed, sometimes from hour to hour – and you have a great deal of baggage. Come, boy, do not look so distraught. We, too, are going to be moving soon – I want to make a start while everything is moderately quiet. We will leave in a great caravan – I have all the servants and their families to move as well!"

"Will we be going by sea, Fram? Yusuf Dyal says there are difficulties. Manika had moved to stand close to Fram, who answered her soothingly.

"Manika, I cannot promise you a simple journey, but leave that side of it to me. All I ask of you is that you organise the servants and the packing."

"Of course I will do that, and I promise I will not trouble you with questions if you will tell me when you have decided which way we will travel. Delhi seems such a long way off now." "Delhi is exactly where it was, my beloved. To worry only makes things seem worse than they are. Trust me." As he was speaking, Fram looked across at Yusuf Dyal and Sher Ali was convinced that he had seen an expression of dislike cross the older man's face. "We must not make Tiger's friend here bored with discussion of our plans," Fram continued. Nawab Sahib, we usually foregather on the *chibutra* at sunset before we dine. I expect you would like to go to your room and have a bath and change to refresh yourself after your journey. Rama, show the Nawab Sahib to his room, please."

Yusuf Dyal made no argument. He smiled, thanked Fram for his kindness, and followed the old servant out of the room. Very soon after this, Manika, her forehead still creased with thoughts that were not relaxing, made her apologies to Sher Ali, saying as she was leaving, "I do not have to show you to your room, Tiger, you are in your usual quarters. Sher Ali thought of how many, many times he had stayed with the Dinshaws in this house, always welcomed as a son – and he was sure he saw tears in Manika's eyes as she left the room. He was sure that, like him, she was sorrowful that those days were now over.

"Fram," Sher Ali spoke. "I suggested to Manika that when we leave, she should come with us. I am sure that I can put off our departure for a day, and take Manika to Madore where she can stay until things have quietened down. Surely there is no need for this upheaval."

"Tiger, you are speaking from your heart, not listening to your brain. You know quite well that things aren't going to settle down for some years. Do you want us to stay here, facing trouble, and perhaps worse than that, for five years? It will take at least that for this country to quieten down, as you put it. I could perhaps face it, but not with Manika, she would worry herself to death. As to her going to stay with you, no. It is a kind thought, but I will not allow it. I ask you to think of what has happened in the last year. Have you forgotten the bloody massacre of those days?"

"But Fram," said Sher Ali, "that time is past! There have been no killings on the railways for some months."

"True. The trains are well guarded now with armed police and there are troops at every station as well. But the latest news is not good, inter-communal rioting has started up in some of the hill villages, and there have been killings on the roads – the blood lust on both sides has not yet been satiated. Madore is still quiet, but Manika's presence in your home might spark off a riot – if one is not an orthodox Moslem, one is a target. A Parsi lady, with her pale, delicate features can look very much like a high-caste Hindu to eyes crazed with fanaticism, and there are many fanatics, make no mistake about that – in all religions. Think no more of that plan, Tiger."

As he spoke, the sound of the sunset call to prayer from the distant mosque sounded clearly in the room. Fram smiled sadly, saying. "How often I have heard that cry from the mosque, heard it with pleasure and reverence. Now it fills me and many others with fear, it could be a tocsin. Go now, beloved boy, and make your prayer. Add my petition to yours – let peace come to dwell among us again."

Without a word, Sher Ali left him and went to join the others, among them servants who were of his religion, praying in the garden. He made his prayers with fervour, not knowing that bright, wondering eyes watched him through the lattice-work covering a nearby window.

Nine

Arina watched Sher Ali praying, and prayed herself, murmuring the prayer she had learned when she was received into the faith as a three-year-old child.

"In the name of Allah the Beneficent, the Merciful. Praise be to Allah, Lord of the Worlds, the Beneficent, the Merciful, Owner of the Day of Judgement. Thee alone we worship, thee alone we ask for help. Show us the straight path. The path of those whom thou has favoured. Not the path of those who earn thine anger, nor of those who go astray."

As she said the last words of the *surah*, Arina saw that Sher Ali had also finished his prayer and was walking away. The fact that they had been praying together seemed to her to be a tie between them, something she had not felt before, and she almost called to him, but Chunia was telling her to come away from the latticed window to finish her dressing, and Arina, obedient to a voice she had never forgotten, went to her at once.

She stood deep in thought as the two women, Chunia and Sushi, chose the discarded clothing with no reference to her Arina's thoughts took her a long way. She had so much to learn about this new life. Already she had learned a little. She felt that she was emerging from dreams and shadows of her grandmother's past, escaping from memories that she was not sure were hers, reaching, perhaps, for realities. Suddenly she felt there was nothing to fear, she was in her own country, even if it was still unknown in this new guise, it was still her home.

She came out of her thoughts and began to take an interest in what was going on.

Chunia had been dressing her as a child dresses its favourite doll, choosing each garment carefully. At last she was satisfied. A long green tunic over full green trousers. Little green velvet slippers, useless for any walking except on deeply carpeted floors. Chunia stood back, looked, and approved. "That is well, my child. Now here is a gold chain for your neck and jewels for your ears. These things belonged to the mother of your grandmother. Here is a veil, a cloud to lightly veil beauty. Eh, it is good that you were taught to wear your clothes as one accustomed to the best. Now," said Chunia, satisfied with her work, "now, look at yourself and take pleasure as one who cares to please the eyes of others."

Smiling at the old woman, Arina looked into the mirrored walls of the dressing-room. She blinked, and looked again.

Shadows had gathered, it seemed, and then parted, to let in clear light. Who was it who stood there so still, looking back at Arina? A stranger from a past she had never known. A girl with long dark hair, with gold gleaming at her throat, and green fire at her ears. Who was it, wide-eyed, silent, green-robed?

A breath, a whisper, sounded in the room.

"Muna!"

The mirrored walls seemed to shiver as if a powerful wind had blown through the room. For a moment, time and space had lost meaning, had no place here. Chunia stood as still as her mistress, while shadows moved and wavered in the reflecting walls.

"Love is stronger than death – hold thou to that."

It was Manika's entry that changed the atmosphere, brought the present back to the room. She tapped at the door, and swept straight in and exclaimed with pleasure.

"Arina! The dust and travel stains all gone, and what beauty is revealed! You look like the Zeena I remember, and yet it is not altogether Zeena – someone else, who is it? I never saw

Gulbadan Begum, your mother – or Yasmin the beloved, your grandmother's mother. Chunia, who does she look like? You must know – is it Gulbadan Begum?"

Chunia, picking up discarded silks and helping Sushi put them away said firmly, "She looks like all the women of her family. Who else, Lady Sahiba?"

All three women looked at Arina, who was still gazing into the mirror as if she was looking for someone – something – a lost, half-forgotten face, a crystal voice, words once spoken still sounding down the years? As if some enchantment had touched her too, Manika said slowly, "I once saw a portrait – long ago. Where did I see it? I cannot remember, all I know is that you are the girl in that picture – it seems so—"

Arina turned away from her reflections and said quietly, "Tell me – who is Muna?"

The two maid-servants were silent, exchanging glances, waiting. It was Manika who answered after a few moments. "Muna? Muna the Beautiful. She was a very famous lady, I think there is some family connection, I must ask Fram, but it is her portrait I was thinking of. Years ago, when my mother took me up to Chikor, we went one day to a neighbouring state, to meet the old ruler, Jiwan Khan. The portrait was on the walls of the old palace. The portrait of Muna, the Rose of Madore. That is who you resemble. I can see her now – why did you suddenly think of her?"

"Because I think she was there."

Before Arina could answer, Chunia came forward. "Ayee, child, do not frighten yourself and the lady! It is nothing, Lady Sahiba, she is not used to the mirrored walls, she saw herself reflected, what else? And she is tired and saw her reflection and was amazed – that is all! Muna was never here."

Manika was frowning, and looked very shaken, but her voice was steady, and she tried to smile as she said, "Well, Arina my dear, now you know who you look like. Your resemble a beauty, the golden Rose of Madore. Come, let us join the men on the *chibutra*, and taste the evening air. The wind has fallen, and there is no dust. It has been a tormented day. This is not the season for dust storms, but nothing is as it should be, it seems. You will soon be away from the dust and all the worries of this place – the closer you get to the hills, peace comes to you. As you know, I am not a hill woman, I was born by the sea in Bombay, but I long for the hills and the peace one finds there. I wish with all my heart that I could come with you. I felt as if my son was bringing home a daughter to me, when Tiger told me he was bringing you here. Now I will not even have the joy of seeing you married – how strange life has become."

"Oh, I wish you could come with us – I do not understand why you cannot come." Arina was speaking sincerely, but suddenly stopped, staring at a man who was standing beside the door in front of them – an armed sentry, who stepped forward to open the door for them.

Manika nodded, saying, "You are shocked to see that, Arina? I am, too. Every outside door of this house is guarded by armed sentries – all ex-service men from the Punjab regiments. At night there are twelve men on duty and the garden is patrolled night and day. So far we have only been troubled by threatening letters, except for my old amah, Agnes, who was stoned and badly hurt in the bazaar. Friends of ours, an Armenian family, had their house burned to the ground, and other friends are to leave this place for good. We are going too – and that is part of the reason why we cannot come to your marriage. Do you understand? You will have heard of the terrible times that attended the partition of India. Everything is still unsettled, no one knows what will happen next. What madness all this seems! But I should not be speaking of it to you. Do not think of it – thank God it will not touch you and Tiger. I must say no more, I am putting shadows across what is to be a happy celebration tonight. Come, my dear Arina, I see Fram and Sher Ali, arguing as usual – and the other man is a nawab of one of the newly named provinces, East Pakistan. He came with messages from Gulrukh Begum. I was hoping for a pleasant family evening until he arrived like a black crow, bringing bad news. But we had to ask him to stay, once he was here. I will leave Tiger to tell you the new plans."

She smiled across the wide *chibutra* towards the three men, her arm round Arina, saying, "Tiger, look what I have brought you – you do not deserve her, bringing her over those roads in that terrible car, but she has recoverd herself, and is going to ornament our evening with her presence."

The men all stood up. Sher Ali had changed his clothes. He could no longer be mistaken for an Englishman or, indeed, for anything other than what he was: a handsome prince of Pakistan – in what looked like a particularly evil temper.

Arina stared at him in alarm, barely noticing that he was now wearing a bright green turban and a green brocade *achkan* over Punjabi trousers. He looked taller than ever, and towered over his host, Fram-ji Dinshaw.

However, the other man, now rising to his feet, was as tall as Sher Ali and equally handsome. He was wearing a dinner jacket, but no one could mistake him for an Englishman. He was unusually dark skinned for a northerner, and his eyes looked black, though it was difficult to tell. She could only give him a swift glance, as Fram, also wearing a dinner jacket, had come up to take her hand and welcome her.

"Indeed Manika, you are right – here is the light of our evening and the cause for this happy celebration. Arina, welcome back – the last time I saw you, you were very small indeed. A little girl of three, and in great distress. You wept miserably for Chunia, left behind in Madore, but you do not remember those tears, I hope, now that everything has come so right, you are back in your own country to begin a new life – and you even have Chunia, the faithful one, with you at last. We wish you lasting happiness."

As she thanked Fram gracefully, thinking what a charming old man he was, Arina saw the gentleman she was to spend her life with, approaching rapidly. She had a strong desire to run away, what on earth was the matter with him, he looked so angry?

She saw a confused Manika glance at him, and Fram also looked surprised as he said, "Tiger – you may speak with Arina for a few minutes, then I am going to take her away from you."

Oh yes, thought Arina, please take me away, and the sooner the better! Any feelings of being close to Sher Ali had now gone. This was a furious stranger – how could she be expected to cope with him alone, to marry him? He seemed so changeable that she could scarcely recognise him from one minute to the next. Now he was in front of her, bending towards her. He could not be about to disgrace her by kissing her in public, surely not? In fact he looked more likely to bite her. She had to force herself not to step back as he leaned closer.

"Where is your veil?" he asked, through clenched teeth. "Cover your face at once, we are not all family here! How dare you come out without a veil."

She had forgotten all about her veil – it had fallen back from her head and was lying on her shoulders, so fine that it was difficult to see. With shaking hands, she pulled it up, and drew it across her face, only leaving her eyes free – or did he expect her to cover them as well? There was probably a rule about it. Her hands felt as if they did not belong to her, but it was rage that made them tremble, not fear. How dared he speak like that to her, in front of a stranger? This marriage was not going to take place, that was quite certain.

She would speak to Manika, she would understand. She would stay here with them, and when they had arranged a passage for her, she would return to Scotland and her grandmother. She faced Sher Ali, gave him one flashing, furious glare, then pulled her veil up so that it covered her eyes as well, and, turning her back, she walked away towards Manika.

Angry as he was, Sher Ali could not help smiling to himself as he watched his bride-to-be walk away. The little cat had come out from behind her elegant beauty. As she stepped out on to the *chibutra*, Sher Ali couldn't believe how beautiful she looked! He had stared in silence, forgetting to go forward to greet her and present her to Fram, forgetting everything at the sight of her, floating towards him in her green silks, and then he had heard Yusuf Dyal draw in his breath in a lascivious sigh, and heard him murmur, "Wah! what a pearl."

Dyal! How dared he! This was Sher Ali's affianced. Dyal should not have set eyes on her, but should have turned away his head. Oh, what has my grandmother done, sending this libertine down to ruin what should have been a perfect, family evening! And what was Arina thinking, displaying herself in all her beauty, like a dancing girl of the street, bareheaded, barefaced, not even making a token gesture at drawing up her veil as a modest girl should? But then, she had meant nothing, I am sure, thought Sher Ali. She is innocent, she who was taken from her own country and her own family and sent away to be brought up by *that* woman whose name must not be mentioned in the palaces of Chikor, Pakodi and Panchghar – *that* woman, Zeena, who had already brought shame and disaster to those princely states. She had obviously not told Arina all that she should have, had not taught her the necessary customs of a well-bred girl.

But I was too harsh. Arina did not know that there was a stranger present I should not have spoken to her so roughly, thought Sher Ali with remorse. I should have taken her to one side, and told her quietly – I believe I frightened her again, her hands were shaking as she pulled up that totally useless – almost transparent – veil. A veil like that was perfectly adequate for a family gathering, but not for a party where there were strangers that vile man Dyal – who should not be here at all. He made me lose my temper – I was brutally rude to Arina. The look she turned on me had no fear in it,

85

only rage, and hatred. I must put that right before the evening is over, she must not go to her bed hating me. I must make my peace with her, tell her about the change in our plans for tomorrow, ask her to forgive me, explain that I am not angry with her, but with the liberty that that swine took, daring to look her in the face!

Sher Ali hurriedly turned away from thoughts of Dyal, he was getting worked up all over again. He would speak to Arina now.

Arina was walking in the garden with Fram. He had seen the stormy distress in her eyes as she turned sharply away from Sher Ali, and walked towards Manika. He was afraid that she would burst into tears. Manika had sent him an appealing look, and he had intercepted Arina, taking her hand and saying, "Arina, come with me and see our strange garden."

Now she walked beside him along the paths of the garden. It was a very stylised garden, set out in geometric flower-beds, with paths paved in old bricks now faded with time into a pale rose colour, laid in immaculate herring-bone pattern. The flower-beds were brilliant with marigolds and zinnias, and many bushes starred with the white flowers of jasmine made the air sweet with their scent. They strolled in silence, and slowly, her hand held firmly in Fram's warm grasp, Arina grew calmer. Her decision was still firm, she would have to leave and go back to Scotland. It seemed the only way to avoid marriage with this remarkably difficult man, but all the same she had a lump in her throat, it was hard to think of leaving this longed-for country. Also, for a short time she had felt great happiness in what had seemed to be a close understanding with the man she was contracted to marry. That feeling of closeness had gone, and emptiness had been left in its place. She felt she had lost someone very important to her, a man who mattered more than any other person had ever mattered. Yet, she told herself, perhaps she had wandered back into one of her dreams, perhaps that man had never existed except in her mind, perhaps he was only a figure in an old picture after all.

She sighed at this thought, and Fram looked down at her. "That was a very sad sigh, my dear. Are you feeling homesick, missing your grandmother, the beautiful Zeena?"

"If I was," said Arina sadly, "I would be in trouble if I said so!"

"What do you mean?" asked Fram, standing still to turn and look at her. Under his kind, puzzled look, Arina decided to tell him the truth.

"I am not allowed to speak of her to her family or anyone else. To her family she is dead and buried, and I must never mention her name."

"Is that what Tiger told you?"

"No. He just gets angry. My grandmother made me promise that I would never mention her name – I am breaking my promise now by speaking of her to you."

"You poor child, and I suppose Tiger has been brought up by Gulrukh Begum to believe all that old nonsense too. That old story should be allowed to die and be forgotten. But of course, up in those high hills, cut off for half the year when the snow closes the passes, old stories live on and grow in the telling. To be honest, dear Gulrukh Begum, as she has aged, and grown old in widowhood, has become deeply entrenched in the old customs and old beliefs. But she loved Zeena very much, and you will find in time that she will be unable to refrain from asking for news of her cousin, and all will be normal. As for Tiger, do not allow yourself to be distressed by him as he is at present. Poor Tiger, he is suffering from that very tiresome disease . . . he has a bad attack of jealousy. He and Dyal have been rivals for most of their lives, Sher Ali has always hated him. Now on top of the old rivalry, there is jealousy over you. Very difficult for Tiger to handle. You must be patient with him, and do not be hurt if he is sharp with you. Oh, Arina my child! You two have so much to learn about each other! And one of the things you must learn is patience."

"And Tiger – What does *he* have to learn?" said Arina, beginning to feel ruffled again.

Fram laughed. "Sheathe those little claws, Arina. He has much to learn, and the most important thing is that he must admit to himself that he has fallen in love at last."

Arina shook her head. "In love? With me? I cannot believe that. He seems to dislike everything about me, I disappoint him, I think. And yet . . ." She paused, remembering how Sher Ali looked when he smiled, his kindness when he saw she was frightened in the car, and his tender concern for her when she was nervous of arriving at Sagar House. That changeable man?

"I do not know what to believe, I think that he is like the animal he is named for, uncertain and dangerous."

"Poor Tiger. You make a hard judgement. Wait and see, as time passes, what you will find in the man you will marry."

But Arina was still shaken by her last encounter with the tiger. She said sadly, "I could wait and see, but I think it might take a long time to find out what he is really like. Suppose I discover that I am right in my judgement and that I am then tied for life to a man I do not like. What then?"

"That is a risk you are both taking, Arina," said Fram gravely, and for the first time Arina thought of Sher Ali's side of this contract, to take a bride he had NOT chosen for himself – surely that was hard? He had seemed to accept the situation, but what if he was not content with it? Perhaps that accounted for his changeable behaviour. She would have to ask him, make him tell her the truth, then if he did not wish to marry her, surely they could work it out together? She would ask Fram if he would make it possible for her to speak to Sher Ali alone, as soon as it was possible. She turned to speak to Fram and saw Sher Ali walking towards them.

Having made the decision to make his peace with Arina,

Sher Ali had gone over to where Manika was talking to Yusuf Dyal, and asked where Arina was. "Fram has taken her into the garden to show her the only rose that has flowered this year – go down and join them, Tiger."

Smiling unpleasantly, Yusuf Dyal joined in. "Yes, do go down, old boy. It is most amusing to see the famous Tiger ensnared by a girl. Incidently, I would not spend too long in a wooing if I were you. Someone else might step in and pick the fruit you covet. If I ever saw fruit ripe for the picking, I saw it tonight."

The words, the tone, the suggestions were so vile that Sher Ali could hardly keep his hands from the man's throat. Only Manika's presence kept him from committing murder, and Yusuf Dyal knew it, leaning back against the balustrade of the *chibutra*, smiling and completely at his ease.

"What a very unpleasant remark, Nawab Sahib!" Manika's voice was cold. "I am surprised that a man of your breeding should say such a thing. We have the pleasure of considering Arina to be our daughter, I should watch your manners if I were you." She turned her back on Dyal and whispered quickly, "Tiger, calm yourself – the words of a fool are not important, they leave no mark. Go down to the garden, Fram will show you where to take Arina so that she sees the precious rose. I wish to speak a little longer with the Nawab Sahib, then I may join you." There was icy anger in her words, and Sher Ali had never seen her so troubled.

He did not wait to hear what she was going to say to Yusuf Dyal, he allowed himself one look at his enemy's discomfited expression, smiled unpleasantly, and walking away, went down the steps to the garden.

He saw Arina with Fram, so slowed his step but was close enough to them to hear Fram saying, "That is a risk you are both taking, Arina," and see Arina stand deep in thought. What were they talking about? What were those thoughts that were making Arina look so sorrowful? Would he ever know what she was thinking? They did not look like friends taking an easy stroll through a garden – they looked so serious. However, as Sher Ali came up to them, Fram smiled.

"I wondered when you would come, Tiger. Is Manika coming, too?"

"I think not – she stayed to have a few words with Yusuf Dyal, that son of Eblis. She may come down after that, I think."

"Ah," said Fram, "A little plain speaking, perhaps? I had better go and either soothe ruffled feathers, or ruffle them still further, depending. I leave you to enjoy the sweet air of the garden with Arina. There is a rose I have been guarding to show her, a sweet white rose."

The two now left facing each other were not at ease. Arina did not lift her eyes. If she had looked up at Sher Ali, she would have seen regret and embarrassment in the eyes that had blazed at her earlier.

Sher Ali found himself annoyed by the veil that he had insisted on earlier, the veil that had caused so much trouble. Although the veil was light and transparent, when it was stirred and blown into folds by the mind, it shadowed her face, and hid her eyes. If only she would look up! Softly, he said, "Please will you look at me, Arina Begum, and tell me that you forgive my bad manners?"

Arina looked up, registering the tone of his voice rather than his the words, saw his expression and, without stopping to think, said what she felt. "I can forgive you, if you will forgive me for being what I am, Tiger."

She had never said his name before. This was a wonder to him, hearing his name in her voice, which he had already noted as soft and attractive. He was silenced by how gentle his name sounded when uttered from her lips. Then he saw that his silence worried her. "I don't understand you. What is there about you that I have to forgive, soul of my soul?"

90

He had switched into his own language and she answered it in the same tongue.

"I am what I am, Lord. Not what you would wish me to be, if you had the choice."

"What do you mean? What choice."

He looks at me, she thought, as if I have gone mad. How can I continue talking about this embarrassing subject if I am going to have to repeat everything twice? She looked away from him and said, "The choice – the *liberty* to choose the woman you want for your wife. The kind of girl you want – I do not know what you thought I would be, but I can see that I have not pleased you."

"What have I done? I have brought you sorrow for no good reason, because of that misbegotten dog, Yusuf Dyal. What have I made you feel, what are you trying to tell me? Do you want to be free of this marriage, I will set you free of it, if you so wish – only tell me your thoughts and wishes, Arina."

"My thoughts," said Arina, convinced now that this contract was as difficult for him as it was for her. So, he was so willing to break the contract because he did not want her – she was not what he would have chosen. How terrible that suddenly seemed to her. Did she want to break the contract? Go back to her grandmother in Scotland, away from this country, changed now perhaps, but still her country, the place where she belonged? Her blood and background spoke clearly and she did not know what to say to this man standing in front of her, waiting for her answer. She had been silent too long for Sher Ali to bear.

"Arina, please tell me – do you wish to break this contract?"

She looked up at last, meeting his eyes. She looked away again and said, "If you want to break it, then do it. You are a man, you have the right to choose freely."

In the name of Allah the Compassionate, thought Sher Ali, how long are we going to play this game? Is she playing with me? What does she want me to say? Her eyes are hidden, for all I know she is weeping – or laughing. Her voice – is it always like this, with a break at the end of every sentence? I can listen to this no longer. "Arina! What do you want me to do? What should I say?"

"Oh, *I* don't know!" said Arina, wishing he would take the decision from her, wishing he would stop staring at her, would say something she wanted to hear. She was desperate now. "I don't know *what* I should say."

"Thanks be to God," said Sher Ali suddenly relieved. "Say nothing, do nothing, listen to me for a few minutes. Forgive my evil temper, there was a reason for it which I will tell you one day. Trust me when I say to you, that you *are* my choice – let me be *your* choice. We are fortunate that we have met like this, and spoken together. Let us learn about each other now in this precious time – and then, through the length of each day, we will come close together in love. Will you let it be so?"

Arina did not know how to reply in words. A vast happiness had filled her – she felt close to the tiger once again.

She stood before him trying to find the words to express her relief, but he could not wait. He could not see her face, and at that moment her beautiful eyes were more important to him than anything else. He stretched out his hand and gently lifted back her veil.

"You told me I should not do this – what do you say to me now?"

She answered, without looking away from him, "No one will ever have a better right."

Sher Ali smiled. "That is all I need to hear. Come, my heart's pleasure, let us find the rose Fram spoke of – and go up and join them."

Ten

M anika and Fram watched them coming up from the garden towards the steps and Manika said, "I think all is well. Tiger has made his peace and has been forgiven. She is holding the rose."

"Thank God. I thought everything was going to be over before it had begun."

"Oh no. There is no question of that. They are both already deeply involved with each other – love is waiting in the wings, my dear. I can see the signs."

"Well," said Fram, with a sigh, "I do hope you are right. The only thing I saw coming was a mammoth quarrel – and a young girl rushing back to Scotland. Why on earth did Gulrukh Begum pick that fellow to bring her message? Well, never mind that now." He got up and went forward to meet Arina at the top of the steps.

"Come and have a drink, my dear. Did you enjoy the evening air, and my poor garden? With the sea winds that we have it is difficult to grow anything."

"And I have picked your only rose – I did not want to, but Tiger said—"

"I told her that the rose had been grown for her – the scented Persian rose. Was I right?"

"Perfectly right – I grew it for you to give Arina. It seemed that the rose knew which day she was coming, for this morning it came into bloom. Now, let us have this celebration drink, and start the evening properly. See, the

93

first stars are coming out – it will be dark soon and we will have to go in."

Arina saw Manika suddenly shiver. "How I hate the dark," said Manika, and Fram put his arm round her at once.

"No, you do not hate the dark, Manika, you love our evenings – we usually sit out here because the evenings are so pleasant, but this is the time of year when the sandflies and mosquitoes are bad, so we go in and keep the screens across the windows. Come, let us sit here until the lamps are brought out, and Manika will tell you the legend of this house and the white rose."

It seemed that her husband's arm about her shoulders was all that was needed to remove the look of fear and anxiety from Manika's face. Would the day ever come, Arina wondered, when Sher Ali's arm round her would be all the shelter she needed? It had not come yet. Apart from the time when he had held her hands for a little while in the car.

He was now looking at her, and she hurriedly turned away, glad of her veil between herself and his penetrating stare. But after a moment, she looked at him again, and saw that he had raised his glass, and without speaking a word, and looking straight at her still, he drained his full glass and put it down.

Was he drinking to me, Arina wondered, or was he looking at me to find something to criticise? But Fram was smiling to himself, as if he knew something quite different.

"How I wish you were not going so soon," said Manika. And Arina herself wished that they could stay longer. This place was beginning to feel like home. Ahead of her in the mountains of Azadpur was a family she should love, and who should love her, but she was not very sure of this, and wondered how difficult it would be for her to adapt.

"Must we really leave tomorrow? Is there a reason for our sudden departure?" she said, and Fram turned to look accusingly at Sher Ali.

"Have you not explained the situation to Arina, Tiger? You

really are too bad. Arina, my child, you have to go because
there has been a message from Gulrukh Begum, saying that
there has been rioting in Faridkote and, as the road to Azadpur
goes through the town, it has been decided that your wedding
should be held in Madore, in the old Chikor palace – and
sooner than we thought."

Sher Ali, looking irritated, said. "The message was brought
by Yusuf Dyal. I wish my grandmother had picked up the
telephone in Madore and spoken to me herself, it would have
been better than sending messages by that untrustworthy—"

Fram, seeing the frown gathering on Sher Ali's face, interrupted quickly, "Well, perhaps the telephone lines are down.

"And I suppose you will have to go by train?" asked Manika.

Sher Ali, diverted, said at once, "Oh no – I would so much
rather take Arina by road, in the big car of course, so much
more interesting. What do you think, Fram?"

"Well, it is a more interesting way to travel, of course, but
can you be sure of finding accommodation for night stops?
These days it is not so easy – most of the Dak bungalows were
burnt down by rioting *goondas* along the roads."

"Oh no, Tiger, please go by train," Manika begged. "We
know they are well guarded now – don't risk the roads, that
man Yusuf Dyal says they are dangerous."

"I can imagine what *he* said. He is an alarmist and a coward.
Where is he, by the way? I thought I heard his car start up and
leave when I was in the garden with Arina. It sounded as if
he was in a tearing hurry, fleeing from the devil. Is he, alas,
coming back?"

Manika did not answer, she looked down, her fingers
twisting and turning the heavy ring she wore. Fram laughed.

"He was fleeing, all right. Fleeing from a little plain speaking. I know that he is no friend of yours, Tiger. It is strange
that of all the people Gulrukh Begum could choose from, she
chose him to bring an urgent message. She must know that
there is ill-feeling between you both?"

"Oh, yes, she knows. But he probably talked her into it, with promises of a quick delivery – where women are concerned, he can talk his way into anything, and Gulrukh Begum, with respect, is not the wisest woman in the world."

"Well he won't be back again. Manika's plain speaking is very plain indeed, and I spoke my mind, too. We do not care for him, he comes of a bad family. But let us forget him – he upset Manika, and that I will not have. My dear, put him out of your mind, don't think of him – I can see that you are still distressed. Please put this episode – that is all it is – out of your mind."

It was a few minutes before Manika looked up and said, "I am distressed. He looked so evil as he left. I wish I had not spoken to him as I did, but he displeased me so much when he spoke of Arina. Now I am afraid that he will pay me back in some horrible way – he looked so vindictive." She drew her shoulders together as she spoke, as if she was flinching from a blow. She was looking out into the garden where the shadows had gathered into darkness.

Arina remembered how she had said, "I hate the dark."

"Can we not forget this man, Manika," Fram said. "You are talking nonsense, frightening yourself. What can that man do to harm us?"

"Oh, I do not know," said Manika on a long sigh, "I only know that I felt something very bad about him. He has a snake's eyes, cold and dangerous. He will do something to avenge his loss of face before us – I know he will."

Sher Ali said firmly, "Manika, he can do nothing. Do not be afraid of him, he has no power, he is not liked by the men in government now. His right to his state and to the *guddee* of Sagpurna has not been ratified yet – and he has to go down there at once to talk to the senior members of whatever passes for a council of ministers in those new small states in the south. He will be lucky to get his inheritance, I understand that the people of Sagpurna do not want him – there is another claimant.

Forget him – Gulrukh Begum should not have sent him here, he brings bad news, just by coming himself."

Fram heard the tone of Sher Ali's voice roughen as he said those last words. The young man's brows had drawn together in a formidable frown, and he was almost snarling. Fram saw Arina's head turn and, although she had her face covered in folds of her veil, he saw her draw closer to Manika, and was sure she was nervous. The name of Yusuf Dyal alone was enough to make Sher Ali furious again. Quickly, Fram said, "That is quite enough about Yusuf Dyal – as far as we are concerned, he is dead."

"I wish he was. I shall certainly kill him the very first chance I get. It is time that that family is wiped out completely," Sher Ali was spitting his words.

"Oh, Tiger, do not make yourself angry again, about nothing. And please do not make statements like that. It will do you no good, and when you look as you do now, you closely resemble the animal you are named for, a noble animal, but very terrifying. Not at all a social animal, a creature difficult to love, really." Fram hoped that his words would convey a warning to Sher Ali, to frighten and disturb Arina again would not be conducive to an evening of celebration, and might very well make her desperate to return to Scotland.

If Sher Ali heard the warning in Fram's voice, he paid no attention. He said, unpleasantly, "I wish I was that animal. Then I could hunt down my enemy and kill him. He has insulted me unforgiveably by what he inferred about my future wife, and by insulting me, he has insulted her. Arina Begum, I apologise if I am causing you pain again, but I do beg of you, please, to remember in future that modesty in a woman is her protection against predatory men. Did no one teach you anything in Scotland? You were in the care of . . . of a woman who would have known the importance of such things."

Fram heard what he thought was a sigh, but it was so light, so soft that he could not be sure he had heard anything. He looked towards Arina and his wife, and saw that the white rose was lying on the floor between Arina and Sher Ali. Fram moved to go and pick it up, but before he could do anything, Arina, with a swift movement, tore her veil from her head and threw it on the ground.

"It seems that I do not please you. I am immodest, I have not been brought up as a well-bred girl. I am not at all the type of woman you desire. So, I will make you free of this contract, which must be very unpleasing to you. Now, in front of witnesses, I say you are free." She turned to Manika and said, "Lady Dinshaw, please excuse me for making a public display, but it is necessary. I cannot be what I am not – I was well taught, and well raised by my dear grandmother, but I do not meet Sher Ali's high standards. If I may stay with you just until I can arrange for a passage back to Britain, I will return to my home." Turning to look at Sher Ali, her eyes blazing, Arina said, "I do not know why you bothered to say what you said in the garden. You did not mean one word of it."

In the silence that followed her words, one word came back to her. "Home!" The word struck her heart. Home was not back across the oceans. Home was here, in this country to which she had dreamed of returning. This was her true home, her blood and ancestry spoke clearly to her. Here she belonged and this man, Sher Ali, despite his unpredictable temperament, was part of her future – whatever she said or did. If he was not to feature in her future, there was no future for her. Her hot anger had drained away, leaving her cold and embarrassed, unhappy, and alone. What had she done?

Then two warm arms embraced her, she was enveloped in the loved and memory-bringing scents of sandalwood and jasmine. Manika held her close, saying, "Daughter of my heart, how can you leave us? This is our day of happiness in a time of great trouble, you have brought us pleasure. You are our loved Tiger's gift to us, to bring you safely home after so long away, and now you think to leave us, because of a few foolish words? No, you cannot go, and no one has heard anything you said – nothing is broken."

"Except my life, if you go," said Sher Ali, coming to stand close beside them. "I have asked your forgiveness before, I cannot ask again. All I can say is that you are already in my heart, my heart is your home. Stay with me, teach me the things you know, and I will try to teach you of love – *my* love for you, which you have planted in my heart, it has been growing with strength since I first saw you. Never speak of leaving me again, light of my heart, stay with me."

These words, spoken so firmly in front of Manika and Fram, were to them an amazing declaration of love and determination, amazing because they were spoken by a man who never revealed his emotions. Indeed, on this day he seemed to have opened his heart and displayed, not only burning hatred, but a love of enormous depth.

To Arina, Sher Ali's words were balm to her very hurt feelings, and they were also a vow – a declaration made before his closest friends. Could she believe him? Yes, because Manika and Fram had heard him. But what could she say in return?

All three were waiting for her to speak, but she could not find the courage . . .

Sher Ali bent down and picked up the precious white rose and held it out to her. "You dropped your rose, piyari. Do you want it, or were you throwing it away?"

Now she could speak, now she could pick up her veil – Sher Ali had made both possible. "The rose fell from my hand I will never throw it away." And she bent to pick up her veil, and draw it over her face, saying, "That was thrown down in anger. I regret, I must learn patience myself before I teach you."

As Sher Ali handed her the rose, he spoke gently. "And what of love, my golden heart?" But Arina pretended that she had not heard him. Love was part of dreams and fancies still, she could not speak to him of love, love was still a stranger.

Sher Ali waited for an answer, but she remained silent, so he waited no more.

"I will ask again later, Arina. I am already being taught patience," he said, and wished that he could see her face. The veil was firmly in place, even though she did not need to be veiled now, there were no strangers, but he was not going to ask her to lift it. Was she smiling behind that cobweb, or was she frowning and still displeased – his little cat! The shadows of the darkening evening, combined with the veil, made it impossible to see her face. He was sure that she knew that he wanted her to remove the veil, and was waiting for him to ask. Let her wait, he thought, I too have my pride.

Sher Ali moved restlessly, and Arina lifted the rose to her face as if to smell it, and Fram, watching said, "Can you smell the rose through your veil? I know that the scent strengthens with the night, but don't you wish to remove the veil now, we are all family here?"

Arina seemed to hesitate, and Sher Ali, pride now satisfied, said, "Please do lift your veil, Arina, and enjoy the evening air and the scent of the rose." And, he thought, let me enjoy looking at you in peace – it seems we have done nothing but fight since we met.

She threw back her veil, and sat, looking intently at the rose. Manika came and sat beside her on the cushions, and Fram spoke, "Now, my love, while the scent of the rose is all about us, tell Arina the of the rose and how it came to us."

The glasses were refilled, and sitting in the shadows.

Manika's soft voice started the story. "It should start, '*Ek tha raja* . . . Once there was a king.' All the best stories start like that. This king lived far away in the north, beyond the mountains of Chikor. He was a young king, unmarried, and he was told by his old mother that he must choose a bride. She had selected five princesses and told her son that he must choose one of them. They were girls from good families, with health and youth and beauty as their dowries. The king made it clear that there should be no haggling over money. He was a man of wealth and was satisfied with his fortune, needing nothing more.

"They were not all girls from the hill families. Several of them came from distant places. There was a daughter of a Chinese merchant prince who lived in Bombay, and a Persian princess whose father was a diplomat in Kabul. All five girls were brought to the palace of the young king by their parents. In order to save the girls from embarrassment the king sat in a screened alcove, and one by one they were sent in to walk through the room. They would not know that they were watched by the king, but of course they did know. The news ran through the *zenanas* of the various states and kingdoms from which they had come, and was spoken of in the bazaars of Bombay, Delhi, and Madore, and every woman wanted to know who would be the chosen one.

"On arrival at the palace, the girls were taken to the women's quarter, and were prepared for their showing. Silks, furs and velvets, jewels and golden ornaments – and the most seductive perfumes that could be found – were used to adorn them. Then – individually – they began their walk through the big hall, and the king watched from behind his screen, saying nothing. All but one had completed their walk, but the Persian girl was late. The road from Kabul was long and tiresome, and there were enforced halts where land slides had blocked the roads. When at last her party reached the city, and arrived at the palace, the girl had not yet been told why she had been brought on this journey and thought that her father must be coming to see the king on some diplomatic matter. So of course she was surprised when her parents left her with the women of the *zenana*, hurrying away without saying anything.

"The first four girls had already been viewed and there was no time to bathe, dress and adorn the Persian girl. She was hurried into the room where the king waited. She did not know what she should do, or why she was told to walk through the room. The dust and sweat of the journey were still on her, her long red hair was dishevelled, and she was unveiled and confused. She stood in the room and waited for someone to come and tell her what to do. The king looked, and looked again. He was holding a white rose in his hand, and suddenly the perfume of the rose was all about him. He stood up and came out from behind the screen and went close to the girl and, taking her hand, he placed the rose in her fingers and folded them over the stem of the flower. He asked her what her name was, and she told him she was called 'Gul-rang'. The king sent for his mother, who came swiftly, and the king said to her, 'I have found my love, I will take this one, and no other.'"

Manika paused and looked, smiling, at her audience, and Arina said, "Did the Persian girl know what this meant? Did she know what was happening?"

It was Sher Ali who answered. "If she did not know then, she would have known quite soon – when the festivities began and the singers and dancers came to entertain the guests."

"But then," said Arina, "'when the festivities began' it would have meant that she was married, and it would have been too late. Poor girl."

Sher Ali looked as if he was considering something that he did not care for. "What do you mean, Arina? Too late for what?"

"Too late to say anything – married so quickly, with no time to learn about him. She had no time to say that she did not wish to marry. Perhaps she had already met the love of her heart. She should have given back the rose, if it was a signal of love. She had perhaps already received a rose from someone else. But she was confused, she did not understand, no one had told her anything. Then there would be no way out for her. It was too late."

Oh, God, thought Sher Ali, she speaks as if she has felt so confused – perhaps this is why she is so cold to me, so reluctant

– what happened in Scotland, with her in the sole care of that woman? Of course, she has a lover – no, she is still untouched, I swear it: her eyes, her mouth, Oh, God, ready and waiting. But surely her heart has been taken – this is terrible, she should have been brought back here sooner.

I shall go mad. Why do I have to learn about what love is for this girl, who is already ensnared? Now what should I do? Perhaps it is not too late, perhaps away from him, she will forget. After all, she came out here, knowing she was going to be married. She came to do her duty! And I? If I had seen her, not knowing, given the chance to choose – what would I have done? I would have chosen her. Of course I would, but she has chosen some beefy football-playing Scotsman, God help me. Oh, what trouble that Zeena has caused.

Sher Ali had risen, and was walking restlessly. Fram thought he was looking for another drink, and said to Manika, "What time do you think we will eat tonight? Have we time for another drink?"

Manika, too, had been watching Sher Ali pacing up and down in the shadows, and wondered what was worrying him. She made a fairly shrewd guess, but decided not to ask. She said, "Fram, of course there is time for another glass of wine if you want it. I will go in and organise dinner. Arina, would you care to come in and I will finish the story inside. I must go in anyway, to find out why the servants have not brought the lamps – they are very late."

Arina was about to stand up and follow Manika but Sher Ali, who had come to an abrupt halt beside her, said, "Arina, you speak as if you can understand the girl from Persia. You feel for her – why?"

Arina was surprised by the question – surely he knew why? Looking up into his face, unable to see his expression because it was dark, she said, "Tiger, I feel for her – she had come a long distance, was given a rose by a man she may not have loved to find herself faced with a marriage with no time to think about it. I, however, have been more, fortunate – at least I know what is going to happen to me." She hesitated then, and blushed.

She turned quickly to Manika, "I am ready to go in with you, Manika, longing to hear the end of the legend."

"I will tell you – and better than that, I will show you something to do with the legend which prove to you that love is lasting. Come with me."

Sher Ali started to say, "Oh, wait a minute, I want to talk to Arina," but Fram's voice calling to Manika over rode his words.

"Manika, don't send lamps – the stars are so beautiful. We will sit here with our drinks and come when you call us."

"I have never known Fram be so interested in the stars," said Manika, as the guard opened the door for them, and they walked through into the house.

Eleven

As the door closed behind them and the guard stepped back out of earshot, Sher Ali turned to Fram. "There you are. You heard her yourself – she doesn't love me. I feel sure that *that* wretched woman, who had no morals herself when she was young, has allowed Arina to meet someone else, and she has lost her heart to him – what am I to do now?" Fram's answer came out of the dark shadows, his tone was cool and firm.

"Tiger, I will tell you what you have to do. Pull yourself together and start behaving like a man instead of a hysterical woman. You must learn not to speak about Zeena Begum like that. I blame your grandmother for your most unfair attitude. Zeena Begum is a charming and honourable lady, who has brought Arina to a delightful well-mannered maturity, which is more than can be said for your grandmother's effect on you. You will antagonise Arina if you continue to be rude and insulting about the grandmother she cherishes. Stop and think a little. You realise what the family – notably Zurah Begum – were arranging for Zeena? A marriage with your friend Yusuf Dyal's dreadful old uncle. She was seventeen, he was over sixty and steeped in every form of depravity you can put your mind to. Do not denigrate Zeena, whom we all love and whom Arina adores. Right, that is the first thing.

"The second thing is this: you have said, before us, that you love Arina. Very well said, but now try and show it by ensuring that you don't distress her, and do not constantly imagine vain

105

things. Arina is a young girl, posted out here, and presented to you like a birthday gift. Remember, she is a human being, and has her own ideas about life. Tell her that you love her, that is good, but *make sure you show* it, too. Have you kissed her yet?"

"Great heavens, no! I think she would very likely scratch my eyes out if I did. In any case we have never been alone for longer than twenty minutes."

"It does not take twenty minutes to kiss a girl, Tiger."

"You are laughing at me – I wish I could see you, this voice out of the darkness is like a consultation with the Delphic oracle – could we not have a lamp?"

"I prefer not."

"I have never known you longing for starlight, Fram."

Sher Ali's voice had changed, he was alerted by some tone in Fram's voice. "What is wrong, Fram? Why this darkness?"

"Because we present too good a target when we sit up here illuminated by lamps."

"Target? Are you suggesting someone may take a pot-shot at us? I don't believe it—"

"Not us. Me. You are quite safe, you are a believer – one of the faithful. And you had better believe it, Tiger. Sammy Narona was shot dead sitting beside his mother on just such a *chibutra* as this one – and you know what a short distance lies between their house and ours. They have gone, the family packed up and left – and that is why we are going too."

"Good God. Then why have you kept Manika here? Never mind packing up, get out – or at least get her out. If you won't let her come with us, then put her into a hotel in Karachi, while you close up the house – wouldn't that be more sensible?"

"For one thing, she won't leave me – and even if she would, are you sure she would be safer in a hotel? There are some strange things going on in the city – organised demonstrations against the capitalists who have been cruelly oppressing the workers. I think she is safer here with me."

106

"In spite of the sharp shooters?"

"Yes. At least we would be together."

"Fram, don't talk like that. Please, both of you come up with us – you said yourself, we are quite safe. With us, as our family, you would be safe, too. No one would attack you in Chikor or Pakodi – we have people from every religion you can think of there, all living together perfectly peacefully: we have two temples in Chikor, and a mission station and a church; and in Pakodi we have Sikhs and there is a *gurdwara* for them, a temple for the Hindu residents, also a church – with a large statue of the Virgin Mary outside. Come and build a tower of silence, I will give you the land. Come and live in peace with us."

Fram smiled and thanked him. "You are a generous man, Tiger, and if all was as it used to be, we would come. But, Tiger, how long is it since you were last up among your mountains in Azadpur? You have been out with your regiment for a year, as I remember."

"Yes – that was a bad time. We had only just got back from service in Java, when all the trouble began. Well, it is over now, and I am on leave at last. But I have not been up in Azadpur, as you say, for a year. Why?"

"I think you may find things have changed a bit. I hope everyone is still living together in peace, but I don't care for the sound of these riots in Faridkote, that is rather close to your part of the world. Tiger, have you thought that you may be recalled to your regiment?"

"No, I have not. I won't even allow it to cross my mind. I shall desert, I tell you, if that happens. I haven't had any leave for eighteen months – none of us have. Now we are having staggered leave and this is my turn. I must get Arina safely back to Madore. This is really why I have not been upset that the wedding has been put forward – if we are married soon, I can take her down to Saranabad with me. But now I am truly worried that she seemed to think it so cruel that the Persian girl was married so swiftly."

"Tiger, you have not told Arina that the wedding has been put forward by Gulrukh Begum? Oh, you are too bad, really. You must tell her yourself. Take her into the smaller sitting-room when we go in – tell her there. Tell her you are delighted that you will be able to be married sooner than you thought, say you hope that she is pleased, too. Put your arms round her, for God's sake, and let her *know* that you love her. Don't keep talking about it, *show* her."

"I think you are suggesting exactly what my grandmother feared I would do – I can't take hold of her, she'll imagine rapine and heavens knows what."

"Well, you've got to tell her, I can't act as a go-between. There's the bell – come on Tiger, we must go in."

Once they were in the house and away from the men, Arina and Manika had got no further with the story of the rose. Arina was full of questions she had been longing to ask, so Manika took her into the small drawing-room and they sat down.

"Manika, please tell me – I thought I heard Fram say that we were going back directly because of trouble in Faridkote, that we are to be married in the old Chikor palace sooner than you had thought. How soon – when in the marriage to take place? Manika, thinking quickly, said, "Tiger has not told you? I think it will be almost as soon as you reach Madore."

"I see," said Arina slowly. "Can you tell me why?"

"It is because of the trouble that seems to be starting all over again: inter-communal rioting. Hindus and Sikhs against Moslems – or, in some places, Moslems killing Hindus and Sikhs. Did you not hear about this terrible situation when you were in Scotland?"

"Yes, I remember hearing that there were problems once the British had left – it was on the wireless, but then Zeena Begum said it would not concern us. She said the mountain people were at peace still, and she turned the wireless off."

"Zeena Begum was quite right – as far as I know, Azadpur

is at peace. But Faridkote straddles the only road to the Lungri Pass, which you have to cross to reach Azadpur."

"Could we not wait in Madore until the trouble settles, and then go on to Chikor?"

Manika bit her lip, listening to the worried note in Arina's voice. Was the child so anxious to delay the marriage? That did not seem to be a hopeful sign for the future. "Indeed you could wait there, but there are several reasons why it would not be a good thing. The most important point is that Tiger is on leave at this time – if the troubles spread, or get worse, he will certainly be recalled from leave, and your marriage would have to be postponed, perhaps for months. The troubles we have here tend to get worse instead of better. And the next important point in that the invitations to the festivities for your marriage have gone out. Many of the guests are princes from distant states – not all Moslem. In any case, it would be unwise to hold a large gathering of important people if things were very bad – think of the journeys these people have to take to get to Madore, never mind Azadpur. Then, if the passes are closed, you will have rulers unable to get back to their states, not a good thing when everything is in uproar. That is why the wedding has been put forward, so that your guests can attend and then get back to their duties before anything worse happens. Dear Arina, you do understand, do you not?"

Arina looked down at the rose in her hand. Her face was very sad, and Manika leaned forward to put her arms round the young girl.

"Arina, my dear child. Tell me, do you want to break this contract? I think it will break Tiger's heart if you do, but if you really feel that you can't go on with it, then Fram and I will help you. But you must be sure. It is, as you know, a very serious matter."

Arina took time to think before she answered. She held Manika's hand tightly as she said, "I do know what a serious matter it is considered here in India – I mean Pakistan. But to be married very quickly to someone you do not know at all is also very serious. You see, I thought that I would have perhaps a month at least, to get to know Tiger – and for him to get to know me. It is important, I think. Did you marry in such haste?"

"No. But I could have done, willingly. I was in love with Fram almost as soon as I met him. You had a most unfortunate beginning. All the fault of that stupid old woman in Pakodi. We should have gone to meet you, brought you back here, then Tiger could have come down and met you with us – that would have been easier for you, wouldn't it?"

"Oh yes, that would have been perfect – it was, I think, as hard for Tiger to meet me like that as it was for me to meet him."

"No. Not so hard for him. He was, I should judge, fascinated at once – and now it has gone further than that. Tiger is in love with you. Make no mistake, he is totally head over heels. I know him very well, I can tell."

Arina did not look as if she believed Manika, but all she said was, "Do you really think so?"

"Arina, I do not *think* so. I am quite certain. It will be very hard for him if you do want to break the contract."

"I think that the only thing that will be hurt is his pride – I don't imagine any other girl has turned away from him." Arina spoke with certainty, and Manika was shocked.

"Arina, do you have no feelings for him at all? You sound as if you really dislike him. I think you are being a little unfair. After all, he is not entirely unknown to you. As a small child, you adored him. Followed him everywhere. Do you not remember that?"

"I think it was the horse, and the bird with bells on its feet . . ." Arina paused, with a sudden memory of a very tall young man who had filled all her dreams for so long. What was the reality – was he Tiger, this man so unexpected in temper, so wooing in speech? "Oh Manika, I do not *know* him at all. He seems to be three people: the memory of the boy from my childhood; a tiger who flares up with no warning and very little reason, and then this gentle, charming man who tells me he would choose me, that I am in his heart. How am I supposed to believe him when he is so changeable?"

"Dear Arina, I do understand. Tiger is volatile at present, but he will never let you down – and he will never lie to you. Try to understand him and be patient."

I don't feel patient, thought Arina. Nothing is as I imagined it would be, even the name of this land I have longed for has been changed. I am lost, but there is nothing I can do. I would break my grandmother's heart, if I were to break this wretched contract. I understand it now. I am here, in her beloved country, because *she* cannot come back. She can only return through me – I mustn't let her down. There is no way out for me.

"I am the Persian girl," she said aloud, and Manika knew what Arina was saying, and was glad. Arina was not going to ask to be set free. But how sad she looked!

I can say no more, thought Manika. Now it is for Tiger to help this girl to happiness. "Arina, I promise you that all will be well. You are at the beginning of a happy life. Let us now think of other things, such as food. You must be starving. I am going to call the men, I know that dinner is ready. Come with me, we will go into the dining-room, and wait for the Tiger and Fram there. Ah, here's Fram – we'll wait for Tiger and then go and eat."

"But not quite yet, Manika. I want to show Arina something," said Fram.

Over Arina's head, Manika's eyes met her husband's warning glance. So this was important? She let him lead Arina out of the room, and saw them cross the hall and go into the smaller receiving-room. He showed Arina in and, without pausing, closed the door and came back to his wife.

"Tiger has to speak to her – alone. He must—"

"Well, I hope he makes a better job of communicating

his feelings than he has up till now. That girl is miserable – she can't understand his changeable behaviour, and does not believe that he cares for her. I hope this does not end in another fight."

Behind the closed door of the receiving-room, Arina confronted Tiger with astonishment. "Fram said he had something to show me, but he has gone."

I have been brought here for a reason, she thought – now, now he will tell me that he wishes to put an end to this stupid situation, and I shall have to tell him that I agree. Then what do I do? I shall stay with the Dinshaws as long as they will have me.

Arina straightened her shoulders and faced him, her eyes steady, waiting for him to speak.

She faces me as if she is waiting for an attack – am I a monster to her? Take her in my arms? I would sooner embrace my colonel – she looks just as unyielding. Fram is mad. He does not understand women at all.

They stood facing each other in silence for some moments. The silence stretched, and Arina began to feel that something had to happen or she would start laughing, or worse, possibly weep. She said "Tiger – has Fram brought me here because you wished to speak to me alone? You have something you would like to say to me? Please tell me. I think Manika and Fram are waiting for dinner."

He looks terrified, she thought, what on earth is wrong with him – oh goodness, has he had bad news from Scotland? Her voice trembling, she said, "Tiger, there is something wrong – please tell me."

Now I have frightened her again. This is a foolish endeavour. He cleared his throat and said, "Arina, there is nothing wrong except that I am a fool. I find words difficult, but I must speak."

Now she looks as if she is waiting for execution. Oh I can't bear this. Tiger stepped forward, pulled Arina roughly into his arms and began to kiss her. She fought him, her thoughts flying about in her head, she battled against with the strength of a healthy young girl, and Tiger struggled to hold her. She relaxed in his arms at last, and his grasp became more gentle, his kisses less bruising. He heard her say, "Tiger" and he released her at once and stepped back.

They were both breathless and, for different reasons, considerably startled. Tiger, rendered speechless by the force of his own feelings, thought that he had been too rough – how she fought.

Arina was shocked by her own confused feelings – was this how a man showed his love? She was shaken by the feeling that had he not released her then, she would have stopped fighting, because the urge to fight had been replaced by another very strange urge. She began to try to order her dishevelled state. Her silk shirt was ripped at the neck, her hair was in a tangle, her whole body felt bruised and in a tumult. She looked at him and saw that his face was scratched – as she looked, he put his hand up to his face. "I am bleeding," Sher Ali said, looking at his fingers. "You are a little cat."

"You should not have done that – is that usual?"

The question made him laugh. "Quite usual," he said. "That is why you wear a veil – in case some madman behaves as I just did. But it is different for me."

This made her angry, it assumed too much, she thought. She repeated, "You should not have done that."

"Really? Should I not? Do I ask forgiveness now, my golden heart?"

She looked away from him blushing and said, "I have lost an earring – and how can I go back to Manika and Fram like this?"

He looked with mounting pleasure at the disordered beauty before him, and smiled.

"You can rejoin them without any shame. How else would you expect to look after you have been embraced and kissed?

113

As a matter of fact you looked much worse when you arrived here. Tell me, do you believe me when I tell you that I love you? Did my arms and my kisses tell you more clearly than my speech? Because I do love you. You are my life, my pleasure, my longed-for companion – and so it will be for ever." He spoke in their own language – she listened to him, one silver phrase after another.

Arina felt her heart still beating erratically, her breath shortened as he spoke. He moved closer and took her in his arms again, and this time she did not fight, she returned his kisses, and it was not she who moved away from him this time. He slackened his arms and stood looking down at her.

"Now, my dearest little cat, go to your room and let your maid arrange your hair – love is a dangerous pleasure when it is mutual. Can you tell me yet that you love me?"

"I will tell you but not now."

She disappeared, quickly through the door of the hall where Sushi waited.

Chunia and Sushi made eyes at each other, but neither made any remark. Arina's shirt was changed, the solitary earring removed and replaced with a different pair. And when Manika hurried in to see if all was well, Arina was dressed and ready, and she followed Manika out and down to the room where the two men waited for them.

As she followed Manika down the hall to the door of the dining-room, Arina felt that she had only just arrived at Sagar House. The first part of the day now seemed to be a dream, this was reality, this moment was the beginning of her life in Pakistan. It was a strange feeling, but pleasurable. She entered the room with her head up, sure of herself, and then met Sher Ali's eyes, stumbled, and blushed scarlet.

Manika had told her that this room was part of the old house. Arina did not raise her eyes to see the high, painted ceiling, where the moon and stars were represented. The floor under her feet was made up of different colours of marble. There were beautiful carved and fluted pillars at the side of the doors and the high-arched windows. The brocades that hung before the windows were Syrian, embroidered with birds and flowering vines. The lighting came from tall candles set in silver sconces. However, for all that Arina noticed of it that night, the dining-room could have been a ruin.

The food was as perfect as Manika's well-trained and practised cooks could make it. But Arina ate like a bird and tasted nothing. She drank thirstily from a silver goblet, yet saw nothing of its beauty. The room was ornamented for the celebration of her coming but Arina was in a different world. She sat quietly in the company of the other three, saying nothing unless she was addressed, and even then she answered, her mind on other things. She glowed with happiness.

Sher Ali watched her with delight. She burns, he thought, she is a flame in an alabaster vase – she is alight with happiness, and it was I who evoked this feeling in her. Please God, in a few short weeks we will burn together in a fire that will light the rest of our lives. I am crowned with her joy.

Fram, who had been trying to talk to Sher Ali without success, lent across and put his hand on the young man's arm. "Tiger, my dear fellow – you are not listening to me! I asked you a question. How much leave have you actually got?"

"I have a month – and only four days have gone. But I think I must get us to Madore as soon as possible, so I am afraid it is the train for us." He turned to Arina. "Do not be disappointed, I promise you I will drive along the old roads later, after we are married, and everything has settled down. Though I cannot promise you the Taj Mahal – we have lost that."

"Oh, have we?" said Arina, bemused. "I did not know."

"Yes. The Taj is now in India – and Kashmir is in an uproar, so we cannot go there."

A shadow had fallen over his happiness, so Arina said quickly, "But someone told me that Chikor and Pakodi, and the mountains and valleys there are more beautiful than those in Kashmir." And at that Sher Ali smiled and turned back to speak to Fram.

"I do not know the name of the man who decided where the borders would go, but he was no friend to Pakistan. He handed over all the main centres of manufacturing to India, the headwaters of the Indus are lost to us – the the lifeline for our agriculture – but we will succeed whatever the other side has, we have the men and the will, the brain and courage of Jinnah."

"As you say," said Fram, "the whole future of Pakistan rests on that one man's shoulders. I cannot help thinking that he should have waited a little, perhaps trained others to take on some of the load – he is not a man in good health. We can only hope that the Quaid-i-Azam Mohammed Ali Jinnah lives long enough to see Pakistan through these very troubled times. Thank God you also have a first-class army."

"No!" said Sher Ali with force. "Leave the army out of this. The army must be put in reserve for the defence of this new land. It must not be used as a policing force, nor wasted in any foolish border squabbles. I am sure that our Indian brothers-in-arms are saying the same thing. What a ridiculous state of affairs this is! It is inconceivable to think that any one of us wishes to go to war with his schoolmates, companions from Sandhurst – friends with whom we have been in the same battalions? The British government has not done well by our army – the army it has used in so many wars. No, Fram. Let the politicians finish the job they have begun."

While the talk flowed between the two men, Manika and Arina remained silent, listening. Manika wanted to hear Fram's views of the future. Arina was simply spellbound.

Here, in this Tiger, this stranger, was yet another, a third man. A man of patriotism, of pride in and concern for his country, a sober, thinking man. Suddenly she remembered that he was almost thirty. The same age as her father would have been if he had not been taken by the earthquake.

She seldom thought deeply about her parents, especially about her mother – so young, a flower cut down, Zeena had told her. She had no memories of her mother at all – Chunia's image had been superimposed on hers. The word "mother" meant Chunia. She had heard more about her father of course – the boy born to Zeena Begum, the child who gave her a reason to to live after her young husband had been killed. Had her father been like Sher Ali? Handsome, full of laughter, arrogant, courageous, quick-tempered and passionate in love?

Who am I describing to myself, thought Arina, looking through the candle flames at the alive, resolute face of Sher Ali, as he spoke of his native land. He spoke of Pakistan as if he spoke of an adored woman. Had her father felt this passion? He had been determined to come here, she had been told so much by Zeena Begum. Everything he did and learned was for one purpose – to come back to India and be part of his father's old regiment. Did he too have the dream of a separate country, a Pakistan?

She sat listening, wondering, thinking. She was beginning to see a man whom she hadn't thought existed, the man behind the arrogant Tiger. Something grew and began to take shape within her mind and heart, as she sat beside Manika in that beautiful room.

The candles were guttering out and, when the servants brought a second batch, Manika stopped them.

"I think it is time we retired, Arina – you must be so weary. You have been very quiet."

"Poor girl," said Fram. "She has not had much opportunity to be otherwise."

"No, how impolite of me," said Sher Ali, "I have been monopolising all of the conversation. Arina, forgive me, I see Fram so infrequently, and I value his opinion so much. I forgot myself, but I did not forget you. All the time, you were there in the back of my mind – you were so deep in

117

thought that I longed to know what you were thinking. What were your thoughts, my soul?"

"I was listening to you both," said Arina. "There is so much that I do not know about the happenings here in Pakistan – I have so much to learn." And not only about Pakistan, she thought, so much to learn about *you* – but I am learning now.

When, with Manika beside her, she said goodnight to the men, Fram kissed her warmly, and Sher Ali took her hand and lifted it to his lips and then for a moment to his heart. Manika saw Arina's eyes and wondered if a long train journey was going to be too much for both these young people to support. She decided to tell Fram to book a purdah carriage for Arina and both the maids.

When she had kissed Manika, and Chunia had risen from her place on the floor at the foot of the bed, Arina found that the earring she had lost had been returned to her. Sher Ali had put it in her hand, with the rose – but she, feeling his lips on her fingers, had felt nothing else.

Undressed, bathed, her hair brushed and plaited for the night, Arina was glad to be lying on her pillows.

Chunia slept as soon as she lay down and Sushi, lying on a pallet in the dressing-room was asleep soon after, but Arina lay awake for a while, thinking over the day that seemed to stretch back a long way . . . She turned her thoughts to her grandmother, and imagined the letter she would write to her in the morning, and so, between one thought and another, holding the fading rose, she eventually drifted into a deep sleep.

Twelve

A rina, totally exhausted, slept peacefully and dreamlessly. She did not hear the bell that rang and continued to ring until at last it was answered. She slept on until the hurrying footsteps in the hall and the steady knocking on a door close by woke her.

She sat up, wide awake when a voice she recognised spoke sharply, to be answered by Fram, saying quickly, "Tiger, wake! There is a call for you, it is urgent."

Blinking sleep away from her eyes, Arina saw that Chunia was up, standing with her head pressed to the door. Staring at her, Arina saw with dawning alarm that Chunia was holding a very serviceable dagger. Arina scrambled out of bed and ran to stand beside her. "Chunia! What is happening?"

Chunia put a finger to Arina's lips. "Shst! Be quiet. I listen." Obedient to an authority that had ruled her earliest years, Arina stood quietly, her brain seething with suppositions, all of them frightening.

Still dark outside, no gleam of light came through the shuttered windows.

Chunia moved from the door, putting her knife away in a sheath that Arina had not noticed before, hidden as it was under the folds of her sari. She said quietly, "Child, I think something bad has happened. I could not hear properly, but the little that I heard makes me feel that it would be good if you dressed quickly while I go and find out more. Be quick, piyari, and do not fear. Sushi is with you, you are not alone."

119

Sushi looked shaken and Arina wondered bleakly how much help she would be if marauders broke in. As far as Arina knew, Sushi did not carry a dagger. Perhaps it would be sensible if she herself carried a knife! How very odd life was becoming. She began to hurry, the bathing and dressing process was not prolonged. Sushi still looked strained, indeed Arina saw that the woman's hands were trembling, and tried to cheer her. "Come, Sushi, do not be afraid – this is a civilised place, no one will harm us."

Sushi shook her head. "This is a bad place. How could we be safe in a house built on a tomb? Let us go to the hills, Huzoor, before we are all killed."

"Oh, Sushi, what are you thinking? We are leaving today – and do you think the Nawab would have brought us to an evil place? Of course not."

Sushi looked unconvinced and went to the window, peering out through the shutters, and turning back to say, "Alas. It is still dark, the moon is down and there are no stars – a long night, a night of disaster."

"Stop it, Sushi! You will bring us bad luck if you say such things. Listen, I can hear the *muezzin* calling from the mosque. It must be nearly dawn. Cease your complaining. Come and help me do my hair."

Arina was sitting in front of a mirror having her hair plaited when Manika hurried in. "Oh Arina, you are up and dressed – you have heard of the dreadful curse that has fallen on us all? May God pity us."

Her face was tear stained, and Arina was shocked to see her so distressed. "Manika – what is it? I have heard nothing. Please tell me what has happened."

Manika tried to speak, but had to stop to catch her breath before she could utter the words. Her voice breaking, she eventually said, "Arina – Jinnah is dead."

As Manika spoke, it was as if the words had some terrible power of their own. All the lights went out and the room was

plunged into a darkness so complete that it seemed tangible –
black velvet against the eyes.

Arina heard Sushi repeating the words of a prayer, and put
her hand out to take the woman's hand and hold it as much
to comfort herself as to comfort Sushi. Jinnah? For a moment
she had no idea who this man was. A member of the family?
Or of Manika's family? Surely not – unless he was a very
close relative, there was no reason for this excessive grief.
Jinnah – the name reminded her of something, seen or heard
somewhere else?

Manika was speaking out of the darkness. "It is the end of
Pakistan. Without the Quaid-i-Azam, Pakistan is nothing – a
child without a father – and what will happen to us when chaos
rules? Oh God! I cannot bear to think of what will happen."

Quaid-i-Azam. Of course, Mohammed Ali Jinnah! The
Governor General of the New Nation – the Inspirer, the
Founder, the Father. Indeed, the darkness round them was
more than lack of light, it was a darkness of the spirit.
And Arina shuddered within herself, afraid of her future in
a country that might go into extinction before it had taken a
firm hold of life.

A line of light grew around the edges of the door, and then
Chunia came in carrying an oil lamp. "It is a power cut,
they say."

"Well, we will hope that is what it is – and not a nationwide
expression of mourning. Manika sounded calmer." Arina,
forgive me for my earlier hysteria. I am ashamed, but this has
been a great shock. It should not have been, for Jinnah was a
very sick man. He was seriously ill with TB. I think he must
have been keeping himself alive for the sake of his precious
Pakistan. Death has overruled him. May he rest in peace without any memories of what he has left behind, for the situation
will now be terrible, I am afraid. Arina, Fram sent me in to tell
you that you must leave at once, while the whole of Pakistan is
in mourning, there will at least be calm until he is buried."

121

Leave at once? Go where? Arina's heart sank.

"The mourning will give us a little time to get you to the safety of the northern hills." Manika continued. "Fram is arranging for you to go from the station of Kiamari – one of the outer suburbs of Karachi – as the city will be impossible. Everyone will be trying to get here for the funeral. It would be no good, he says, for you to wait for the mail train to Madore. He wants you to get as close to Madore as possible today. He thinks there may be a suitable train from Kiamari to Multan where you can change on to a slow train direct to Madore. Or perhaps you could catch the Karachi mail the following day. Anything to get you out of here. Fram is very worried about you being in this city at present. Jinnah's birthplace, you know. There has already been some rioting and the authorities are expecting pandemonium once the funeral is over. Fram will drive you to Kiamari and organise tickets for you and the two maids."

"Do we go alone?" asked Arina, her spirits quailing. Where was Tiger? she wondered.

"No, no, of course not. Three trusted men will go with you, two of our own guards and Alam Beg, one of Tiger's menservants. All fully armed, of course. Oh, Arina, child of my heart, I would not send you away from me if I could help it. But you are in danger here with us, is it not tragic? There are bound to be a great many demonstrations against anyone who is not Moslem – and even peaceful well-ordered demonstrations can very easily turn into riots, killings and worse. Fram says that you will be safer anywhere than here with us. So please – come with me now and have some breakfast, and then Fram will take you to the station. Chunia, pack what you will need for a few days because, my dearest Arina, Gulrukh Begum will have everything you need waiting for you. This is a blessing for her, to be receiving you into her care sooner than she expected."

Chunia, a light veil in her hands, was standing beside Arina, listening critically to everything Manika said. As soon as she finished speaking, Chunia arranged the veil over Arina's head and said firmly, "Lady Sahiba, there is one small matter, if I may speak. Multan is not a good place for the Begum Sahiba to wait. It is very close to the border with India."

"Chunia, that is not so. It is more than a day's journey to the border." Manika spoke sharply, but Chunia paid no attention.

"Huzoor, it is between two rivers, there is a ford there, and it is easy to cross the border at Gunganagar. It is not a good place, Multan, for a woman to wait alone on a platform. Better we leave the rail *gharri* at Dera and go from there, a few miles only to Mianaghar, a place I know well."

Manika was aghast. "But how will you reach Mianaghar? There is no railway station there."

"No, Garib Parwar, no railway there. It is only a small place, only a few miles—"

Manika shook her head. "No, Chunia. You cannot do that. I will not allow it. Dera Ismail Khan is in a tribal area. To go through such a territory on foot – women alone – is forbidden. No one goes there without a special pass."

Chunia's head went up, her only eye flashed. "This is stupidity, Lady Sahiba. I who speak, I will take my child into the territory, it is my country. My mother's sister married Jubal Khan, the *sirdar* of that part, and now his grandson is *sirdar* in his turn. We will have no trouble. In any case, those laws of going here or there or not going – wah! They were made by the British Raj, who greatly feared the tribesmen. The British Raj are gone – and with them went the laws. They no longer speak."

Manika was surprised at the passion shown by the old woman. "Chunia, forgive me if I ask you a question. How is it that you, with the name of Chunia, claim to come from one of the tribes? I did not know you were of Islam?"

Chunia smiled and shrugged, saying, "I learned early to dissemble. Zurah Begum, that child of the evil one, bought me from my parents in the bazaar of Kazarshah, above the hills of the border, north of Chikor. My parents, being poor, were glad of the money she offered – they had three daughters to marry off, and I was small and a weakling in those days. But my mind was good and Zurah Begum found me useful. My name was Zarah, but Zurah Begum did not care for a servant having a name so similar to her own. She named me Chunia, the name of the dhobi's donkey. It did not matter. I was fortunate to be chosen to take care of the ruler's daughter, Zeena Begum, and later to take the place of my beloved Arina's mother. Do not worry for Arina Begum. In that territory you fear, she will be safe. Believe me, Lady Sahiba, Multan is a place of danger. I myself will tell the Burra Sahib, he will see that what I say is true."

Strangely, against her will, Manika felt that the old woman was right, as long as Arina was with Chunia, she would come to no harm. Chunia had proved her devotion to Zeena at great cost to herself, and her devoted love to the baby Arina was remembered by all. Manika bowed before the old woman's determination. "Very well, Chunia – or should I call you Zarah?"

Chunia cackled. "Nay, Lady Sahiba. After so long? I will make my prayers to the great God who is above all gods – and invoke the guardianship of the heavens for my child. Take her and make her eat while Sushi and I prepare for the journey – the short way to safety, inshallah!"

Breakfast was laid in a smaller room than the dining-room of the night before. Lit by candles and oil lamps, it might have been a room in Zeena Begum's old house in Glen Laraig. Covered silver dishes were set out on a sideboard, a bearer waited at the table, pouring either tea or coffee, bringing fresh toast – even a jar of Cooper's marmalade was there, in its labelled jar. Suddenly beset by homesickness, Arina drank coffee, but found it hard to eat anything. What would her grandmother say to this departure before dawn, this sudden journey to what Chunia said would be safety. Danger in this beautiful, luxurious house? It seemed very strange – and *where* was Tiger? Arina waited with growing impatience to hear his voice – or to be told where he was. Finally she could wait no longer.

"Manika – please, where is Tiger? This must be terrible news for him, too. What has happened to him?"

"Oh, I am so sorry – I should have told you before. Tiger has been recalled to his regiment. All leave is cancelled."

"So he has gone?" Arina's heart had fallen into a dark pit of misery. To go without even a farewell! Love me? What rubbish. He loved nothing but his regiment. Just like her grandfather, who had rushed off and left her grandmother, alone in a strange place. It seemed that she was living out her grandmother's life. She said, half to herself, "History repeats itself."

But Manika was still talking. "Of course he has not gone! Tiger is on the telephone, trying to contact his colonel and explain his predicament. He does not want to leave you alone."

The world became a different place. But at once Arina said, "He must not be troubled about me. I shall be safe with Chunia. You heard what she said. All I have to do is get off the train and go with Chunia to Mianaghar and wait for a suitable train. I am not at all worried about it, if Chunia is with me – and all those guards, and Sushi."

Manika shook her head. "You may tell Tiger that and see what he says. Tribal territory! My goodness, I wonder if that story she told us is true. Had you heard it before? I understood that Chunia came from Ladakh."

"I have heard some of that story – my grandmother said that Chunia was bought from her parents as a slave by Zurah Begum. My grandmother told me so many stories though . . . But I do know that Chunia and Sushi are related. Chunia used to wear a blue bead and a small silver charm locket with the secret name of Allah inside it and she and Sushi did not pray before idols as the other women did. I trust Chunia with my life, as my grandmother did. I do not care if her name is Chunia or Zarah. She is my mother, Manika."

"And I am your third mother, you are truly the daughter of my heart, as Tiger is the son of my long dreams. Why should I feel unfulfilled because neither of you are born of my body? You are both children of my heart. If I die tonight I die a woman fulfilled, the mother of dreams come true." Manika leaned across to put her arms round Arina, and for a moment they sat warmly embraced.

It was then, in that moment of closeness and comfort, that Arina heard the voice for which she had been waiting. Sher Ali's voice, coming nearer, and Fram answering, and then the two men came in.

With a sinking heart, Arina saw that Fram was filled with anxiety, and Sher Ali looked furious.

As he entered the room, Fram was saying, with vehemence, "Tiger, you cannot do this – you will be court-martialled for desertion, if not shot! Please listen to me."

"No Fram, I will not listen, I have listened enough. I have done my best to contact my regiment. It is not my fault that all the telephone lines are down between here and Abbottabad. The colonel – or possibly the adjutant, Bukshi Mohammed, will think that I have already left for Madore, and will try to contact me there. I will *be* there in four days at the latest. I will deliver Arina safely into the hands of my grandmother and start telephoning from there.

"Old Bukshi is a friend of mine, he will cover for me. I will then start off for wherever the regiment is – who could blame me for this?"

Fram sounded exhausted as he said, "Oh Tiger, don't be a fool. Your colonel will blame you when he gets through to the Shell people again. It was the managing director of Shell who telephoned to you, wasn't it, having already spoken with your colonel and having told him that he would contact you at once?"

"I will tell Colonel Jahan that the Shell man did not speak to me personally, that the message was received by you after I had left with Arina Begum to take her to safety. Surely old friendship is worth a small lie in, these circumstances? After all, I did not give him my name, I was just a voice on the telephone."

"Tiger, please do not be foolish. You are jeopardising your whole future. You cannot do this."

"There is only one thing I cannot do. I cannot let Arina travel alone. I will take her to Madore, nothing you can say will stop me. In fact we are wasting time now. Arina, have your maids packed for you? Are you ready to go?"

Manika said firmly, "Tiger, you will now eat something, and so will Arina. If you eat, she will. Fram, please sit down and have some coffee, and tell us what is causing all this excitement. We have already arranged for Arina to go this morning, with Chunia and Sushi, the guards and Alam Beg. So what is all this drama about?"

Tiger, with his mouth full attempted to reply, but Manika held up her hand. "No. You eat. Now, Fram, tell me."

Fram shrugged, hopelessly. "It's a question of the trains. There has been a hold-up at Shardana, so the trains will only run as far as Dera. They say that the mail will go, heavily guarded but not until tomorrow night. I think it will be quiet until the Quaid-i-Azum is buried, so it is vital that we use these few days to get Arina away to Madore, and Tiger back to his regiment."

Tiger drank some coffee, pushed his plate away and said quietly, "I will take her, and be myself in Abbottabad before anything starts. Please, dear Fram, understand how I feel. Would you let Manika set off alone at this time?"

"No. But Manika is in double danger – Arina is travelling in her own country, and her religion is not threatened – in fact

I think she would be safer without you. With your temper as it is, you could easily start trouble. She can go as far as Dera and wait there for the mail – Arina, can you do that?"

Arina had found her security, only to lose it again. But she was sure in her mind that Fram was right in what he said. With her dutiful maidservant, travelling to a place known to Chunia, set against Tiger running into trouble and being court-martialled out of his beloved regiment – of course she was sure of what she should say and do.

"I can go safely. Tiger, you have not heard what has been planned – Chunia has family at Mianaghar, and that is close to Dera. We will go to Mianaghar and wait there for the mail, and go on to Madore. Then I will wait there until this is over, and you will be free to come."

As she said the words, it all suddenly seemed very easy, rather pleasant in a way – she would have time to prepare for the wedding and the parties afterwards. It would be exciting to wait for her bridegroom in the old palace in Madore, with the beautiful garden that she could vaguely remember. "I will be able to ride," she said suddenly, smiling at the thought.

"You are all mad." Tiger said. "Look at her – she has no idea at all what she is facing. How can I let her go alone? Chunia, Sushi, Alam Beg, what security can two old women and an elderly guard give her? How far is Dera? I mean by road?" Fram felt a sudden spark of hope.

"It is two or three days' journey – over rough roads. What are you thinking, Tiger?"

"I am thinking that I will take Arina up as far as Dera, wait with her until the 'Karachi Mail' comes on its way to Madore, put her on it, and then continue my journey to Abbottabad. Who could quarrel with that? You will not have to tell lies for me, Fram, you will be able to say with truth that I am on my way."

"You will only get as far as Dera, Tiger. You leave her there – and where do you go?"

"Fram, you are determined to throw cold water on me. Do you not recall the old route to Abbottabad? At Dera the rail branches off, crosses the Indus, and continues on, up to Pindi. I get off at Pindi, there is a small road to a place called Hassan Abdul, where I can get transport to Abbottabad. Easy." He smiled across at Arina.

"And if the regiment has already been sent to some other place? Then what?"

"Then I follow – just as I would at the end of my leave. I am sure that my battalion will still be sitting fretting in the depot, not having been sent anywhere. I know what it will be like – there will be no action for us, and I will get another short leave, and go to Madore, taking the route across the hills, and be married in joy and celebration, and take my wife back over the passes to let her meet those brother officers and their wives who were not able to join the festivities. Now, please could we stop discussing what Arina and I are planning to do, and *do* it? Arina, go and get your entourage together, and we will go. Fram, my dear friend, will you sink your fears for my future, and drive us to Kiamari? It is about half an hour's journey from Karachi, I think, so we will be able to get the eight o'clock train to Dera easily. It is now only six a.m.. Let us take advantage of this early hour and go."

Watching him, Arina knew that he was holding his temper in check with difficulty. It gave her pleasure to find that she could tell what he was feeling. He is, she thought, very dismayed and saddened by the disaster that has befallen his country, with the death of the man who had made the dream of Pakistan come true. I wish I was not being so much trouble to him. I am certain that if it were not for me he would dash off to join his battalion at once – and yet I am so proud that he is worried about my safety, and is willing to risk a court-martial for my sake! I should be ashamed, I am a selfish, demanding woman, thought Arina, who had not ever felt grown-up before. Now, I am really ready to be married, she thought.

This man, this Tiger, was slowly becoming inseparable from the man of whom she had always dreamed. She was in fact, ashamed to be so full of happiness in the face of this national grief, but she did not want to lose the feeling. She gazed at Sher Ali, with her heart full.

"Well," Sher Ali said, noticing Arina's gaze. "Are you going to sit here for the rest of the morning, or shall we start on this aggravating expedition?"

"Aggravating" is the right word, thought Arina, rising quickly with a flush painting her cheeks. He must be the rudest man I have ever met. Do I really want to start off on a journey during which he will be my companion? No, I don't, and if it weren't for Manika and Fram, I would refuse to go, but they are both so worried and unhappy that I must behave. She hurried to her bedroom, but there was no one there.

"They are outside, by the car. Chunia has everything you need, including your veil. Don't be angry with Tiger – he is very worried, and determined to keep you from danger. You must believe his love for you – be patient."

Patient! Arina did not dare to respond. She kissed Manika goodbye, and felt that she was leaving her one and only friend, and climbed into the back seat of the car, crushed unhappily between Chunia and Sushi, with Alam Beg on Sushi's other side, trying to keep himself to himself and his eyes to the front, while Chunia, sternly admonishing, wrapped Arina's face and shoulders in a thick veil. Sher Ali was sitting in the front seat beside Fram.

"This is ridiculous," said Fram, who was now looking over his shoulder at his unhappy passengers. "You cannot sit in such discomfort. Sher Ali, take your own car, let Arina sit beside you. I will follow you, and I will drive your car back. I will take one of the drivers with me to bring my car back."

So it was that Arina found herself alone with Sher Ali sooner than she had expected, sitting beside him in a large, black car that she first remembered seeing parked at the docks. She was surprised by the arrival of Chunia, who with an expression of grim determination, climbed into the back of the big car, followed by Alam Beg, wearing a belt with a holster unfastened to show the handle of a revolver.

Arina wondered if Chunia was wearing her dagger.

Sher Ali glanced over his shoulder. "There are more to come, Alam Beg?"

"Nay, heaven born. We are all."

"Thanks be to Allah the Beneficent. Let us go."

The car started off with a roar, and Arina sat back in her seat and wondered if the ride was going to be as frightening as her first drive with Sher Ali.

The sun had not yet risen. The sky was a delicate apricot shot with pink, and the sea, an unbelievable shade of green, lay like a coloured mirror alongside the road. It was a beautiful morning, and it seemed ridiculous to be driving in a car with an armed man – and, no doubt, an armed woman. She glanced sideways at Sher Ali, and found he was looking at her – very briefly, as their eyes met, the car lurched and he looked away at once.

"I suppose I have made you angry again?" Sher Ali asked. "You are asking yourself why you are here, going somewhere with a man you do not even like – you must be asking yourself that. Why can I never read your thoughts? Will we ever be close enough to understand each other?" He spoke perfect English. At least, she thought, he wishes to keep our affairs private.

Once more, Sher Ali found himself waiting for an answer, wishing that he could stop the car and shake an answer out of her. And if I did, she would scratch my face, and Alam Beg would have to shoot Chunia or she would be at me with a dagger. At last Arina said "I can't remember your question – it has blown away with the speed we are travelling at."

Sher Ali pulled the car over to the side of the road and stopped. He turned to her and said, "I have a great desire to shake you. If you were already my wife, I would do so."

131

"Thank you. You have at last given me a good reason for refusing matrimony."

"Does that mean that up until now you have felt that you might very well marry me?" He was smiling, that heart-breaking, charming smile that altered his whole expression, and suddenly made her lean a little towards him without her knowing she was doing it. He saw her involuntary movement and stopped his hand going out to pull her closer with a self-control he did not know he possessed.

"I have already told you. In spite of various trying facets in your character, I will not break my word. I promised that I would marry you. As long as you want me to be your wife. Do I have to keep repeating this? Will it not grow tedious?"

He didn't wait any longer, and he started the car, pulling back on to the road. Then, with his eyes focused on the road before him, he said, "'Want' is a word not to be used lightly at this moment. I did not understand what all the meanings of that word could be. I am a man who wanders in a desert, thirsting, with the water close at hand but forbidden to drink. Yes, I want you as my wife. As my companion, the mother of my children, the one who shares my life . . ." He paused, and added, "I asked you if you could tell me of love and you did not answer. Can you tell me now?"

Arina hesitated, and Sher Ali waited, his eyes on the road, then he sighed and said, "Is this the sort of moment when you always take to serious deep thought? I am not used to this – I expect an immediate answer. Tell me! Tell me about love – mine for you is self-evident. And yours for me? *Tell* me!"

"Tiger, please. To answer such a question instantly, without thought, would be an insult, it would mean that your question meant nothing to me. I need to think about my answers, and try to see into the meanings of your words, which you use so freely. Sometimes I wonder—"

"What do you wonder, bird of my heart?"

Arina felt her own heart quicken and change beat. Her

breathing shortened as she said, stammering a little, "I wonder whether you mean what you say – or are these the words you always use when you talk to girls?"

Now I have made him angry again. Oh, are we never to have a conversation without one of us losing our temper? But this time, to her relief, he answered her calmly, and with a thread of amusement in his voice.

"Arina – I have not had very many conversations with girls of your class, except my own sister and, with sisters, you do not talk of love. You are going to speak to me now of love? You are going to say that you love me?"

"Tiger. I cannot say that I love you. I do not know you – you do not know me. We only know what we see: I like very much what I see, but love – Oh Tiger, what is love? I do not know this love that everyone speaks of so loosely. To my grandmother love brought nothing but sorrow and loneliness. Tiger, she used to weep in the night, I would hear her sometimes. Is that love, to be away from your own land, and weep alone in the night?"

Sher Ali wanted to look at her, he wanted to stop the car and pull her into his arms and kiss her again, but, ahead, he could see the distant shapes of houses. Time was his enemy, they would arrive at the station before he could do anything. He said, taking one hand from the jerking wheel of the car, to take her hand.

"Arina, love can bring sorrow, but it can also bring the greatest happiness in the world. I promise you love and happiness. As long as I live, I will keep you from sorrow as well as I can. Life can be painful, you know that, but you will find out what joy can be discovered in loving. Let me tell you now, in our own tongue—"

It was too late, they were bumping over cracking tarmac and the station was ahead of them. No time to say anything more, and with the audience sitting all ears behind, no doubt, there was no time to snatch a kiss.

Sher Ali kissed Arina's hand, palm and wrist, and terrified his passengers with a sharp turn and a near miss as a lorry reeled out of the dust in front. At last though, the car came to a halt in front of the rickety buildings of Kiamari Station. Five minutes later, while they were still unloading, Fram arrived with his passenger, Sushi and two other men.

"Tiger, as you see, Sakhi Mohammed is with me – he is intent on going with you."

Sakhi Mohammed, the tall young man in uniform, who had been with Sher Ali at the docks, saluted his master, and bowed over folded hands before Arina, saying quietly, "The Nawabzaida Sahib knows that I go where he goes, always. It was an oversight that I was not in the car with him."

His eyes were turned to Alam Beg, his look was not friendly.

"Do not imagine vain things, my brother," Alam Beg said at once. "I am not here to take over your duties. I have my own duties. I am honoured that I have been ordered to guard, with my life, the safety of the mother of future kings. I serve the Begum Sahiba Arina of Chikor – who else? Hold no *zid* against me, brother!"

Sher Ali was watching the two men with a smile in his eyes, then he said quietly to Fram, "See – faithful servants both, and they will be at each other's throats in a few minutes." He stepped forward and touched Sakhi Mohammed on the shoulder. "Enough! Two days of war, snarling at each other? Be ashamed, old companions as you are! You are both of equal importance, here for only one reason, to do your duty faithfully. Who else could do it more faithfully? Enough chatter, go and find a first-class purdah compartment and load the baggage. I will bring the Begum Sahiba once you tell me you have a place for her. Fram, have you the tickets?"

Fram had gone forward already, the tickets in his hands, and Chunia and Sushi and the two men were quick to follow him. They vanished into the mass of humanity that surged up and down the platform outside the train. Men, women, children, hobbled goats, chickens in wicker baskets, and amazing piles of luggage balanced on the heads of porters created what looked to be an impenetrable barrier through which Arina dreaded trying to get. She saw women, carrying babies thrusting their way through the crowd. She thought that they were like sheeted ghosts, veiled from head to foot in heavy white cotton *burkahs*. The sight of them made her uneasy. Surely her veil was sufficient – or should she be wearing a *burkah*? She turned a nervous glance to her companion, convinced that somehow she would have offended him yet again. He could not see her face, the veil was thick, but she was sure he must have noticed the *burkah*-clad women. But he did not look angry, he was smiling at her.

"We are never alone," he said "I have so much I want to say to you – and just one thing that I long to hear you say. We are going to be apart for how long? Only Allah knows, but I will ask for permission to come back to you in Madore as soon as I can. Do not forget me, my heart of gold – keep me in your mind, as I will keep you. Look for me in your heart every day, for I will not be able to send word to you. Remember me."

She wanted to say that of course she would remember him – her affianced lord – for how could she forget him? How strange he was. One minute so arrogantly sure of himself, the next . . . What, who, was he? Still a stranger. She was about to tell him she could never forget him, but the noise level of the station was suddenly augmented by a series of loud blasts from the train's engine.

"That is our train and it is about to leave. Where are those fools? Arina! Follow me at once."

He began to push his way into the crowd and Arina hurried to keep up with him, taking advantage of what little space he made as he ruthlessly shoved and pushed people aside to clear his path.

Thirteen

It seemed to Arina that she was never going to get through the tightly packed, struggling mob of laden people, who were between her and the open carriage door which she could just see beyond Sher Ali's head. With her eyes fixed on that lodestar, she pushed and wriggled until, at last, she saw a hand stretched through a gap towards her, which she seized. She was pulled through the last few bodies, and found that Fram's hand had rescued her.

Sher Ali was there, but he was busy talking to two fully armed and purposeful-looking guards. Alam Beg was there, standing four square in front of the compartment door, and behind him she could see Chunia and Sushi, dim shadows in the darkness of the shuttered compartment.

Arina had a sudden frisson of fear as she looked into the dark compartment. It seemed haunted by more than one shadow – who else was travelling with her? She had an almost overwhelming desire to beg Fram to take her back to the clear bright air of his house by the sea, but he was now engaged in conversation with Sher Ali. Fram looked as unhappy as she felt, worried and uncertain. She was sure – in fact she *knew* that he considered this journey of hers to be madness. She was certain that if she said to him, even at this last minute, "Please, Fram, take me back – I am sure that something terrible is going to happen," he would do his best to free her of this journey.

I am being foolish, she told herself, this is my own doing. I agreed to make this journey, and I would be a great nuisance to Manika and Fram, to everyone, if I changed my mind now.

She said nothing, stood beside Fram and Sher Ali and, when he turned to her and took her into his arms and kissed her forehead through her veil, she felt his warmth through the chiffon that covered her face. She clung to him, leaning her head against his broad chest, clenching her teeth against the words she wanted to say. But he felt her tremble in his arms, and said at once, "Arina, what is it, my dear – what is wrong? Tell me."

But she held back the words. This sense of impending disaster was only in her imagination, brought about by all the warnings and fears of others. She had to remember that Tiger was not afraid of any evil happening, she had to learn to rely on him, and not be the cause of concern for these kind people, Fram and Manika. They had become so close to her in such a short time! She could hear Manika's voice saying, "you are the daughter of my heart", and she herself had been too busy worrying about Tiger to make a proper, loving reply. She said now, standing in the safe circle of Fram's arms, "There is nothing wrong – only that I hate to say goodbye, dear Fram. Please, will you tell Manika that she is has a special place in my heart. I think that my mother, if she had lived, would have been to me what Manika has become – a loved friend, as well as a mother. Tell Manika what I say, Fram, please. Don't forget – tell her as soon as you can, I want her to come up to us in the hills. Tell her I love her dearly. She must come."

Fram was very moved. "I will of course tell Manika. Tiger has always taken the place of the son we could not have, and now you have filled the other empty space in our lives, our dear daughter."

He gently loosened her fingers, which were holding on to his hands, embraced Sher Ali, and left them out of sight in the crowd in seconds.

Arina found herself standing close to Tiger, looking up into his face, and was glad to see that he looked as if he had hated saying farewell to Fram. She was also glad of her veil, because her eyes were full of tears that she did not want him to see. To weep when she was going off on a journey with him would certainly throw him into one of his rages, the last thing she wanted. She wondered how they were going to be able to talk together, with Sushi, Chunia and other servants in the compartment. But at least they could sit together, and perhaps come closer in understanding. She knew that she was almost ready to say what he wanted her to say – she would be dishonest if she continued to deny her love for him. If only they were alone, she could say that she had now discovered the country of love. The flame was lit, and burning – he had taken her heart, she could truthfully tell him that. But whether her love would be able to grow against the uncertainties that his changes of mood aroused in her, she could not tell.

The crowd on the platform seemed to have increased, the engine whistled ear-piercingly and a man ran past shouting and waving a red flag.

"Thanks be," Sher Ali said, "we will be moving out shortly. My heart's gold, you must get into your compartment and then I must go find my own – not too far away, I hope."

"But – but – aren't you coming with me?" Surely it couldn't be that he was not going to be with her for this journey?

"Light of my heart," his look was one of astonishment, "I cannot travel with you. This is a purdah carriage, for ladies only. In any case, we are forbidden to travel together before we are married. Your name would be shamed for ever if we were to spend a night alone together! Let me help you in. I shall miss this train if I do not leave you now, but I leave with sorrow, so do not be unhappy. I shall think of you every minute that we are apart."

The engine whistled again, and Sher Ali almost threw her into the compartment, shouting to Chunia to lock the door.

"And keep the shutters up and locked until we are well away from this station – I should wait about twenty minutes before you open them." He looked one last time at Arina's veiled face, he was sure that he had been very close to hearing from her what he longed to hear, and he cursed the constant interruption this courtship seemed to undergo, and also the hard fact that they were never alone together – nor were they likely to be before marriage.

It was at that moment, as the train jerked and began to move very slowly, that Arina put up her hands and threw back her veil and looked, smiling, into his eyes. He could only meet them for a breathless second before he had to jump down and run along the platform towards Sakhi, who he could see waving at him frantically. He heard, behind him, the slam of the door as Chunia did as he had told her. And then he reached his own compartment and tumbled into it with the help of Sakhi Mohammed's strong arms.

Left behind in the dark and airless box of the purdah compartment, Arina watched Chunia slam the door shut in the face of a man who was determined to push a woman and two children through the door, paying no attention to Chunia's shriek of "Reserved, reserved – fool, get away."

Arina was horrified, she put out her hand to stop Chunia, but the old woman paid no attention to her, the door was shut and locked and, at the same time, Sushi was busy checking all the windows.

"Chunia, that was a woman with children. She has a perfect right to come into this purdah compartment, there is plenty of room."

"Nay, child, we do not want a village woman and her brats in here – we have paid to have this space to ourselves. It is always the same on these slow trains, there are never enough purdah carriages and, on this train, no other first-class compartments – and those people were not first-class travellers."

Arina looked about at the carriage that was reserved for her and her two maidservants. It was large, it seemed to her, but then she had nothing to compare it with, never having travelled by train anywhere before. There were four beds, two folded back against the side of the compartment, two below. Two chairs, a mirror with a small shelf in front of it, a central fan, two windows on each side, three doors – one of which led into a very small room with a basin, a shower and a lavatory.

The two women had already unpacked, a bed had been made up, Arina's toothbrushes and soap were laid out on the shelf above the basin, and she saw Chunia carefully covering the made-up bed with a clean cover – it looked as if they had been settled in for some time.

Arina asked how long they were to be on the train. Chunia held up one finger. "It will be one night, and one day, we arrive at dawn tomorrow." It sounded a very long time to have to spend shut up in a little box. Chunia assured her that they would open the windows very soon. "But the dust is very bad, you will see. I have unpacked for you a travelling dress – I will change your clothes for you after the next station, then you will have clean clothes to put on for Dera where we leave the train."

And say goodbye to Tiger, thought Arina with a sinking heart. There would be no private farewell, their meetings and partings always seemed to be made in crowded places, surrounded by interested observers. She began to wish that they had made better use of the short time they had in the car, they could have ensured privacy by speaking English . . .

She sank into a reverie, thinking back over all the things that had happened since she arrived – when? Only the day before! So much had happened, so many unexpected events – she felt that she had already been in Pakistan for years. She had a family – not just a grandmother. She had Chunia back, and she had Fram and Manika, so close that they seemed to have always been part of her life. And Tiger – the man in the picture, and the boy with the hawk and the horse, the angry man, who flamed with rage with no warning, and the man who looked deeply into her eyes and made her heart race when he called her by loving names that no other man had ever used to her.

Was he truly a man in love? Had he learned to use those words to give pleasure to some other woman? How did one find answers to these questions? Why could she not trust him? She suddenly spoke her question aloud, perhaps Chunia could answer her?

"Chunia, why can I not trust Sher Ali?"

Chunia took no time to answer. "It is because you have never met a man's love before. You find it hard to understand a man's way of loving. The Nawab Sahib is in the full flush of his first love. He has not wasted the love of his heart on any other women – you are fortunate. Do not question it. It is rare indeed to be the first love of such a man. Take pride, and enjoy your good fortune." Chunia shook her head, frowning and smiling at the same time. "It is his luck that you are so young for your years. You are like a child of fifteen or sixteen years. Your grandmother did not spoil you with too much useless information. Better you learn about love from your husband. I have always said this – no one else's words can teach you of love. Listen and learn from your husband – and do not question so much."

"So marriage without choice is good? How can you say that, Chunia, you who know the full story of my grandmother's life?"

Chunia was silent for a few minutes, long enough for Anna to recall that it was her grandmother's love, and her desire to escape from an arranged marriage that had almost cost Chunia her life, and had left her a woman old before her time, her beauty gone, with only one eye.

Oh, how could I have been so thoughtless, to ask her that, to reawaken the past?

"Oh Chunia, my dearest old one, forgive me, I did not think

before I spoke – my grandmother owes you so much, you have given so much to our family."

"Ssht, ssht! What is all this pother? I gave nothing that I did not wish to give, and I would do the same thing, if the same situation had arisen again. But you, my beloved child, your fortune is written in your eyes – a life of joy and contentment. Now, enough of this. You have lived under the shadow of your grandmother and her sorrows for too long. Of course it is hard for you to believe in love! Love, the strongest, most powerful emotion, brings different things to different people. You are at the beginning of your life – forget the sorrows that are not yours. Look to the sunshine of your days, and be happy in your future, which is so bright."

As if to underline what Chunia had said, Sushi had pulled down the shutters and brilliant sunshine streamed in through the dusty glass of the train windows. There was nothing to see outside, nothing but sand, rocks and a few thorn trees – nothing moved in the landscape that stretched unbroken as far as the horizon. But the light was clear and the compartment felt less like a box surrounded as it was with so much open space.

Arina sat looking out, but not for long. Sleep overtook her, and she did not wake when Chunia put a pillow under her nodding head, and covered her with a light shawl.

Further down the train, three carriages away from the purdah carriage, Sher Ali had reached his compartment and was staring, horrified, at his companions. Two were English, brother officers of his in the same regiment, but a different battalion, the other was Yusuf Dyal of his own battalion. Sher Ali could not believe his eyes.

"What in the name of all angels in hell, are you doing here?" he said in Urdu, totally ignoring the welcoming words of the other two, Tom Fraser and Dick Walker, who were both very surprised by his angry entrance. Like most of the regiment, they had imagined that these two officers were great friends.

The long love that in my thought doth harbour

The Long Love

Yusuf Dyal showed no signs of distress at Sher Ali's greeting. Instead he laughed. "What am I doing? Much the same as all of us, I suppose – going back to the regiment, leave having been cancelled. But of course, you are particularly unfortunate – at least the rest of us have not been torn from the bosoms of our nearest and dearest." He turned his smile and guileless eyes to the other two, saying, "Poor old Tiger was engaged in taking his fiancée up to Madore to their wedding. Can you beat *that* for bad luck!"

"Oh no, poor Tiger, that is a bit hard. Where have you left her?"

Before Tiger could answer, Dyal said, "Oh she's been left in the lap of luxury, hasn't she old boy? All Tiger's friends and relatives are either very rich, or royal, so his future wife will at least be comfortable, though lacking the excitement of Tiger's presence, poor little thing."

Both Tom and Dick agreed that this was very hard luck. It would, they both thought, explain Tiger's rudeness to his old friend Yusuf Dyal. Certainly Yusuf did not appear to have been distressed by Tiger's manner. He smiled happily as he said, "Dear boy, don't be too unhappy – though having seen your bride, I can understand your feelings, by God I can. You must be, as they say, on tenterhooks. Tell you what I will do – I will speak to the colonel, tell him how you are placed, and wring an extra couple of weeks' leave out of him for you. After all, what is the point of having one's uncle as colonel of the battalion if one cannot make use of him for a friend? Leave it to me."

Seething, Tiger tried to ignore the first part of Yusuf's remarks and said, "Since when did Colonel Lanfield become your uncle? An act of adoption?"

Yusuf Dyal shook his head, looking amazed. "My dear fellow! You are behind the times! Old Lanfield has gone – it was, of course, very sudden but the good colonel has taken early retirement. I don't know all the ins and outs of

143

it, but what I do know is that my uncle, Nasir Dyal is now commanding our battalion. So I can put in a word for you – easiest thing in the world."

Dyal looked so delighted that he had the ability to help his dear friend that both Tom and Dickie congratulated Sher Ali on the fact that he had such a friend to straighten things out for him. Neither of them appeared to notice the implied slur on Charles Lanfield that Yusuf Dyal had made. Sher Ali, on the other hand, wondered what chicanery had been employed to get rid of Colonel Lanfield – a man revered and popular with all of his regiment. However, he had enough on his mind to deal with – he would worry about the happenings in the battalion later.

Right now, he thought, one thing I must prevent is this accursed Dyal discovering that Arina is on the train – he didn't seem to have seen their arrival at the station. Perhaps the crowds had hidden it from this end of the train. Or did Dyal have some idea . . . ? Had Sakhi Mohammed been questioned, had he said that his master was attending the arrival of the Begum Arina and seeing her safely into the purdah compartment? No, Sakhi Mohammed would have said nothing about the Begum. He was to be trusted completely.

Sher Ali felt that Dyal knew nothing, but he would have to make sure it stayed that way. Which meant that he would not be able to go down and speak to her – he'd have to keep away from that end of the train. He could not explain to himself exactly why he felt it so essential that Arina's presence on the train be kept a secret. It was nothing to do with Tom and Dickie, the feeling of suspicion that he had was directed entirely at Dyal. Every time he looked across the carriage and saw Dyal, he was shaken with rage – but, as well as rage, he felt fear, something he had never experienced before. He was conscious of a feeling of real terror whenever he thought of Arina in connection with Dyal, and he could not understand this. Now he hated Dyal with more virulence than he had ever felt before. But terror? This was new.

He looked at Dyal and saw in his place a coiled and venomous snake – the apparition was so sudden, so real, that he started to his feet, glaring across the compartment, and feeling for the gun at his hip.

"Here, steady on, Tiger, what is it? What have you seen?" Both Tom and Dickie were on their feet, looking in the same direction as Sher Ali, towards the door of the compartment. The window was not shuttered, though the glass was in place to keep out the dust. The two Englishmen looked automatically at the window, but Dyal had seen Sher Ali's eyes fix on him, and he was afraid to move.

Sher Ali heard Tom's exclamation, his hand touched the cold end of his revolver and his sight cleared. The coiled snake was gone, he saw only Dyal's frightened face.

"There doesn't seem to be anything out there, Tiger, what did you think you saw?"

Sher Ali, taking his hand from his revolver said quietly, "I saw a snake. A deadly snake." He kept his eyes firmly on Dyal as he said, "And what did you see, Yusuf?"

Yusuf Dyal was pale, but said, steadily enough, "I saw nothing – nothing at all."

"You lie, Dyal. I think you saw something. I think you saw death." And he turned away, going over to stand beside Tom. "Well, whatever I thought I saw, it seems to have gone now."

Tom went back to his seat beside Dickie. "Whatever you *thought* you saw, Tiger, I am glad I did not see it. It made you look like death on the prowl – wouldn't like to meet you on a dark night looking like that, I can tell you. No pussy cat – you had the look of the real thing."

Yusuf Dyal was very quiet for the rest of the two hours before the train came into a wayside station and stopped. It was hard for Tiger to stay in his seat. After a few minutes,

Dickie, who had jumped down on to the platform, came back to say that the train would stop in this station – Gorahghat – for about twenty minutes.

"I'm going to stretch my legs. Coming Tom? Tiger?" Tom decided he wanted to walk, and Dyal got up without saying anything, and the three of them went off down the platform. Sher Ali saw Sakhi Mohammed outside, and beckoned him over. "Sakhi – go down to the purdah compartment and tell Chunia that I cannot come down. Tell her that Dyal is on the train – tell her to keep the shutters down. Dyal must not know that the Begum is on the train . . ."

"I go, Lord," said Sakhi, and hurried away, and Sher Ali sat, desperate with anxiety until he saw Sakhi coming back. But Sakhi only rolled his eyes, without speaking to him, and climbed into his own compartment. But Sher Ali understood when he saw that Dyal and the other two were coming back down the train.

Sakhi was certainly a man of intelligence, thought Sher Ali, and was grateful that he had a man with such good sense and quick understanding.

The two Englishmen had bought fruit, large golden Kulu apples. "I wonder how these got here," said Tom, "I imagine that they came by pretty devious ways, the Kulu valley definitely appears on India's list of possessions. No other apples like them – have one, Tiger?"

Tiger shook his head. "No thanks – I am going to put my head down for a bit."

He knew that he had to get away from the sight of Dyal, or he would do something foolish. He climbed into one of the two top berths, and stretched out. He tried to clear his mind of everything except the memory of Arina's face as he had last seen her, and, with her image before him, he slept at last, dreamlessly and deeply. But suddenly the peaceful world of slumber was shattered by a terrifying nightmare.

The snake was back, coiling and uncoiling in shiny, patterned loops along the edge of the berth on which he lay in silent fear. Into that silence came a voice – Manika's voice – saying, "He has a snake's eyes." And Sher Ali woke with what he thought was a shout of "Dyal!" and found that he was whispering his enemy's name, and sunset was gilding the walls of the compartment. He had slept through the whole tedious day – there was only the night now before Arina reached safety.

Fourteen

For Arina the day had gone slowly, she had been waiting to see Sher Ali at the first station where the train would stop. But then the train stopped, and he did not come. Sakhi Mohammed appeared on his own, had a short conversation with Chunia and left at once. Chunia then closed and locked the door, and Sushi put all the shutters up again, and it became very hot and airless. Arina begged for a window to be opened, but Chunia refused, firmly.

"Sher Ali has sent a message to say that we are to keep the window and doors locked while we are in the station – and his orders must be obeyed, or he will send me away from you."

Arrogance again, thought Arina, already disappointed, now angry as well. "I will not allow him to send you anywhere, Chunia. Where I am, you will be, and I don't understand why I can't have the shutters up, so that I can at least see out. And why did he not come? He said he would come at the first station – he is not a man of his word?"

"Do not be foolish, Arina. You must learn when to bend your head before authority, and when to fight. If you do not learn the lessons of life yourself, then how will you raise your son who one day will – may Allah keep that day distant – have to rule with wisdom?"

Arina felt her temper beginning to flair. Chunia was so old – no doubt she was still living in the past. Things must have moved forward since those days. Arina tried to speak calmly, but it was not easy to remain cool when she was so hot and uncomfortable and – yes, she admitted to herself – bitterly disappointed. "I suppose Sher Ali can change his mind, come to see me or not come, just as he feels, and does not have to be courteous enough to send me a message, an explanation. I suppose that is how he will behave as a husband. Well—"

"Arina!" Chunia interrupted, holding up her hand. "Watch your tongue. Do not say things that you will regret afterwards. Better to keep your tongue between your teeth when you are displeased. Always remember who you are."

"How can I forget when you remind me all the time? I am not Arina, I am not a girl, I am a *thing*, I am only valuable as the mother of a future ruler – a son for the crown. And what happens if I have a daughter? I suppose I am cast off, and Sher Ali takes another bride, and I become her son's washerwoman."

Arina's eyes sparked with angry tears, and yet underneath the rage was a sadness, a great loneliness – a life lived like that, without Tiger! It looked bleak.

Chunia came to stand beside her. "When you speak so, you sound as though you are someone of very little importance. Just a very silly girl, too young for your years. Come, I understand. You are hot and sweating, and very disappointed not to see your lord. That is why you are speaking angry nonsense. I will make you feel better. The train will leave in a short time. Before it starts, let me take you in here and help you shower. We will wash the dust out of your hair, then you will feel better."

Mutinously, Arina said, "He is *not* my lord."

Chunia paid no attention, though, and hurried her mistress into the little room, barely big enough for two. She took Arina's clothes from her and turned on the shower, getting soaked herself in the process. She bathed Arina and washed her hair, her hands firm and disciplinary. While Chunia was doing this, Arina saw her maidservant's left hand and remembered the story of how it had become so badly broken, so misshapen, and was ashamed of the way she had spoken.

Chunia had been willing to lose her life rather than allow Zeena Begum to fall into the hands of her enemy. Her broken hand, her blind eye, spoke of her constant, unshaken loyalty and courage.

"I am ashamed before you, Chunia. You are right. I spoke foolishly because I was so disappointed, I wanted Sher Ali to keep his word to come and see me. Forgive me. I have no right to speak so to you."

Chunia smiled, wrapped Arina in towels and said, "There! You see, I told you that you would feel better. Be very sure of one thing, Sher Ali had good reason to avoid drawing attention to this purdah carriage. There is someone travelling who must not know you are on the train – Yusuf Dyal is sharing Sher Ali's compartment."

Arina felt a shiver of unease – that man did seem to bring distress and disorder to her new family. She remembered Manika had shuddered at the thought of him. He had caused Sher Ali to be enraged with her, and now he had made her lose her temper. He certainly seemed to be a person of bad omen. She dismissed the thought of Yusuf Dyal from her mind, and instead of dwelling on him she thought of something more important.

Sher Ali had good reason for not coming to see her. He would have come, she was sure, if it had been without danger. That thought healed all hurts, but now there were other concerns . . .

When, at last, the train jerked into movement, Arina was dressed in a clean blue cotton sari, and was sitting in a chair while Chunia combed out her long hair, and soon Sushi unlocked and pulled up the shutters and Arina could look out and enjoy the passing country. They were still in desert country, barren and sand coloured, with nothing to break the monotony but occasional rocks, shaped by an endless wind that raised whirling dust, blotting out the landscape and pattering against the glass of the windows like fingers tapping on the panes. Arina longed to see some life, animal or human – anything to take away the feeling of desolation she was experiencing as she looked out at the treeless scenery before her.

"Is it all like this?" she asked. and both Chunia and Sushi assured her that it would change in the morning.

"We will be in sight of the mountains and the river. By sunset you will see the river – we arrive at dawn and you will see the mountains then. We will be at Shahbaiya by sunset, we will stop there, and Alam Beg will bring us food from the station restaurant. We will stay at Shahbaiya for perhaps two hours, many people will be eating in the restaurant. Then the train will only stop four times through the night – at Sindipur, Channa, Daryakot, and Karakot. After that, at dawn, we reach Derastan, and that is where we leave the train. Between Karakot and Derastan the sky will be growing light, and you may see the blue dome of the tomb of the Rani of Karakot. It is very beautiful."

The word "tomb" brought a feeling of horror to Arina, and she shuddered, turning back to look out at the empty desert. The thought of anyone being buried so far away from any town or dwelling made her want to weep. What comfort would a blue dome bring to the Rani lying under it, without the sound of a human voice? The depression that began to fall on Arina was so unusual for her that she could not bear it. "Poor Rani" she said, "To be buried in the wilderness . . ."

"When in the sleep of death, no sound could cheer her, or disturb her dreams. Does this thought disturb you, Khanum?"

"Yes, it does. I know it is foolish to say so, but it makes me very sad to think of her lying there alone."

"Then you would rather lie where the Persian girl lies – below the house of the Dinshaw family?" Sushi asked quietly.

"*Ayii*, what a thought that is! There is no good fortune in such a building – nothing but grief can come of such a place."

"What do you mean, Sushi? The Dinshaw house? Do you

mean Sagar House? Is the Persian girl – the girl of the rose – buried there?"

"Sushi, you would have done better to have kept quiet at this time." Chunia spoke calmly, but there was a coldness in her voice, and Sushi lowered her eyes and did not reply to Arina's question.

Arina looked at Chunia and said, "Manika did not finish the story of the Persian girl – is that why? Is her tomb in the house? Why?"

"It is not part of the house. Over the years, various members of the family enlarged the house and it spread until the tomb, built many, many years ago was included under some of the rooms. And no one has ever thought anything of it, except that the tomb is honoured and tended by the members of the family. As to the reason for the family building near the tomb – why, the Persian girl is of their blood. The Dinshaw family are Persian, merchants of wealth and renown – there is no question of ill luck falling on any member of that family. There is nothing strange about a tomb being close to a house. Sushi, you speak like a person from another *jat* – what is it with you?"

Sushi looked ashamed and embarrassed under Chunia's glaring eye. "I was foolish. But while I was in the house I felt sorrow coming, and there were shadows of the past everywhere. Did you not feel it, too, my sister? Perhaps, as I grow old, I grow foolish. I do not wish my fears to burden you, Arina Begum, especially not at this time which, for you, should be one of roses. Forgive my foolishness."

"There is nothing to forgive, Sushi. I have my own fears and shadows. Chunia, did you not feel anything there?"

"Nay, my heart of gold, I felt nothing there but joy, joy at seeing you safely back among your own people. Let there be no shadows to mar your happiness, my bird. As Sushi says, this is the time of roses for you. Think only of your marriage, and all the festivities that will attend it."

The words were brave, and Chunia was smiling, but Arina saw her hand go up to touch the silver chain at her throat, and the blue bead beside it, and thought she heard a softly breathed, "Inshallah".

Arina said the words to herself, and wondered what it was that had cast a shadow over this day. Perhaps the nation's sorrow over a good man's death had touched her, too, although she was still virtually a stranger in her own country.

Looking out at the desert land that stretched away to the horizon in veils of blown sand, Arina's eyes grew heavy and eventually she fell asleep, the hours passing with ease.

Chunia and Sushi moved closer together, and whispered to one another, speaking of the next few days that would lie between them and their arrival in Madore – if all went well. Chunia saw that Sushi was still worried, and she herself felt that Dyal's presence on the train was not fortuitous.

"This is not good – that son of the devil, Yusuf Dyal, was supposed to have gone by the mail to Peshawar. He has some plan, I am sure. When we stop in Shahbaiya, I will try to speak with Sakhi Mohammed. It would be good if he came with us, and let Alam Beg go with the Nawab Sahib."

"But he is the prince's bodyguard, sister. Does he not have to stay with the prince?" Sushi could not believe that Chunia could alter the arrangements of the entourage so easily, but Chunia had no doubts.

"The Nawab Sahib is not in any danger – the danger is close to us, I fear. I will send a message to Sher Ali himself, he will think as I do."

When the train drew up at Shahbaiya under a blazing sunset sky, Sher Ali saw Alam Beg come down the train and go into Sakhi Mohammed's compartment. His companions were getting ready to go to the railway restaurant, but he declined to go with them. "Sakhi Mohammed will bring me something – I'm not very hungry."

Yusuf Dyal smiled. "Lost your appetite – hungry for hya-cinths instead of bread. That girl is a spellbinder, if she can take your appetite away."

There was laughter in his voice, and Tom and Dickie did not notice the controlled anger on Sher Ali's face. They only heard what they thought was harmless levity.

"Come on, Tiger, you've eaten nothing all day," said Tom. "This place is supposed to put on a very good chicken curry – worth having a look."

Sher Ali managed a smile and shook his head. "You go ahead – I shall have a drink here, and I may join you later."

He did not know how he had kept himself from getting up and strangling Yusuf Dyal, as he heard him say, "Yes, come on you two – leave him to dream of his marriage night. From what I saw of the girl, it should be a hot one. She is what we call a—"

"Oh, shut up, Dyal, you are asking for trouble, you've gone far enough," Tom interrupted.

Sher Ali could hear Dyal laughing as he walked down the train with the others, and then Sakhi Mohammed was with him in the carriage, telling him that Chunia was worried. Sher Ali did not hesitate. "Of course you must go with them. And Alam Beg. I do not need anyone, Gokal can do up my bedding roll, and bring my tea in the morning. You will make, of yourselves, a wall around the one who is to be my wife." And, he added to himself, the light of my life. Now I understand the meaning of those words. The light would go out for ever if anything happened to her.

Sahki Mohammed poured a whisky for his master, and Alam Beg had already been to the station dining-room and brought a *tali* of chicken curry and two folded chapattis wrapped in a clean napkin. Sher Ali, with Sakhi Mohammed standing behind him, drank his whisky and asked for another. The curry was good, the chapattis freshly made. He saw Alam Beg standing outside and told Sakhi to send him back to Chunia. "He can tell

Chunia that she will have you both – and will only lose Gokal for as long as it takes him to roll up my bedding and pack my shaving gear. If I do it myself, Dyal will wonder where you have gone, and then he'd start asking questions."

"Lord, I know, the son of Eblis hates you. *Ya illah!* Give me the word, and I will make him sleep for a long time – and who can say how a man catches cholera out of season? He is a great eater of mangoes – it is child's play," said Sakhi Mohammed.

Sher Ali grinned at him, but shook his head. "Nay, Sakhi, I will deal with him – but later. I will have no truck with poison – that is a woman's game."

"I can find you a woman who will do it for a jewelled nose ring, Hukam. Say the word."

"Leave it, Sakhi. Guard my life's happiness, and we will talk again – when we are in our own place – about the short life of Dyal. Go now, I will not rest easily until I know you are on guard down there."

Alam Beg had already gone, hurrying through the crowd when he saw Yusuf Dyal coming out of the station master's office. There was something furtive in the man's appearance. That was a wallet he was putting away into an inner pocket. What could he have been buying? Perhaps he should go back at once, and tell Sakhi Mohammed what he had seen. But at that moment Chunia opened the door of the purdah compartment a little way, put her head out and called to him to bring food for them.

Well, even if they had taken from him the responsibility of guarding the Begum Sahiba, at least he could still look after her comfort! He was offended at the way he had once more been superseded by Sakhi Mohammed – with no apparent reason. Of course, he thought as he waited on the women in the compartment, I am an old man, that is true, but I would have died for the Begum.

Everything he did for her was an honour – and he was

155

willing to do *anything*. When they had finished eating – and the Begum ate so little – he took the *talis* away, and went back to make up the Begum's bed, and to lower the upper berth and make a bed on it for one of the maids. He brought fresh iced water in an earthenware pitcher, and then remembered to tell Gokal the junior guard, to go down and take Sakhi's place. But the one thing he had forgotten to tell anyone was the most important thing of all: Dyal suspiciously coming out of the station master's office. That slipped his memory completely, as if it had never happened.

Far away in Karachi, Manika and Fram were talking of Arina.

"Fram, she is our daughter in everything but blood. I always felt that pull towards her, now it is stronger than ever. I do wish we had insisted that she stayed here – and now she is on that crazy journey. All caused by that silly old woman Gulrukh, sending messages by that horrible man. How could she! She knows perfectly well that he is the nephew of Tariq Khan who was, of course, a sworn enemy of the Chikor family." Manika sighed.

"I can't understand that either. After all, the telephone is working perfectly – I have just rung through to Dera to book the ladies' waiting room for Arina and her maids. If there is any hitch with the mail train to Madore, she will at least have somewhere to wait, in case Chunia's family are late coming for her. So many things that can go wrong! I wish we had kept her here. I think I shall telephone Gulrukh Begum, and tell her that she must send a car to Dera to meet Arina. Surely that will be possible."

Twenty minutes later, Fram came back from making his telephone call – now more worried than ever. He wondered if it would not be better to keep his news from Manika, but she saw his face before he was ready and said at once, "What is it Fram? Something is wrong?"

"My dear – yes. It is bad news. I got through to Gulrukh without any trouble. Manika, she didn't send a message by Dyal. She has not seen him for months. She will send a car to Dera as soon as she can. There has been inter-communal rioting in Madore. It seems that that is about the only true thing the man told us."

"But why did he lie? Oh Fram, I am afraid. I think he is planning to ruin Tiger's marriage"

"Yes. I think you are right. I am going to send a telegram to Sher Ali, care of the station master at Shahbaiya. The train waits there for at least two hours. It is worth trying."

Fram worded the telegram as simply as possible.

No verbal message sent by your grandmother. She will send car to Dera as soon as possible. Trouble in Madore may cause delay. Suggest you stay with Arina until car arrives. Fram.

"That will have to do, Manika. Now, please do not worry. Tiger will deal with this."

Yes, thought Manika, if the message gets to him. There is nothing more we can do.

Walking down towards the railway restaurant, Dyal saw the purdah carriage. "Look, chaps, a ladies-only – I wonder who is travelling in there, with all the shutters closed. Some favourite wife – or mistress, more like."

As he spoke, the door opened just wide enough for him to see an old woman in white and, behind her . . . Surely that was Sher Ali's girl? So she was on the train, and Sher Ali had said nothing about it. Dyal smiled to himself.

Dickie had looked into the compartment too, just as Chunia looked out. "Well, it is a very old lady anyway. But how hot that compartment must be! Why on earth don't they open the windows, how stupid." As he spoke, he saw a man approach the old woman. "Surely that is Sher Ali's man, isn't it? Talking

157

to the old woman – I wonder if his girl is travelling with him, I must ask. I would like to meet her, if she is going to be a wife in the regiment."

"Yes, do ask him to bring her down to our compartment, Dickie – he'll very likely kill you. If the lady is travelling, she is in purdah, and she certainly won't be brought anywhere near us. I should avoid the subject if I were you," said Tom, "Don't you agree, Dyal?"

Dyal did not seem very interested. He excused himself, saying "I'll have chicken curry, Tom. Order it for me, I have to make a telephone call, I won't be long."

Dyal had heard rumours that the mail train from Derastan to Madore was being held up. If it was, Sher Ali's girl would have a long wait on Dera station. He had already begun to improve on the plan he had originally made. That girl was Sher Ali's soft spot. Through her . . . Oh, what I might inflict on the Tiger, thought Dyal, what vengeance I could inflict on the Chikor family.

He went into the station master's office, produced a well-stuffed notecase, and asked if he could use the telephone. Eyes on the notecase, the station master agreed at once. Dyal made his call to Dera station. All was well, his men, horses and mules were already there, the goods had arrived and were under guard, very satisfactory. He finished his call, and was paying the station master his illegal fee when the man asked if he was travelling with another Sahib, named Sher Ali. "I have a message here for him."

Yusuf Dyal could not believe his luck. "A message? I will give it to him, station master-ji – he is an old friend of mine."

The message was handed over, and a few seconds later Dyal was reading it. He tore it up and threw the pieces to the wind, and walked on into the restaurant where Tom and Dickie were awaiting him.

Fifteen

How long a night could be! Arina woke from a light sleep each time the train stopped, thinking that they had at last arrived at Derastan. She feared the day ahead – not because she was going to unknown places. Chunia knew this part of the country and that was enough for Arina. What she feared though, was the inevitable parting from Sher Ali. He seemed to be the one stable element in all these shifting events. Apart from that, she already missed seeing him, and she longed to learn more about him, as if he was a book that she had started to read, that she was fascinated by, and that was going to be taken from her before she had turned more than a few pages. Arina tossed on her hard berth, and longed for dawn.

Sushi had raised the shutters so that Arina could see the night sky through the blurred glass of the windows. The stars were there to be counted, instead of sheep, but even counting stars – the flocks of the night – she did not fall asleep. Only three more stations to pass and they would be at Derastan. Surely Tiger would come down the platform to say goodbye to her? He could not let her go without seeing her again – not if he truly felt as he said he did. Or if he feels as I do, thought Arina, ready now to admit to herself that Tiger was more than a book to read. He was the man she loved, known, or unknown. He was in her heart, and she wanted to tell him so. She wanted to see his smile, and more than anything she longed to be in his arms again – and feel his kisses.

She was dressed in clothes that Chunia thought suitable for

a travelling lady of rank – lightweight cotton, the colour of the jade earrings and bracelets that Arina was wearing. Her hair was woven into two long braids, tied with green silk ribbons, with bells – little silver bells fixed to the ribbons. Like that bird, thought Arina. Tiger's bird that used to sit on his hand, with a green hood, and bells. For a moment, she was a child again, begging for a ride on his magnificent horse – and being refused. She thought, with a small shiver of delight, that Sher Ali would not refuse her now.

Chunia, laying the light veil, like a green mist, over her shoulders, saw the sparkle in her eyes and said, "Aha, you have happy thoughts, my bird! You smile like a bride." And Arina blushed and looked away from that one seeing eye in Chunia's wrinkled mask.

Arina was ready a good half-hour before they were due to arrive at Derastan. She saw that the sky was growing lighter by the minute. She saw a mirage of blue, far on the horizon, the dome of the queen's solitary tomb, and out of her own uncertainties, she sent a prayer for that long-dead queen's soul. Someone who loved her must have raised that tomb. Would that love have lasted through the years, through death and whatever came afterwards? A voice seemed to sound in her heart, answering her questioning thoughts, a voice she had heard before. "Love," said the crystal clear voice, "love is stronger than death. Remember, my daughter, no love is ever lost."

Arina started, and put her hand on her heart. Where had she heard that voice before? Whose was the voice that spoke to her so clearly? She thought at once of Manika, though it had not sounded like her. Manika, who had never finished the story of the Persian rose, dear Manika, moving gracefully through the many rooms of Sagar House, surrounded by the shades of the past. Arina wondered if Manika felt those ghosts round her, and heard long-ago voices. Had they been Manika's words? Perhaps Manika, in some earlier life, had been her mother?

160

Who could tell. But somehow, she knew that the voice was not Manika's. She had connected it with Manika, because she had heard the voice before in Sagar House. But before, she had time to remember when that voice had spoken to her, the train had pulled into Derastan, and all thought but one left her: would he come?

Sher Ali had spent most of the night awake, thinking of Arina and dreading the morning when he would have to say goodbye to her for an unknown period of time. He did not consider that Chunia was a suitable guardian, even backed up by Sakhi Mohammed and Alam Beg. He, himself, should be with her. He fell asleep at last, but was wakened by the noise of the train coming into Daryakot station. He saw that the sky was growing light, and got up quietly. His companions were all asleep.

Dyal seemed to have gone to bed fully dressed, and he was worried about this, wondering what villainy Dyal could be planning. But he did not have time to think about anything but getting dressed before the train reached Derastan. He was shaved and clothed, and ready to jump down on the platform as soon as the train pulled into Derastan. He ran down the platform and, when he reached Arina's compartment, he found Alam Beg preparing to assist Arina down the three deep steps to the platform. Without ceremony he pushed Alam Beg aside, and took the hand she held out to him – wishing that she would trip and fall into his arms. His touch was enough, Arina missed the last step and fell. For a breathless moment, he held her close and it was hard for him to let her go. He kept hold of her arm, and led her through the jostling press to the only empty bench on the station. He did not care who saw them now, this might be his last sight of Arina for some time.

"Arina, don't say goodbye to me. Those are words I never want to hear from you. I will get back to you as soon as I can. Fram will have spoken to Gulrukh Begum, and you will be met in Madore – Sakhi Mohammed will see that everything is made easy for you. I hate leaving you like this." He leaned towards her and gently lifted the thick veil of heavy cotton that Chunia had put over her head, and threw it back. "I must see your face once more before we part."

Arina, her heart breaking, tried to smile at him, but it was difficult – so little time, so little privacy! Passengers were hurrying to board the train, the engine had already given two ear-shattering blasts of the whistle, and the guard was walking down the train slamming doors and shouting.

Tiger had told her not to say goodbye, but why was he speaking in English? When they spoke Urdu together, they seemed, to her, to be so much closer. Was he trying to distance himself from her? She looked into his eyes and knew that he was not, he was staring at her as if he was trying to memorise her features. Oh Tiger, that is how I look at you, and for the same reason. I love you so – how has this happened so quickly?

"How long will we be apart, Tiger?" she asked, speaking Urdu.

"When you speak Urdu, even such a question sounds sweet. But I can give you no answer, bird of my heart, except to tell you that every minute we are apart will be a century. I see now that time has no kindness – when we are together it moves so fast, without you it drags. Arina, beloved, I must go."

With one last look, he stood up, leaving her, and she had said nothing that she longed to say. The thick veil fell behind her as she sprang up and hurried to catch his sleeve.

"Tiger, wait, I have something to say to you. I have learned a lesson about love. Oh, Tiger, this is not the time and not the place I would choose, but I must tell you. I think of you all the time, and I do not wish to be apart from you. Is this love? I think it must be – I have never felt like this before."

He looked down at the hand on his sleeve, bit his lip and covered her hand with his own. "Not the time, nor the place, light of my heart. We are crossed by ill-starred events. I have never wanted anything so much as I want you, want to take you in my arms, want to cherish you. Yes, this is love. I, too, am learning about feelings desires I have never known before."

Bareheaded, taken quite out of herself, Arina looked up at him. "Then, I can say that I love you with all my heart. May we kiss?"

"In the name of Allah the Merciful! Nay, my dear love, here we may not kiss. Even to hold your hand in public is to risk disgracing you. Arina, you must go away from me. I have to leave you yet I cannot walk away. I am only a man, in love. Walk away from me, then I will go."

"I will do that for you but tell me again, I cannot hear you say it enough . . . Is it true?"

"I love you, Arina. You are my life. Keep me in your heart, as I will keep you. Now go."

The railway guard was at Sher Ali's elbow, the engine gave piercing scream, and Arina stayed where she was. The tiger gave her one last desperate look, then walked away without looking back. She lost sight of him very quickly as he walked among the crowds. Presently the train started with a jerk, and moved slowly out of the station. Arina's world was empty.

She did not know how long she stood looking at nothing, but time no longer mattered. Chunia hurried to her side, picked up the fallen *chador*, saying, "You will not need to wear this now," and folded it over her arm. "Child, do not weep. This is a dark day, but tomorrow and tomorrow, and the world will be light again. Come with us."

Arina, because Sher Ali had told her to veil herself, pulled up the light veil that lay over her shoulders and covered her face with it, to hide the tears she did not want to shed, but could not stop. Sakhi Mohammed was behind her, Chunia beside her – together they got her through the press at the gate and out into the blazing morning sun.

Some little distance from the station, there was a great tree, throwing a pool of shade over the rough sandy ground. Here,

Arina saw, were gathered the rest of her company. The two armed guards, Sushi, and some small pieces of baggage. Apart from the tree, nothing broke the flat plain that seemed to stretch for miles. On the horizon, Arina saw a ragged frieze of mountains, the emptiness struck at her heart, spoke to her of loneliness. She sank to the ground, ignoring the rocks and the dry sand, anxious only that they should start the next part of her journey, make time go quickly, let this separation between her and Sher Ali be over. She looked up at Sakhi Mohammed, considering him to be the leader of the expedition, and asked when they would start for Mianaghar. But it was Chunia who answered her.

"As soon as my relatives come with the horses. I have sent Alam Beg to tell them that we are here, they should come at once."

"Horses?" Arina asked, "I thought that we were going to walk?"

Chunia shook her head. "I have given this some thought. It is not fitting that you arrive at the house of my relatives like a village woman, walking, and tired, and covered with dust. No. So when I spoke to the Burra Sahib, I asked him to make one telephone call to the station master, and tell him to send a message to my nephew who is the Khan of Mianaghar, and tell him to send horses for the Begum and her party. Soon they will come. Sit, piyari, it is cool here. Sit and be at ease, there is time."

Arina felt a strong reluctance to sit and wait. She felt that Chunia was taking a great deal for granted. Had she *really* asked Fram to telephone the station master? It sounded very unlikely. She glanced up at Sakhi Mohammed, who she thought looked as dissatisfied as she felt. Chunia had moved over to sit beside Sushi, both women appeared relaxed and cheerful. Sushi was smoking a *biddi*, Chunia had opened her little brass box that held all the things she needed to make "pan" – a fresh green leaf, Arica nut, powdered lime, powdered tobacco. A pinch of all these ingredients were wrapped into the green leaf, and then Chunia popped the resulting little parcel into her mouth and sat chewing peacefully. Presently, Arina knew, she would move a little aside and spit discreetly. She was not looking in Arina's direction and Arina seized the opportunity to question Sakhi Mohammed about the likelihood of any horses coming.

"Begum Sahiba, I know not. I know that the old one did indeed speak with Fram Sahib, and he said that he would telephone this station as soon as he returned to Karachi, to his house, after taking us to Kiamari. But about horses, I do not know. As to how long we may have to sit here, that I do not know either. It would, Begum Sahiba, be better if we walked, but truth to tell, I do not think that the old one could walk three or four *kos*. We must wait a little and see what comes."

Arina looked over at the two maids; Sushi looked tired, but Chunia frail and old. She had been looking at her beloved Chunia without seeing that time had passed, and Chunia was no longer the strong, active woman she had been, even though she was crippled. Now she was a very old woman, and looked fragile and tired. Sakhi Mohammed was right. Three or four *kos*? It was impossible. They would have to wait.

The patch of shade grew small and they moved round to the other side of the protecting tree. The shadows were beginning to grow long – it was afternoon, and Sakhi Mohammed grew as restless as Arina.

"Where are those horses coming from, old one?" Chunia answered him with the studied calm of one who was not feeling calm at all.

"They come from the village of my nephew, where else? I sent Alam Beg, he knows the village, and it is not so very far away – maybe four *kos*. I do not know why it has taken Alam Beg so long. It is possible that the station master did not send a message, or my nephew was away – or even the horses, they perhaps are not brought in from the fields. I think it would be good to send one of the guards, Gokul perhaps, to find out what is making this delay. Gokul! Come here."

Sakhi Mohammed held up his hand. "No," he said. "We send no one else. I will go and speak with the station master and see what he says."

He strode off, leaving Chunia very ruffled, and Sushi looking on the dark side.

"There are no horses," she said, "it was foolish to have waited under this tree for horses that will not come. Now we are going to walk in the full heat of the afternoon."

It was not only the afternoon that was sultry, Chunia was looking furious, but fortunately Sakhi Mohammed came back before open war broke out between the two women. Sakhi Mohammed looked worried. He told Arina that the station master had indeed received a message from Karachi. "He sent the message to Mianaghar by a band of travellers who were going in that direction, but the message was only sent this morning after our train had come in. Therefore, old one, I think you are right, and your nephew is away from home."

Chunia said at once, "Then what has happened to Alam Beg? He should have returned at once."

Sakhi Mohammed nodded. "Very likely he is still on his way. Old one, the station master told me that Mianaghar is three *kos* from here. Tell me, the house of your nephew – is it within the walls of Mianaghar?"

Chunia said reluctantly, "It is outside the walls. But only a short way."

Sakhi Mohammed nodded. "It is a fort. I know the place. My battalion made a punitive expedition there some years ago. The fort of your nephew's people is a good four *kos* further on. In all, the distance we have to cover is over sixteen miles. Old one, you will stay here with the baggage, we will start off now, and inshallah we will reach you nephew's fort before dark. We will send transport then for you."

166

He turned away from Chunia's furious expostulations and called the two guards over to him. "Gokul, go you now to the station master and tell him we will be grateful to borrow the carrying chair he offered me, and the two men to carry it. Karim Dad, you carry the baggage to the ladies' waiting room."

A carrying chair – Arina knew, with a sinking heart, that she would be forced to ride in it. Over sixteen miles. In a skirt and stout shoes she could do it easily. In silks and velvet slippers and veils – oh no.

Chunia sat still looking miserable, but she had to admit that this was the only solution. Sushi would have to look after the Begum Sahiba. She began to give Sushi directions she did not need when the arrival of the carrying chair caused a diversion. The two men who brought it said that they knew the road well. The chair was big enough for two small women. So Arina insisted that Sushi shared it with her. The expedition set off, leaving Chunia to go and sit in the ladies' waiting room with the baggage, and Karim Dad stood on guard outside the door.

The train was moving, gathering speed as Sher Ali ran down the platform and leapt for the open door and Tom's willing arms, which helped him in.

"That was kind of you, Tom. Thank you."

"It certainly was lucky – we were afraid you were going to miss the train, which would have been serious. What on earth did you find to do in that dead and alive place?"

No need to keep Arina's presence a secret any longer, she is safely away, he thought. "I was seeing that my future wife got off the train. She is catching the mail train for Madore tomorrow night."

"Good heavens! We had no idea that she was on the train. You are a dark horse, Tiger. Why didn't you tell us? Did Dyal know?"

167

"Certainly not. I carefully avoided telling him."

Both the others laughed, and Dickie said, "Surely you are not jealous of Dyal, that old cobra! He is not very interested in girls, would you say? We have always had a feeling he had other interests."

Before Sher Ali could say anything in reply, Tom said, "Well, whatever Dyal's interests are, I am afraid your efforts to keep Arina's presence from him have failed – he is bound to see her on the platform. Unless she goes straight into the ladies' waiting room until the mail comes in, provided it *does* come. These days you can't depend on anything."

Sher Ali said slowly, "Just a minute – what do you mean Dyal will see her in Derastan? Where is he?"

"Tiger, he got off the train when you did – in fact, we did not see either of you, we were asleep and when we woke up, you were gone. Actually, we knew that Dyal was going. He telephoned his uncle last night, and was told to proceed to Quetta – the third battalion are there, and he has been transferred. He was very chuffed. His man came in and packed his *bistra* and his shaving things and that was that – we didn't see him to say goodbye."

Sher Ali said nothing, and Tom and Dickie exchanged a puzzled look. Then Tom said, "I don't know what it is with you and Dyal, Tiger. None of our business. But it could be useful that he is in Dera – after all, he is a brother officer, and your fiancée will be able to turn to him if there is any mess up over the mail. He was going to collect a car from somewhere, so if the worst happens, he could be of some use to your future bride."

The thought of Arina being in a position where she might have to turn to Dyal for help was appalling to Sher Ali. But it did not seem to him that either of his companions would understand.

He gathered his thoughts, saw that his colleagues were both looking at him in consternation, and said, "I wonder why you are so convinced that there is going to be trouble over the mail coming in. We checked all that surely, before we left Karachi." He paused, and then said, "It wasn't something Dyal said was it?"

"No. It was the guard. He came down the train warning everyone that news had come in of a hold-up at Sheikapur – a break in the lines. They are trying to put it right, but the guard said he hadn't heard anything more. So really, you should be glad that Yusuf Dyal is there, to be a help to your lady if she needs it."

Dickie, who was looking at Sher Ali while Tom was talking to him, was shocked by the way his hands were clenching and unclenching, and he said, "Just a minute, Tom. Tiger, we are your friends, even though we are not in your regiment. You must put us in the picture. What *is* it with you and Dyal? This is not jealousy, is it? This is hatred. Why do you feel like that about him? We will treat it in confidence, but truly seeing as much of you both as we do, it makes it all very awkward."

Sher Ali turned to face Dickie, looked at him and saw that he was genuinely worried about a situation that he could not understand. They had been together, the four of them, through some very unpleasant events, their time in the desert and later in the jungles of Burma had sealed their friendship. Yusuf Dyal was a brave man, as a soldier he was without fault, courageous and modest.

What can I say, he thought, to those two good friends of mine who are also friends of Yusuf Dyal? Could I bring myself to tell them that, as well as being all that they knew he was, he was also a sodomite, a liar and a betrayer. Could I utter those words and blacken the name of Dyal, as he has tried to blacken mine? I remember the child I was, twelve years old. I remember the agonies of shame he caused me to suffer, I recall the bitter tears I shed. Yes. I can tell them. So that they may understand why I hate a brother officer – how impossible those words sound when put beside the name of Dyal! Yes, I can tell them.

And yet, when he looked up and started to speak, he could not go on. They were both looking at him, how could he make them believe that what he was going to say was the truth?

As Sher Ali sat searching for words, Tom said, "Tiger, you were at school with Yusuf Dyal, weren't you? In England?"

"Yes, yes, I was. We were sent to England together. We are of the same age, we came from what was then the same part of India, from the same background, as far as people knew." His mouth twisted with distaste as he spoke. "That was why we were put in the same dormitory, in adjacent beds."

"I see." Tom looked across at Dickie.

"Did you hate him then?" asked the latter.

Sher Ali stood up and walked over to stand looking out of the window. "No," he said, "I was glad that he was there. We could speak our own language together – I was deadly homesick. I did not care for anything about England."

"What happened then, that made you hate him? You must have been close friends?"

"Yes, we were. He was homesick, too – he would say. I thought – I *believed* him when he used to weep and ask me to take him into my bed. Of course I believed him. We were like brothers, he lay beside me, night after night, and we slept. It was as innocent as two babies lying together. But of course, we were not in our own country. The other boys in the dormitory used to giggle and whisper – and then one night, one of them went out quietly, and called the matron. She saw our two heads on the pillow, went away and called our house master." Sher Ali turned back to face them.

"Well, you can imagine what happened. Terrible interviews, talks of how evil we were. I was only able to bear it because we were in it together, we could laugh at it together. I did not know how seriously the school took it – after all, all we

had done was share a bed, what was wrong in that? I was a
fool. Suddenly, Yusuf joined the other boys when they drew
away from me. I was suddenly moved from the dormitory
and put into the sick room where the matron could keep an
eye on me. The matron was a nice woman, she had always
been very kind. Now she looked at me as if I was some
kind of a snake. I thought Yusuf would be sent to join me,
but he was not. When I asked the matron if he was coming,
she looked shocked. 'Oh really – you think you can carry
on your horrid practices here, do you? Oh, I am so shocked
by you. I thought you were such a charming boy, and all the
time you were corrupting poor little Yusuf, who was supposed
to be your friend. Thank goodness he had the sense to tell the
head. Your uncle is coming to take you away very soon. We
don't stand for that sort of behaviour in *this* school.'" Sher Ali
laughed.

"Little did she know! I doubt if there is a boys' school in
England clear of sodomy. But I did not think of that at that
time. I was shattered by being made to feel ashamed, I was
dirty, something no one wanted to touch or look at and I was
deeply hurt by Dyal's treachery. Well, I was taken away by
my uncle, the then ruler of Pakodi, and he did much to heal
my wounds of the spirit. So does that explain a little of why
I feel such animosity towards Dyal? Don't make excuses for
him – it did not stop there.

"We arrived in the Royal Military College together. At first,
he pretended to be my friend. When I would have nothing to
do with him and told him to keep away from me, the whispers
started again. I was no longer a little innocent boy, however.
I had many friends, and most of them were at Sandhurst. The
whispers did me no harm and I paid them no attention. But
even now, every now and then, I hear a bit of unpleasant
gossip. Filth sticks – I would gladly kill Dyal, but these things
are no longer possible. But one thing you must understand –
the hatred is mutual. Any damage that Dyal can do me, he

will. And if he can he will try to damage me where I am now most vulnerable."

Tom said, "You mean he will try to get to you through your fiancée?"

"Yes. I am, for the very first time, afraid of him."

Sher Ali was silent after this, and presently, Dickie said, "Have you ever spoken of this to anyone else?"

"I spoke with Atlar Khan, my grandfather, but that was all, and he is now dead. I have told no one else. I would not have told you, but I wanted to make you understand that the thought of Dyal offering to assist the girl I am about to marry is not only abominable to me, but it is frightening as well. He is, I am convinced, making some plan, in which she figures. I must get back to Dera somehow. I want you to explain matters to our colonel – tell him everything, tell him the truth, that I am going to see my girl back to Madore, and will come to Abbottabad as soon as she is safely in the hands of my grandmother. Trains permitting, I should be only three days late – Charles Lanfield would have understood, but if it is true that he has gone and Nasir Dyal is now commanding, I am not sure. Do your best for me, will you?"

Both Tom and Dick assured him that they would, and then Tom asked how Sher Ali would get back to Derastan. "There is no train that I know of."

"No. I shall have to see the station master and get transport of some sort – the next station is Akbarighat. I should be able to get a car there. I'll leave my kit with you. Would you give it to my orderly, he'll look after it."

The train was slowing down, and the first buildings were to be seen ahead. When the train jerked to a stop, Sher Ali opened the door and jumped down, waving to the shouts of "good luck!" as he hurried down to the station master's office.

The good luck that Tom and Dickie had wished for him did not seem to be coming his way at first. When he asked the old station master if he knew of a car that could be hired he was told there wasn't one. "Only one car here, Hasrat, and that has already gone with a *hakim* who came in on the mail two days ago, and has been attending patients here."

In despair, Sher Ali said, "Has he already left this place?" The old man shrugged. "Hasrat, who knows what he does, where he goes. But I know that he going to Safed. I heard him tell the driver."

Safed! The name was like a light in a dark place. Safed was only half a day's journey from Madore. If he could only get to Madore, he could be back in Dera in a day, he could pick up one of his father's cars and be in Dera before Arina had to catch the mail. "When did the *hakim* leave with the car?" he asked the station master.

"Oh, early, very early this morning. He wished to be at the hospital quickly. After that, I do not know. Perhaps if you go to the mission hospital they will know when the *hakim* left them. There is a *tonga* outside. If you take the *tonga* to the mission hospital, they can tell you what you want to know. I myself know nothing, and now I must go and wave the flag for the train to go."

Sher Ali was already walking out of the office, hurrying out of the station. A *tonga* – better than nothing. Anything that made him feel that he was doing something that would get him to Arina's side. His prayers were incoherent – just let her be safe in Mianaghar with Chunia and Sakhi Mohammed, just until I get there. Let nothing have happened to her.

The *tonga*, a light two-wheeled vehicle was there, the driver asleep on the ground beside it. The horse, drooping between the shafts, did not look as if it would ever move again. Sher Ali woke the driver, told him to take him to the hospital quickly, the driver whipped the horse into a shambling canter, and drove towards the town of Akbarighat. The hospital proved to be in the centre of the town, a very small whitewashed building with several patients lying on beds under the trees. To Sher Ali's relief there was a car parked outside. As he stepped down from the *tonga*, the fly-screened door of the hospital opened and a woman wearing a white dress and a nurse's veil came out with a man – an English man, presumably the doctor. Sher Ali had taken it for granted that the doctor would be an Indian, and was less hopeful of getting a lift now. But as the man said goodbye to the nurse, and came towards him, Sher Ali recognised him, incredulous at what he saw. Surely this was Doctor Maclaren, always known as the *young* Doctor Maclaren, the son of the doctor who had lived and worked in Madore for many years. The first Doctor Maclaren had been the only doctor that the Chikor and Pakodi families would see. Now this *young* doctor, who must be fifty, had taken up his father's mantle and was Gulrukh Begum's physician. He stepped forward to meet the man, saying, "Doctor Maclaren, this is wonderful luck – do you remember me?"

"Good heavens, Nawab Sahib, of course I remember you. I was talking to your grandmother three days ago. No, no, nothing wrong with her – just a social call. But what are you doing here? I understood that you were on the way back from Karachi, where you had gone to meet Arina Begum. Has something gone wrong?"

As quickly and as clearly as he could, Sher Ali explained the position, ending with, "I am sure you understand, I cannot leave Arina alone on Derastan station for two or three days, with the chance of the mail train not coming tomorrow night."

All the time he was talking, Robert Maclaren was studying him. So this, Robert thought, is the young man who is marrying little Arina. I remember him when he left Madore for England – he has certainly grown up into a good-looking man and, it seems, a caring man. I wish Arina more good fortune in her marriage than her grandmother had. Let us hope the curse that spoiled Zeena's life is finished now.

Sher Ali had stopped speaking, and was looking anxious. Robert Maclaren said at once, "It would surely be more sensible if I drove you back to Derastan immediately, instead of dropping you in Safed. I am in no great hurry to get to Safed and, like you, I do not care to think of Arina waiting about on Dera station for a train that may not come. Let us get started, and we can work out how to arrange things after that."

Speechless with gratitude, Sher Ali got into the car, and the driver turned the vehicle round and began the journey back to Derastan.

Sixteen

In Mianaghar, Rustom, the son of the khan of that district, was awakened early by sounds of an arrival. He heard his father call out in enquiry, and the gate man answer, then he heard his mother getting up in a flurry, and presently she came to him.

"Rustom, go down and see who that is. It may be that Chunia bai has come at last, but if it is she, there are many people with her. Go, and bring me word of who that is."

They had been expecting Chunia bai, their old relative and her mistress, the Choti Begum of Chikor, for the last two days, but no news had come from her since that one telephone call from the Burra Sahib in Karachi. The message had been brought up to Mianaghar from the station master in Dera, there was no telephone in Mianaghar.

Rustom hurried down the steep stairs from the women's quarters where he still slept and found Yunis Khan, his father, talking to a stranger and the outer court full of men, mules, and horses. Yunis Khan took no notice of the arrival of his youngest son, all his attention was given to the leader of the band of men in the outer court.

The leader was very tall, and dark-skinned. But he was also very handsome, and richly dressed, wearing a silk shirt, and loose trousers, with an embroidered velvet waistcoat, and a cap of curled black wool. He was asking for food for his men and himself, and fodder for his animals. He asked as if he expected to get exactly what he wanted. Rustom waited to hear his father direct this man to the *serai*, the place reserved for travellers and their animals in the village. Had the man been alone, he would have been welcomed and given food and drink as a matter of common hospitality to a traveller, but this man had come with ten followers, and mules and horses. Such horses! They were beautiful animals, but the men with them filled Rustom with fear. They were all armed, and the very look of them made Rustom remember stories of bandits and wanted murderers. These men, he thought, had the eyes of wolves, predatory and fierce, and he avoided meeting their eyes.

He was astonished when he heard his father agreeing to find food and fodder for this man and his party. Food was not so difficult, but fodder for so many animals! It would cost a great deal. Also, his father agreed to take the food down to the plateau above Sarghana Pass, eight miles away from Mianaghar, back along the road to Dera. This was a wonderment! Even the man himself looked a little surprised. He repeated his order, and added, "Make no mistake about this. I am meeting friends – there we will be fifteen or sixteen men and four mules. Before sunset, you understand?"

"It will be as you say, Hasrat."

Hasrat! Highness, the title for a Prince! This man must be a prince. His father, speaking respectfully, was now saying, "You are going on to Dera?"

The man shrugged. "Who knows. Is it of some interest to you?"

His tone was unpleasant. Yusuf Khan shook his head quickly. "Nay, Lord. I ask because if you go by the track to Dera, you may hear news of relatives of my family. We are waiting to receive the Choti Begum of Chikor and my wife's old aunt, who is a servant of the Begum."

The man who had gathered up his reins, preparing to leave, stopped and looked over his shoulder. What extraordinary eyes, Rustom thought. They are like black stones in the river bed –

they look as cold as that, and yet suddenly there was a fire in them as the prince looked back at Rustom's father.

"*Who* did you say you were waiting for?"

"The aunt of my wife, and the Begum she serves, the Choti Begum who is to marry the heir of Azadpur."

The man said nothing. With no farewell except a sudden laugh, he nodded and rode away, and his men spurred after him on their beautiful horses.

"Father," said Rustom, watching the dust cloud of their departure eddy and slowly blow away, "Father. That prince, he must be a very wealthy man to mount his servants on such horses. He is not of these parts, is he?"

"No. His lands lie far to the south, on the shores of the great sea. Yes, he is rich. He is also a man of ill repute."

Rustom was full of questions, but his father was frowning and did not answer. When Rustom persisted, his father told him to be silent, speaking sharply, and went into the fort to climb to the *zenana*, the women's quarters in the tower. Rustom followed him, but did not attempt to go with him into his mother's room. Instead he ran round to the balcony outside her room and crouched below the window, and heard all the conversation between his parents. He could tell that his mother, Aisin Bibi, was not pleased.

"Food for maybe fifteen men? Food to be cooked in my kitchen, and then carried eight miles to the Sarghana Pass before sunset today? Where do I find food for so many? What madness possessed you, Yunis Khan, to agree to this? And you have only been paid half? Y'Allah, do you believe he will pay you the rest? He will likely cut the throats of the carriers, and run away when he has eaten. What manner of man is this that he gives such orders to my husband, and is obeyed?"

"Enough, woman. This man is Yusuf Dyal, a prince of the south. His name is known throughout the tribal territories – he sells arms. He is not a man to refuse. In any case, I wish to buy, for a low price, some arms – in these days we need to be able to

178

defend our land and our children. For this reason, if I have to give my wife reasons, we will feed this man and his entourage, and gain favour. As to where you will find food, woman, have you not been cooking ever since we heard that Chunia and her Begum are to visit us? Use the food you have cooked for Chunia, she is not here, but Yusuf Dyal is at our very gates. Kill another goat, if you need it, for Chunia and her mistress. Do not trouble my ears with complaints, I have enough troubles of my own without being bothered about kitchen business. Make haste – remember the food must be there before sunset."

Aisin Bibi knew when to obey. Immediately, she began to call her women round her and give out orders, and presently the women's quarter was full of noise and activity. Yunis Khan left, and Rustom decided to get away too, before he could be captured by his mother and told to do something. But as he hurried down the steps, he heard his father calling him, and knew he must obey *that* call. He expected that he would be told to see to fodder for the horses and mules of Yusuf Dyal. *Bhusa* and corn for the animals would have to be bought in the market in Mianaghar, there was not enough in the store. This was going to be a very costly business, and his father would be in a bad temper. But he had promised to find fodder for fifteen horses, never mind the mules. No wonder his temper was likely to be uncertain. Wearing a worried frown himself, Rustom hurried to his father's room.

But when he stood before his father, Yunis Khan appeared to have recovered his temper. He was smiling.

"Rustom, my son, I have a man's task for you, I am sure that it is time to give you more authority, you will be joining your brothers early next year – inshallah. I want you to follow those strangers, and see if they continue down the road to Derastan, or if they turn off where the track forks for Da Chien. If he turns, come back here, but if he goes on to Dera, then follow him. Try not to be seen, but if by some mischance you are seen, do not run. Go forward and say that you are hoping to meet with the old one, Chunia, and her mistress, and help them on the road. He will not harm you if he thinks there will be people coming, especially women of some rank. I saw his face when I spoke of the Choti Begum of Chikor. There is some connection there, I am sure." Yunis Khan paused, frowning.

"Take no foolish risk boy – do not go past the black rock at the second fork in the track, where it begins the climb. If you have seen no one by then, come home. Indeed, if we are fortunate, he will have met with the Begum, and will turn back with her. Well, well. We can but hope."

Rustom, going off to the stables, had plenty to puzzle over. Why was his father so anxious that Yusuf Dyal should return? So that his father could talk with him over buying arms? It could be nothing else. And to suggest that the man might be interested in the Choti Begum? No boy of Rustom's age, brought up among the men of the tribes, could be an innocent. He knew what Yusuf Dyal's eyes had held. The prince was a man for men, thought Rustom, he would have little interest in women. For a few minutes, he wondered if his father had ideas about his youngest son becoming a royal favourite, bringing riches back to his family. No. His father would not wish for that. Rustom himself wanted more than anything to join his brothers in the Dagshai Lancers. Nothing could take his mind from that. He put a stop to any thoughts of questioning his father, and hurried in to the stables.

Presently he set off on his Tanghan, a little Tibetan horse, as sure-footed as a goat, that his father had bought for him in Leh one year. Rustom was so excited by the task he had been given that he barely looked where he was going, and it was not until he was through the gates of Mianaghar, and out on the rough track that wound through the ravine that he began to remember all that his father had said. He slowed his horse and paid attention to what he was doing. He might have ridden straight into the gang, he told himself, and his shoulders drew together in a *frisson* of fear. He was more frightened of the prince's men than he was of the prince himself. Yusuf Dyal of Sagpurna! It had a fine ring about it. In a way it was a pity that he could not become a palace favourite – and *then* join the army. He had a sudden flashing picture of what his brothers would have to say, and changed his mind at once.

When the banks of the ravine began to be high on each side of him, he rode more slowly and became more alert. He stopped every few miles to listen, but neither saw nor heard anything. He wished that he had eaten something before he had left home – he began to feel both hungry and thirsty.

It was well into the afternoon when he heard shooting. One shot, then a fusilade, then silence. It could be someone from Mianaghar, shooting partridge – or it might not. What had made his father so sure that the men he was following would stick to the track? They could be taking any one of the narrow, rough goat paths that wandered over the hill crests. On those horses? Never. He glanced up at the ridge above him and saw something move. He froze, but it was only a falcon, he followed its flight with with his eyes, then looked back to watch the ridge for what had disturbed the bird. He saw nothing, and reminded himself that a feather blowing in the wind was enough to send a falcon into the skies. He rode on, and heard no more shots, saw nothing until, in the distance, he noticed the black rock. Soon he would be turning to go home, and in spite of being hungry and thirsty, he felt disappointment, and wondered if he should not go a little further, perhaps just a few miles? Otherwise he would have nothing to tell his father. Much better if he just looked around the area on the other side of the black rock. The track ran straight there, and he would be able to see much.

He went round the edge of the rock and was riding down the track when his horse whickered, and Rustom dismounted quickly and grabbed the animal's nose and held its head close against him. Looking up he saw the horses tethered on the ridge, and the man, Yusuf Dyal, kneeling on the ground beside a body. Rustom saw tumbled hair spilling over Dyal's arm, the body must be that of a woman. Rustom moved back into the shadow of the rock, no one seemed to have heard his horse, no one looked towards him. There were many more horses and more men than there had been with Yusuf Dyal in the morning. Most of the new animals were pack ponies, or mules, and they were heavily laden. To Rustom there seemed so many men and pack ponies and mules that it looked like an expeditionary force. He held his breath and stayed where he was, there was nothing else he could do. If Yusuf Dyal turned his head he would be looking straight at Rustom and his horse. Rustom could hear his voice, but not his words. The tone of voice sounded very different from how it had sounded when he had been speaking to Yunis Khan. Then it had been peremptory, now it was soothing, gentle. But presently, still bending over the body of the woman, and without looking up, Yusuf Dyal raised his voice and said clearly, "You! Boy! Tether your animal and come here!"

The shock this gave to Rustom was shattering. His wits scattered, he did exactly as he was told, hobbling the horse with a rope that he always carried. Doing this gave him time, he grew calmer, and he remembered what his father had said, and hoped that he was right. He walked up to Yusuf Dyal, and as he walked saw that the command shouted to him had been as much of a shock to the men around him and up on the ridge as it had been to him. One of them, with an angry exclamation, came running towards him, a knife in his hand, but Yusuf Dyal seemed to have eyes all over his head, for he said firmly, "Hussain! Leave him, it is too late. You did not set guards, I think."

The man stopped dead, looking terrified as well as angry. "Nay, Huzoor, what time has there been for posting guards? The horses need to be watered, and graves to be dug."

"Shut your mouth, fool!" The words cracked like a whip.

The man, Hussain, stood back, now obviously shaking with fear. Rustom saw his terror and became more frightened himself. He wanted to run away, but he could see there was no chance that he would escape – not yet, anyway. "Do not try to run," said Dyal. "What are you doing here? Sent to spy, were you? Sent by your father to see if I told the truth, to see where I was going?"

Rustom found his voice and said quietly, "Nay, Lord. My father sent me to meet the Choti Begum and her servant Chunia bai, who is my aunt. We have been waiting for her for some days now, and my mother is anxious because they are late coming. I must ask you if this is the Choti Begum?"

Yusuf Dyal stood up, and Rustom had a chance to look at the woman on the ground. He saw that she was only a girl, but very beautiful. There was blood on her sleeve and on the front of her shirt. Her clothes were different from the clothes the women of Mianaghar wore, but she was bare-headed like them. Perhaps she was not the Begum, but a servant.

Rustom forgot to be frightened, and repeated his question, adding, "Or if she is not the Choti Begum, but a woman of your household, my family will still welcome her. She is hurt, I see blood. My mother has skill with herbs – I can ride back, and bring two men with a *palanquin* for her, we can take her back to my father's house."

Dyal continued to look at him in silence. The silence stretched and grew frightening, Rustom felt that Dyal was deciding what to do with him, and he knew it was important not to show his fear.

"Only give me the order, Hasrat, and I will ride swiftly. Send one of your men back with me, if you think I lie."

Suddenly there was a lightening of tension, The man standing behind Rustom stepped back a little, and the boy heard him sigh with relief – or was it disappointment? He looked more wolfish than ever as he asked, "What shall I do with this boy?"

This was frightening again, and the answer was more terrifying still.

"There are two things that I have thought of, and I may decide on one or the other," said Dyal. "Hussain, go you and make sure that the graves are well covered with rocks. Boy, go with Hussain, he will give you a glass and a flask. Bring them to me. Let me see how you may shape up as a servant in a good family."

Rustom felt anger driving out his fear. What did Dyal mean, a servant in a good household? If what his father had told his mother was true, this man was a southerner, and of doubtful reputation. I, thought Rustom, am the son of my father and he is a man of good standing. I will not be afraid again. Meanwhile, he was in the hands of wolves, thieves and robbers. He must keep his courage. He felt the man beside him beginning to walk more slowly, and realised they were out of earshot, and out of sight of the leader. What was this wolf going to do? He glanced sideways and, to his surprise, the man was smiling at him.

"Razee ho, butcha! You have caught his eye, you do not have to be afraid – and I am forgiven also. Take a warning, though. Ask no questions, do what you are told, and you will be safe – and perhaps well treated."

Looking over his shoulder, Rustom said quickly, "Those graves – tell me, who lies in them?"

The man raised his hand as if he would strike Rustom.

"What did I say to you? Ask no questions. Those graves are filled, but it would be easy to dig another. Keep your tongue between your teeth, Boy. Here, take the flask and the glass, and keep your eyes to yourself. Be wise."

As he hurried back to Dyal, he heard him speaking. "Rest yourself, Arina Begum. You are safe now, no one will harm you."

Such a soft voice, soothing, tender. He was kneeling beside the girl, holding her hand. When Rustom stopped beside him, Dyal reached up and took the glass, and told the boy to pour from the flask. Then he turned back to the girl, and raised her head on his arm, using the same gentle tones. "Drink, Arina Begum – it is only lime and water, but it is cold and will refresh you."

Arina Begum! So it *was* Chunia's Begum, the girl who was to be married to the heir of Azadpur. Faintly, barely felt, Rustom was conscious of regret. She was very fair. He watched how gently Dyal raised her head again, and knew that his father had been right. This man would do him no harm while the Begum was nearby. He said softly, "The lady is ill. It would be better to let me go and bring my mother back with me. She could come with the *palanquin*, and bring her herbal remedies."

"No. There is no need for your mother to come here, you are going to bring food to me this evening, before sunset. You may bring whatever remedies your mother thinks necessary then. Now, listen carefully to me. You must tell your father that after I left Mianaghar, well into the afternoon, I heard shooting. I made haste down the track and found the Begum lying in the road, and two servants dead behind her. She had been attacked by dacoits who ran off when they heard us coming. I have, of course, sent to men to Dera, to report this shocking affair to the police *thana*. There will be no need for him to send messages, it is already done. I myself will go down into Dera as soon as I have taken the Begum to your family, it is where she was going when she was attacked. I will bring her by easy stages. She is, as you see, very shaken and distressed. We will rest for the night above the Sarghana Pass, so when you return bring blankets for the Begum."

He is lying, thought Rustom – of course he is lying. I am sure that his men did the shooting – he knew he was going to meet the Begum! I must not show that I do not believe him, I must get back to my father and get help for the Begum. He is not going to bring her back to my father. The track to Da Chien goes off just after the Sarghana Pass. He has kidnapped the Begum, and he will take her to Da Chien, and once she is there, who will help her? He met the cold stare of Dyal's eyes and realised that he had been silent too long. There was suspicion in those eyes.

"Lord, it shall be as you say. All will be prepared for you – and I will tell my father that you saved the Begum. Indeed, it was the mercy of Allah that you reached the Begum at this time."

"Indeed it was – and it will be the mercy of Allah the Compassionate that you will need if you are late his evening. Now go – and remember all I have said."

While Rustom was kneeling, taking the hobbles from his horse's forelegs, he heard Yusuf speaking, and looked over his shoulder cautiously to see what was happening. Yusuf was speaking to the Begum, trying to help her to sit upright. He had put his arm behind her to help her, but she was struggling against his hands. Rustom longed to go to her aid, but was too afraid. It would be no help to the Begum if he was killed in front of her. The best thing he could do was to get help as soon as possible. He mounted and, kicking his horse into a fast canter, set off on the rocky track, trusting to the sure-footedness of his mount. He was soon out of Yusuf's sight, but wondered if a sentry had been posted, would he be allowed to pass?

Ahead of him was a rocky outcrop that was a perfect place for an ambush, and it was there that his worst fears came true. A man, rifle in hand, jumped out at him, grabbed for the reins and pulled the horse's head round, so the animal had to stop. Rustom managed to stay in the saddle, but there was nothing he could do. "I go to Mianaghar at the command of your leader – let me pass—"

"No leader of mine," the man interrupted. "Be at peace, boy, I too go to Mianaghar to get help. I saw you riding into trouble this morning." He looked speculatively at the horse – no doubt ready to pull me from the saddle and ride off, wondered Rustom, unable to believe that a man who appeared so suddenly in this wilderness could be anything other than a member of Yusuf's band of robbers. But the man looked to be a different type from the others. He was of a paler complexion, his eyes slanted above high cheekbones. Rustom had seen such men in the bazaar of Peshawar when he had gone down there once with his father – this man was a Gurkha, and a soldier for sure. He could be a deserter, taking service with the man Yusuf.

While Rustom was studying him, the man suddenly ran his hand gently over the horse's nose, and said, "This is a good sort of horse, a Tanghan. They can carry the weight of two men easily – and still make better speed than a man on foot."

Rustom ignored the plain hint. He said, "Who are you? What do you do here, asking for help?"

"My name is Gokul Khagu. I serve the ruler of Azadpur, and am presently travelling with his son's future bride. We were attacked shortly after leaving Dera. I escaped to look for help. I was hiding on the ridge above – I saw you taken, and heard all that was said. If I had not heard you clearly, I would have shot you just now and taken your horse, my need being great. What do you say? Will you take me to your father?"

"Gladly. Mount then, in front of me, and let us go." And Rustom, as he spoke, felt a great weight lift from his spirit. He found he trusted this man, and hoped that his father would too – As Gokul mounted in front of him and the horse began to move, Rustom said, "Are you sure he can carry two of us? I do not want to harm him."

Gokul assured him that the horse would not be harmed. "He will not be able to make such speed as you have made alone, even so it will be quicker if we both ride. If we are pursued, I will dismount and take cover among the rocks and kill as many as I can of those *goondas*, and you ride on. Tell them in Mianaghar that a wounded man, Sakhi Mohammed, lies in a cave among rocks, opposite the old fort, let them call his name, and if it please the gods and he still lives, he will answer so that they can find him."

To Rustom, it seemed more important to get aid for the Begum. The possibility of pursuit frightened him, he clung on behind Gokul, trying to look over his shoulder. The steady half trot, half canter that the horse kept up without showing any distress ate up the miles. The sun was still above the peaks of the Sarghana range when they rode up to the gates of the fort and Rustom shouted for his father.

An hour later, Gokul had finished his story, had been fed, and plans were discussed. Rustom was with his mother while she saw to food being prepared and packed into lidded pots for transport. Rustom had told her all that had happened, had been praised for his courage and quick thinking. When he had finished his large meal, his mother, who had been thinking deeply, went down to speak with his father. Rustom could see that she was not satisfied at all with the part that he was going to play in this rescue. Rustom adored his father, but he was beginning to see that his mother was the power in the house. His father seemed to make his decisions too quickly, his mother seemed to think deeply before she decided anything. As a rule he found this annoying, now he was grateful that she thought about what he was going to do.

"I am going to speak with your father now. His plan is madness, nothing but shooting and dead men on both sides. No, you may not come with me. There is little time. You had better bathe and dress, Rustom – it is almost time for the first call from the mosque, and the sunset prayers. Hurry." She pattered off and he heard her slippers clacking down the stairs. He heard the argument begin, his mother doing most of the talking. She would win, of course, but he wished that he knew what her plan would be.

He went to his own room and bathed and dressed quickly, and buckled on his belt with his most precious possession, his dagger, in a scabbard at his side. The first call sounded from the mosque, and he knelt facing Mecca, and made his prayer short, trusting that Allah the Compassionate, the Merciful, would understand why his devotions could not be lengthy on this one evening. I will pray longer tomorrow, he promised, and then shivered a little, wondering if there would be a tomorrow for him, if all these plans went wrong. He ran down the steps and out into the court, and was surprised to see two laden mules, and his mother sitting astride a third, and his own horse saddled and ready. He looked at his mother with growing apprehension. He had not thought of her as being part of the plan.

"Mother – where do you think to go? You cannot come with me. It is not suitable for you."

It was his father, coming out into the court, who answered him. "She goes with you, boy. Do not argue, there is no time. She has a good plan, one that I did not consider because it endangers you both, but your mother is willing to take the risk for you and for herself. Listen well to what she says, and do as she tells you. Inshallah you will come back safely with the girl. Your welcome will be warm."

There *was* no time for argument. The sun seemed to be spinning down the sky to vanish below the ranges of the higher peaks. Rustom felt his heart sinking with the sun. What plan could a woman make – even a woman such as his mother – that would not be dangerous to both of them? It seemed to him that now he had his mother to protect as well as the young Begum, and without any help from his father. He had imagined there would be men with him. He did not feel adequate to the task of controlling his mother. She had already kicked her mule into movement and was away down the track – was she planning to ride up to those frightening men and begin to order Dyal to give up the Begum? He would likely see his mother lying dead in front of him if she behaved as she sometimes could. He mounted his horse quickly and galloped after her,

When he was riding beside her, she said, "My son, be at peace. I know what I am doing. This is the only answer to the puzzle of how you can take the Begum from that evil man and his servants. Now listen to me, and listen well. It has been a long hot day, all those men will be thirsty and hungered. I have cooked spiced food, I have made fresh bread, and there are several jars of wine, and two of brandy. They will not ask for water, but there is some for the washing of hands. They will drink plenty, not believing their luck to have such a banquet. They will eat as well, with appetite. They will notice nothing, the powder I have added to their food and their drink is without taste in any case."

Rustom was stricken into silence. She smiled into his horrified face. "Eh, my son! Do you think I would kill them? That would be very foolish. But they will sleep. They will sleep perhaps a full night of twelve hours, or perhaps more. They will wake, and wonder where they are, with their heads buzzing and their wits scattered. You do not have to add any more to their food or drink, but I will leave some powder with you, in case the leader wishes to eat different food, or drink of the water. If you need to use the powder, remember only a pinch and another pinch. There is tea for the Begum, it is pure. Do not give her anything but tea, and there is fruit. I have put a glass and a cup and also a small china teapot. As soon as we reach the place, you will build the fires, so that the food keeps warm."

Rustom felt as if he had taken one of his mother's pinches of powder, his head was spinning. Supposing the band had already arrived, what then? But his fears were quietened as they came out above the plateau and saw that it was empty.

"See, we have plenty of time," his mother said. "Light the fires, boy, I will unpack the food and then I will go. We will expect you before dawn, with the Begum. Take that look from your face, boy, all will go well. I know that it will."

She hopped nimbly down from her mule, and in no time had unpacked the baskets and set the flasks of wine and brandy beside the big round trays that would hold the food.

190

Rustom, moving in a dream – or a nightmare, it seemed to him – made three fires under his mother's directions, one fire a little distance from the others, "for the boiling of the water for the Begum's tea. The other fires are for the men to sit round while they eat." He remembered his mother's instructions and lit the fires for the men with a little charcoal and wood chippings that his mother had brought, and then banked them with dried cow dung, from the sack brought on the second mule.

When his mother had seen that everything was arranged to her liking, she kissed Rustom, holding him in a tight embrace, said a prayer over his head and mounted Rustom's horse. She was leaving the pony about a quarter of a mile away and she would send another horse with Gokul, who would be with the horses "in case of need". Then, leading the three mules, she rode off, leaving Rustom alone with the three fires, and the sound of approaching horsemen. He stood up to meet them, praying that all would go well as his mother had said it would, the beating of his heart sounding louder to him than the sound of the horses.

Seventeen

A rina was lying on something soft, someone was holding her hands firmly, and telling her to wake. She could not, for a few merciful minutes, imagine where she was. The voice was speaking Urdu, a man's voice. "Wake, you are safe – it is over." A soft voice, but definitely a man. Had Tiger come? She opened her eyes and looked up at a face bending above her, and knew that it was not Sher Ali, although she could see nothing but a black shape, his head was against the sun. Some kindly passer-by had stopped to give aid, or perhaps this was Chunia's nephew, come at last.

The remembrance of Alam Beg's dead face came into her mind, and Sakhi, falling under a hail of bullets, and, oh, Sushi, tumbled in the dust, with no one to help her. She gasped, losing her breath, fighting to breathe against the fears and memories that had begun to constrict her breast. The misty clouds of unconsciousness were waiting nearby, would fall on her again if she did not fight.

She struggled against the hands that held hers, and the face above her spoke. "Rest, Arina Begum, be at peace. Do not think of anything, let go, and rest."

There was a faint echo of a voice remembered, but she could not recall who it might be. She waited, keeping still for a few minutes, and the man holding her hands called to someone, and presently he put his hand gently under her head and raised it, and put a cup to her lips, saying, "Drink, lady, it is only lime and water but it is cold." Cool and delicious it lingered on her

192

tongue, slipped down her throat. Her sight cleared, her breath came easily. He had spoken English, called her name, so not a passer-by. He must be Chunia's nephew.

As soon as she attempted to sit up, he helped her, raising her, and keeping his arm, strong and steady, behind her.

"There," he said, "that is good. Do you feel better, poor lady? You are not wounded. Thanks be to Allah, you only fainted, and who could blame you. Don't think about it, but just tell me where you wanted to go before these *goondas* swooped on you. Just tell me, and I will take you there, safely."

Chunia's nephew certainly would not be able to speak English like this – almost accentless. Who was he? All the time he spoke, there was some memory troubling her, but she could not think clearly. Looking about her she saw that there were several men standing round, all armed with rifles.

He saw her eyes move, looking in fear and said at once, "These are my men – do not be afraid of anything. You are in safe and friendly hands. It will be dark soon – tell me where you want to go and I will take you there, then I will go back to Dera and get in touch with the authorities and warn them that there is a band of murdering dacoits on the loose in this area. Do you feel well enough to tell me how many people were with you? I shall have to tell the police, so they know about the bodies."

Bodies! Bodies – Sushi could be alive. She had spoken so calmly, of course she was alive. She tried to get up, saying, "I must go – my companion, Sushi, she is wounded."

He was holding her hands again. "Sushi – she was your companion? We have not found her. There is a woman servant lying dead in the road – that is all. Surely you had some men with you?'

Sushi – Sushi dead? But she spoke to me, thought Arina. She spoke so calmly, until I tried to move her – she screamed then. Did she die at that moment, while I was still with her, or did she die alone? Arina felt desolate, Sushi could not be dead.

The man was repeating his question. "Did you have men-servants with you?"

She must answer him. She cleared her throat and said, "Yes. There was Alam Beg, and . . ." She was suddenly conscious of movement behind her, turned her head and saw that several men were standing close by, listening intently. Who were these people who had rescued her? The man beside her saw her look over her shoulder, and spoke angrily to the listening men, telling them to get back. As if they were dangerous dogs, thought Arina, and continued speaking, " . . . and also there were two porters. Are the porters dead, too?"

"I fear that one of them is. The other must have run away. Did you have no one else with you?" Unable to explain to herself why she was reluctant to mention Sakhi Mohammed and Gokul, Arina said firmly, "No, that was all. We were on our way to Mianaghar, to the home of a man called Yunis Khan, who is the khan of Mianaghar."

"Did you see your assailants? I think you must have seen one of them?"

To Arina this seemed an odd way of putting the question. "I saw no one at the time of the shooting. I was not expecting to be attacked. I did not look about me when the shooting began, I was trying to help Sushi. I would like to see her, please – will you take me to her? I cannot believe she is dead."

"She is dead. I will take you to her grave."

At that time it seemed a shocking statement. She said faintly, "She is buried? Already?"

"Yes. We have buried the old man close by. I will take you, so that you may see that all is decently done. My men are raising a cairn of rocks above the graves because of the jackals. Do you feel strong enough to walk?"

"Yes, thank you."

As they walked down the track, she said, "It seems a hasty burial."

"Yes. But it will be sunset in an hour. You understand, we could not leave the bodies lying there all night."

The men who had been behind her had drawn back, and now sat in a half-circle above the track, talking in low voices.

Where could Sakhi Mohammed be? And Gokul? This was a question that for some clouded reason she must not ask. She saw the carrying chair ahead of her, drawn to the side of the track. Two men were adding rocks to the pile, one grave already had its cairn. Her companion pointed. "Your servant's grave is finished. As you were fond of her, you will want to return one day and have a tomb built, no doubt."

She walked forward and stood beside the grave. She told herself that Sushi, her dear Sushi, lay beneath this pile of stones, in this wilderness. She found it impossible to believe. She remembered what Sushi had said that morning, when they had seen the blue dome of the lonely tomb. Now for Sushi herself, there was to be a lonely tomb, where no sound could cheer her or disturb her sleep.

Arina's tears were for both Sushi and Alam Beg, and for herself, so suddenly deprived of her loved and loving servants. She bent and took a stone and placed it on Sushi's cairn and, when she turned away, the men were just finishing the third cairn, and the man who waited for her said, "Come, lady. Do not weep for your servants. Let me take you to your destination – it will be dark soon, I would like to know that you are under a roof before nightfall."

She was dreading having to ride in the chair again, and said so,

"Of course you must ride – how can you walk? You are still weak from the shock you have suffered. Do not be afraid – my men will carry you steadily. I will ride beside you, there is nothing to fear."

"Ride? You have horses?"

"Of course I have horses. I was on a trek into these

mountains when I heard the shooting."

"May I please ride? I cannot go in that chair."

He looked doubtful. "Are you sure you feel strong enough? These are not the type of horses you would ride in Britain."

"I will ride anything – any sort of animal, to avoid ever using that chair again." But how did he know anything about Britain?

He gave a sharp order in a language she did not understand, not Urdu, perhaps it was Ladakhi or Pusht. When the horses were brought, they were small, hill ponies, strong and sure-footed. He helped her mount, placed her feet in the stirrups, and said. "I am afraid that you will be very stiff tomorrow, as you have not ridden for perhaps a month?"

She was too tired and distressed to take in very much of what he said to her at the time, but later she remembered his words. How did he know that she had not ridden for some time? Who was this man, this rescuer? But at this time she said nothing, asked no questions, and was glad to feel the horse moving under her, and to have this man beside her riding down the track that led deeper into the shadows of the ravine.

By this time the sun was declining, but it was still very bright, and as they rode out of the ravine it shone straight into their faces. Arina rode frowning against the glare, a headache beginning to form behind her eyes. She was surprised when the man riding beside her said, "Arina Begum, please wear these," and held out a pair of dark glasses. "You are finding the glare trying, I can see."

He seems to notice everything about me, she thought, as she thanked him and put the glasses on. Who is this man? He is kind and yet I am afraid of him. Why does he seem so familiar? I seem to know his voice – is it because he speaks such excellent English? She turned her head to look at him, and before she could look away, he looked at her and smiled. She was looking directly into his eyes. She was sure then that she *had* seen him before – but where? That smile – of course!

She knew at once who he was. The man who had been talking to Fram on the *chibutra* of Sagar House, on her first evening. The unwelcome guest.

"I am sure that I know you. You are the Nawab of Sagpur?" Arina kept her voice steady.

As soon as she had spoken, she saw a change in his expression. Not anything obvious like a frown, or a smile. Just a difference. His voice sounded different, too, still soft, but something strange – was it surprise? – seemed to sound in his tone.

"Well, you have remembered. I did not think that you had seen me clearly enough that night when we almost met, on the *chibutra* of Sagar House, but I am flattered that you remember. I think that you must be feeling better."

She was still held by his eyes, thought she saw a flame far back in those black depths. She could not look away. This was the man Sher Ali hated, the man that gentle Manika had been very uncivil to and was afraid of. Arina recalled Manika's words: "He has a snake's eyes, cold and dangerous." She shivered as if a cold wind had blown around her. Were his eyes like that? They did not seem so at this moment. There was a smile behind his eyes.

"I think that you are trying to mesmerise me, Begum Sahiba. Believe me, you would not find it difficult, with your eyes – eyes of such strange beauty."

She blushed and looked away, released from his gaze at last. What could she say in answer? Why was she so afraid? This man had rescued her, treated her with kindness and courtesy, had seen to the burial of Sushi and Alam Beg.

But why had he buried them so quickly? She remembered Alam Beg falling towards her, as she tried to get his attention, saw again the ghastly wound in his back, as he lay at her feet. Alam Beg, who had vowed to serve her with his life. Well, he had done so, he must have been dead with such a wound. But Sushi, lying in the dust of the track, blood mantling her white robes. *Had* she been dead, or had those wild-looking men shovelled her into her grave without caring to make sure that she was dead? Arina shivered again, thoughts tormenting her. This man, Yusuf Dyal, who was he? What was he doing in this wilderness of crags and mountains and dark ravines? And why had he not told her at once who he was.

"I don't understand, why you did not tell me who you are. I was afraid that you were perhaps a dacoit, instead, I find I wronged you, and I owe you so much."

To her surprise, he replied in Urdu, as if he took it for granted that she would understand. "Nay, Arina Begum, do not say that you feared me – I would give my life for you. As for owing me anything – you owe me nothing. It is my good fortune that I was in this place at such a time. You needed help, I was there to give it to you. How can there be any debt?"

He smiled at her as he spoke. He was certainly a very handsome man. He had a look of Sher Ali, he was the same type of man, tall, arrogant of bearing, a man of breeding. But what was he doing here? If only he would stop staring at her, she would ask him – she *must* ask him, she needed answers to her questions. What had happened to Sakhi Mohammed, and Gokul? She spoke quickly before she lost her courage.

"I think it was *my* good fortune that you were there, or I might be lying dead on the track, like my servants." She stopped speaking, her question unasked. The names of Sakhi Mohammed and Gokul were forbidden to her, it was so strange and frightening, every time she tried to ask about those two men it was as if a hand was laid across her mouth.

He must have seen the question in her eyes, for he leaned across to her and said, "You were going to ask me something. What is it? Ask anything, my heart of gold."

No! That was Sher Ali's name for her, Chunia is the only other person who can call me that. This man is not a member of the family, he should not speak to me like this. The warning was clear in her mind. He is trying to discover if I had anyone else with me – if I ask about them, he will send someone back to kill them. I must not respond to him by word or look, but I must answer him. She said quickly, stumbling a little over the words, "No, it is nothing, Nawab Sahib. Only, I wondered what brought you to this wilderness, such a strange desert place."

"Is that all? I would give you anything in my power, up to half my kingdom, as they say, and you ask for such a little thing. In fact, there is good Chikor shooting here. I had some leave, so I thought I would come up and see if I could get some quails. Nice little birds, very good roasted over the fire. Does this seem such a wilderness to you? I suppose it does after Scotland. I wonder how you are going to find living among the mountains of Chikor and Pakodi. Very isolated up there, especially when the passes are closed in the winter. Have you imagined how that will be? All those bored women in the *zenana?*"

He spoke mockingly, she thought, and felt a strengthening anger. She said, "Oh, I did not need to imagine anything about my own country. I remember how it was, and long to be back there."

"With your prince, I suppose. Do you think of dear Tiger as your prince? How charmingly you blush, Arina. A flower has been chosen for the Tiger! He is a fortunate man to find such blossom in an arranged marriage – I wonder if you feel yourself as lucky."

It seemed to her that he had changed, that he had up till now treated her with respect. Now, he was no longer speaking as he should to a woman alone in his care. Was he now showing his true nature? She could feel his eyes constantly turning to look at her, and kept her eyes turned away and, suddenly exhausted, she rode in silence – her brain in a haze of broken thoughts, of the happenings of the day – holding herself upright in the saddle with difficulty. He did not speak to her during this time, and when she glanced quickly at him he looked as though he was thinking deeply.

199

After riding in silence for some miles they reached a sort of plateau, looking out over ridge upon ridge of rising hills, and the flash of water, a lake or a river far in the distance. He drew rein, and dismounting, came to take the reins of her pony.

"Arina, this is a good place to halt for a little time – perhaps for the night, as the light is going and the way is rough. I think you are very tired. I sent men ahead to build a fire, then you will have some tea. Let me help you from your saddle."

Desperate to avoid his touch, she kicked her feet from the strange rope stirrups, and would have tried to dismount alone, but he put his hands round her waist and lifted her down. He felt the shudder that she could not restrain, and said softly, "You still fear me – why, I wonder. She did not attempt to reply. He stood, holding her for a moment, looking down at her averted face. Then he released her and stood back a little, but held her arm as if he thought she might fall.

He shouted to someone – "Rustom?" – and she looked about her to see who he was calling, and was astonished at the size of the cavalcade that had accompanied them. She saw that there were laden baggage ponies, too – so many people, so much baggage for a shooting trip?

She saw a boy beside a brightly burning fire, he was unpacking a *kilta*, taking out a cup and a kettle and a teapot. Yusuf Dyal, his hand still firmly holding her arm, led her to where the fire was. There was a rug spread there, with piled cushions. It came to her then that this place had been prepared – the rugs and cushions were inviting, she sank down and wondered if she would ever be able to rise again.

Yusuf Dyal had walked over to speak to some of his men, she saw that they were all studiously keeping their eyes from where she was sitting, bareheaded and dishevelled. Yusuf Dyal was now speaking to the boy, who was kneeling by the fire with a cup in his hands. Not a very young boy. He seemed to be in his teens. Good looking, with great dark eyes that looked kindly at her. He was dressed in clean clothes and an embroidered waistcoat, and his little cap that sat jauntily on his head was embroidered too. Some loving mother's work, she thought. Perhaps he was a young relative of Yusuf Dyal. He was bending close over the boy, giving him some instructions. Then he walked away, and the boy came to her with a cup and the teapot, and she could think of nothing but her dry throat and accepted the cup offered to her so respectfully. The steam that rose from the cup was fragrant, different from any tea she had had before. Could it be drugged? She looked up at the boy, and he looked solemnly back at her, then said softly, "Drink, Begum Sahiba, it is good."

For no reason, she found she trusted him, and drank thirstily and would have asked for another cup, but the boy seemed to have gone away. She could not see him anywhere. She could not see anything very well, she was so tired.

It seemed to have got dark very quickly. She lay resting among her cushions, and did not notice when the cup dropped from her hand. The boy came and picked it up quickly and, as he turned, he found Yusuf Dyal standing beside him.

"How much did you give her?" Yusuf Dyal asked.

The boy shrugged, looking away. "A pinch and half a pinch, as you said. It was more than enough. The Begum was very tired. She will sleep well, and wake refreshed."

"I trust so for your sake, Rustom. Bring some quilts, and make her comfortable."

The boy hesitated, looking up at Yusuf Dyal, met his gaze and ran off at once.

Yusuf Dyal stayed beside the fire, looking down at Arina. Unconscious, open to his seeking eyes, her beauty was there, defenceless, for him to study. Tumbled hair, dust and sorrow, nothing could dim what she was. Her innocence was like a perfume in his nostrils.

Untouched, he thought, a flower still in bud, but coming into bloom. I shall have this white flower, this rose, for myself. No one has touched her, no one will. She is mine. I have found what I looked for in women and could not see. She has the beauty of both girl and boy – the slender strength of her limbs, the strong little hands, and as well the hidden curves that are there, the sensuous lips, the long tilted eyes that turn away in modesty. All for me. I will kill to keep her. Yes. I would even kill *her* if I thought anyone else would take her from me. He felt the throb of a desire that he had not felt before, and as if in answer to his thoughts, the fire flared up and the blaze lit his face, his eyes took colour from the flames and glowed like the embers of the charcoal under burning wood.

The boy returned with a pile of bedding. Yusuf Dyal watched him slide a flat pillow under Arina's head, bend to remove her ruined sandals and tuck a quilt round her. When Rustom stepped back, Yusuf Dyal said, looking down at the sleeping girl. "We will stay here tonight. Look well to her comfort, be careful that she does not throw off her blanket. You may give your sole attention to her." He lifted his gaze from the Begum, and the black gaze was turned to Rustom.

"I will need no attention from you for this night. I will eat with the men, so there is no need for you to prepare separate food for me, if you had thought to make something special, to please my taste?"

Rustom felt a cold chill. What were those terrifying black eyes saying to him? Has this man guessed that I have drugs hidden about me, that I would have drugged his food? No, I am chasing shadows, he would have already had me killed if he had such a thought. In any case, he is going to eat the food my mother laced – with a heavy hand, I suspect. But why does he stare at me?

The boy looked away from the dark unfathomable gaze as Dyal said, "Tell me what does your father imagine you are doing here with me? Will he not wonder why you did not return, having brought the food?" He smiled as he spoke, not a pleasant smile.

The boy forced himself to look back, met the smile with

one of his own, wide and innocent, hoping his thudding heart was not actually shaking him. "My father, Lord? He looks to see me return one day, rich with gold and honour. In years to come."

"Oh ho – does he indeed? So you have joined my service, you expect to stay with me, Rustom? For years to come?"

"I would stay with you, Lord, and serve you well, if it pleases you."

"And return to your father in years to come. Well, we will see how well you please me."

He walked away then, and Rustom, deep in thought, began to feed the fire, hearing a welcoming chorus as the circle round the other fire moved to make space to receive Yusuf Dyal.

The food was being carried over from the cooking fire, a large brass *thali* piled with spiced rice, and another equally large container full of meat. The smell of the spices wafted over to the boy. His mother and the women of the *zenana* had done well. Here, now, was the moment on which everything hung poised.

The boy watched as one of the men brought water to pour over Dyal's hands, and a towel. Rustom's eyes were needle sharp, watching as the men began to eat. The talk and laughter grew louder, they were drinking now. After a few minutes, Rustom relaxed, and ceased to watch, satisfied. He pulled his *posteen* close about his chest and lay down beside the fire to wait, perhaps to sleep a little, close enough to hear the Begum if she suddenly woke and called out, not knowing where she was, poor girl.

But it was the rising moon that woke Rustom. His fire had burned down to a few glowing coals in grey ash. He had slept longer than he had intended. He rose at once, and went to where Arina lay, and bent over her. All was well, she was sleeping naturally. He was glad that he had been able, under the very nose of Dyal, to only pretend to drug her with the powder Dyal had given him. Her breathing was quiet and even – she would wake easily. He left her, and went, barefoot and soundless, to where the men lay around their dead fire. Their breathing was stertorous, they were still deep in their drugged slumber. Good. He went then, with great caution, to look at Yusuf Dyal. He had not moved, and was in the same condition as his men. Satisfied, the boy went back to his fire, and fed it with the twigs he had got ready, until it glowed red and flamed. He put water on to boil, and sat looking at the fire, waiting.

The moon was rising higher, the light was stronger, it was time to waken the Begum, and get her away into safety. The water boiled and he made tea, and took it over to where she lay. He only whispered her name once, and she awoke, staring up at him, puzzled for a moment until the clouds of sleep left her, and she sat up, looking frightened. He said quickly, "Do not be afraid. Drink this tea, and then we will go. He sleeps."

She took the glass of tea, and sipped it, and said, "Where do we go? Can we hide from him?" It pleased him that she was not afraid of him, although she must have thought that he was a servant of Dyal.

"He will not waken for some time. He is drugged. But we must go quickly." He had a very clear picture in his mind of what could happen if something went wrong and Dyal was not held by the drug. He watched the level of the tea in the glass, and as soon as she had finished he took the glass from her and went over to the fire and poured the dregs over it, and then stamped out the embers, and covered them with earth.

She followed him, as if he represented safety. "Where can we go?" she asked. "Where will we be safe from him?"

"We will go to my father – he is waiting for us." He heard her sigh, and realised that she did not know who he was. To her he must seem to be nothing more than a disloyal servant, who was helping her escape because he wanted to get away himself. "My father and mother have been waiting for news of you and our relative, the old one, Chunia, for some days now." He saw her whole face lighten when she smiled. He saw, too, how young she was – only a girl, not much older than his sister Hamida. As he would have done for his sister if she had been frightened or distressed, he leaned towards Arina and took her hand.

"Come," he said, "Fear nothing. The wolves are all asleep, their leader with them and, inshallah, they will not waken for hours. It is not far to walk to where horses are waiting for us, and I promise you, before the moon is down, we will be outside the gates of the fort. Come, piyari."

He led her down the track, and neither of them noticed that he had called her beloved. She no longer doubted him. He was part of Chunia, he was a friend. They rounded a great rock, and there were the horses, not hobbled, Rustom was grateful to see, but safely tethered. In minutes he had helped Arina to mount and, leading the way with the moon as their light, Rustom could feel that success was only moments away.

Eighteen

The sun was setting in red glory when the rattling old car drew up outside Derastan station. All three men were glad that their journey had ended: Kushi, the driver, got out and went to open the bonnet; Robbie Maclaren groaned as he stretched his long legs; and Sher Ali went straight on to the platform, which was deserted. The station master's office was shuttered and locked. No waiting passengers, no one.

Robbie came to join Sher Ali on the platform. "Well, Nawab Sahib, it does not look as if the Karachi mail is expected tonight – or even tomorrow night."

"No. It does not. I hope that Arina has stayed over with the Mianaghar family. In any case, she would not be waiting here. Chunia would not allow that. I think I had better set off for Mianaghar."

"From what I recall of the Mianaghar road," said Robbie, "it is more of a track – and very rough at that. I doubt if the old car would take it, so we shall have to walk, and we better start at once. It will be dark in an hour – we will certainly be doing the last few miles in the dark. Not a pleasant thought."

On the long and tiresome drive from Akbarighar, with constant halts to let the radiator cool, and two separate punctures, a companionship had grown between Sher Ali and Robbie Maclaren. Sher Ali had heard of Arina's life with her grandmother, of her love of horses and her ability to ride. This was naturally fascinating to Sher Ali, who listened intently and, asking many questions, was himself studied and appraised. Robbie liked what he saw and heard, and Sher Ali had felt his friendship. All the same, he had not expected Robbie to accompany him on this last stage of the journey, he had imagined that the doctor would have a rest, and then go about his own business. Sher Ali's expressions of surprised gratitude were brushed off.

"My dear Sher Ali, I like to finish what I start. Besides, I want to see Arina in the country she always referred to as 'Home', though this part of the country is scarcely like the green valleys she was dreaming of. Also, I shall be glad to see you both safely on to the train for Madore. I wonder if there are cars to be hired here, in case the trains are not running. I do not care for the look of the station master's office."

"Well, I am delighted that you will come with me, but I think that we must find some kind of transport. I think that Chunia's relatives live in a small fort outside Mianaghar – it is over sixteen miles, and I think . . ."

Robbie shook his head. "I hope you are not about to suggest that it would be too much for an old man. I am not decrepit yet. I am perfectly capable of walking my twenty miles a day."

"Of course," said Sher Ali hastily, "I am sure you are, but it has been a long day."

"Yes. And a long night before it, with the birth of recalcitrant twins to a fifteen-year-old girl. I am a doctor you know. It will be a relief to stretch my legs, in fact, I am looking forward to it. Shall we start?"

"I still think we should try for transport – horses, that is what we need. It is the time factor that is worrying me. I am supposed to be reporting to my CO tomorrow evening – in Abbottabad. Some hope, at this rate."

"None at all, I should think. In that case, let us go and talk to Kushi, he comes from round here. He may know of someone. I know there used be a grass farm somewhere nearby. Kushi will be delighted to look for horses – he hates walking."

It was the sound of their voices that woke Chunia, lying on the floor of the ladies' waiting room, surrounded by baggage. At last, she thought, they have come back for me. It had been a long day of waiting, and she had felt strongly that she should have insisted that Sushi stayed behind and let her go. She had such a strong feeling of disaster pending that she had been unable to settle, and had, as the day began to move into evening, overruled Karim Dad's objections and sent him off to find out why the others had not returned.

The journey to Mianaghar had begun to appear threatening, a journey from which those who set out never returned. Now hearing voices, she got up quickly, unbolted the door and emerged – just as Doctor Maclaren and Sher Ali were walking past.

Both men recognised her at once. Sher Ali could not believe his eyes, and Chunia herself was staring, astonished. Had she not seen him running for the train this very morning? What had happened, what was he doing here with the doctor? Before she could speak, Sher Ali said, "Chunia! Arina Begum – she is with you?" He was trying to look past her into the room.

"Nay, Hasrat, she has taken the road to Mianaghar. I am ashamed before you. I have been foolish and was persuaded by your man to stay here with the baggage. They said I could not walk sixteen *kos* – I, a hill woman."

Sher Ali interrupted her. "Wait, Chunia. When did she leave? Where are the guards – have they gone with her? Why did she go without you? Did something happen?"

"Your man, Sakhi Mohammed, became impatient, and made arrangements for her to leave. One guard, Gokul, went with them, and Sushi also, and of course, Sakhi Mohammed, as the leader. I, myself, sent Alam Beg ahead – early, as soon as we came to this station – to find out why my relatives were not here to meet us. But he did not return. Then the others left, perhaps an hour after noon, saying that they would send back for me. But no one has come."

Fear and anxiety sounded in her voice, and Sher Ali heard it.

"Chunia what is it? What happened?"

"Thanks be to Allah, nothing. But Hasrat, I am full of fear, I smell danger. Let us follow the path to Mianaghar, and, inshallah, find them safely in the home of my relatives."

"Yes, yes, we will do that – first we must find transport. Tell me, was the Begum walking all the way?"

"Hukum, she had a chair, a carrying chair. She took Sushi into it with her – there were two coolies to carry it."

"That won't have made it a fast journey," said Robbie Maclaren, who had been listening and watching the expressions of Sher Ali and Chunia, both of whom looked very alarmed.

"Come, Nawab Sahib, let us go and talk to Kushi, he may have knowledge of horses," said Robbie.

Sher Ali had one more question. "Chunia, where is Karim Dad?"

"Hasrat, I sent him after them when the time passed and no one came. I sent him to find out what had happened, but he, too, has not returned."

That was all Sher Ali needed. He walked out of the station, and his expression was so full of worry that Robbie Maclaren said, "Look, Nawab Sahib, it is not so bad. They have quite likely stopped on the way – it has been a very hot day. The chair will have held them up. It will have meant slow progress, and you have no idea what that path, or rather track, is like. No need to fear the worst."

Sher Ali shook his head. "On the face of it, no need. I know how the track is – we marched it some years ago. No, it is more than that. Sakhi Mohammed, my man, is totally trustworthy, he would have done exactly what he said he would do. By this time, he would have had time to send back for Chunia. Doctor Maclaren, there is something else. I have an enemy – I am just afraid that he may have caused some trouble. Any trouble he causes for Arina Begum would be directed at me, ever though she would still have had to cope with it. I don't like the sound of things. Let us speak with Kushi, I hope he can help us."

Kushi was leaning against the car, talking to a friend who had a herd of goats and two camels with him. These animals were being guarded by a small boy with a switch and both the boy and his father greeted Robbie Maclaren with welcoming smiles. "Come to our house, Doctor Sahib," said the man, "my family and the mother of my son will be glad to see you. Come and stay the night with us. Darkness will be with us soon – it is too late to travel."

"You are a generous friend, Abdel Karim, I will avail myself of your offer another time. But at present, I need information from you."

"Doctor Sahib, you have only to ask. What I know I will tell you." The tone was willing, the smile warm, but Sher Ali, watching, thought to himself that the answer depends on the information required. This man is expecting to answer some question which might incriminate him. Sher Ali was astonished at the number of people and places about which this doctor seemed to have knowledge. Most unlike the average Englishman – unless of course he was a member of the intelligence services, or that branch of the Indian Police which was called the CID – the Criminal Investigation Department.

"Are the grass farm people still here? Any British officers with them?" Doctor Maclaren asked.

"The grass farm is indeed here, Huzoor. There are no British officers, I think. None came here after the big change. But the Collector Sahib is still here. He is living in his bungalow in Lugard Road. You know him Sahib, Springer Sahib? He and his family are still here. My brother works for him and has heard nothing of his departure."

Robbie thanked Abdel Karim, and turned to Sher Ali. "We are in luck. Donald Springer is still here – I am sure we will get horses from him. He'll deal with the grass farms

210

– I presume they will still have horses. Let us go and find Springer."

Abdel Karim gave stern orders to the boy to guard the animals in his absence, and climbed into the car. Chunia, heavily veiled, made a third in the front seat, and Robert Maclaren and Sher Ali shared the back seat with the small pieces of baggage that Chunia had been guarding.

The district commissioner was out when they called, but Abdel Karim knew the way to the grass farms, which were just outside what had been the cantonment area for the British and Indian troops. It was now empty and deserted.

"The cantonments will be busy again soon, the barracks and stables will be full, and there will be lights in the bungalows at night again, if God wills," said Abdel Karim wistfully. "My friend is a *rissaldar* of the the Dagshai Lancers. He is alone here with only two Lance Daffadars and four *sowars* to keep guard – and grass cutters and *bhistis* of course. He will be pleased to see you."

Rissaldar Wazir Khan, was delighted to see them. He recognised Sher Ali and asked at once if he knew which regiment was likely to be coming to Dera. "We heard tell that the 6th might come back – the Dagshai Lancers. That would be good. But Allah knows any *pultan* will be welcome. This place is full of the spirits of the past. When I shout 'Who goes there!' at night, I wonder who will answer – voices from some long dead men. But there is never any reply." He sighed, looking up at the skies where shadows were gathering as the scarlet and gold of the sunset faded.

"It will be night soon," said Wazir Khan. "We should choose the horses before it is dark. You are riding to Mianaghar, and then to Madore? It is a rough road, a long road, from Mianaghar. Come and choose your horses, Hasrat. I am happy to be able to let you take these animals, and it is good for me to see you, Sher Ali Bahadur."

Sher Ali was looking at the horses Wazir Khan paraded

before him. "Your horses look well, Rissaldar Sahib. These are in splendid shape. I will leave the choice of horses to you. You know what I need."

As the horses were being separated, Robert Maclaren came to stand beside Sher Ali, who said, "This is taking so long. It grows dark. I think of Arina on that rough road. Where will she rest, overtaken by the night? We must go – let us leave as soon as we can. I cannot wait for daylight – I am very worried, Doctor. Neither Alam Beg nor Karim Dad have returned with news. Something is very wrong – I should like to leave as soon as the horses are saddled. I can borrow lanterns from these people here, and it will be moonlight. Will you come?"

"Of course I will come. I have already said so. I am going to call you Tiger – we cannot continue to be so formal. So, Tiger, when you are ready, I am."

Sher Ali took his hand. "Robert Maclaren, you are a true friend – I thank you. Rissaldar Sahib, please saddle the horses. We will start our journey immediately."

Wazir Khan called to one of the Lance Daffadars. "Selim – saddle up. Send Ali to my house, he must tell my wife I will be away for two, perhaps three, days. Let her give him all the food that is ready. You, Selim will come with us, and young Arif also."

As Selim ran off, Wazir Khan said to Sher Ali, "You understand Hasrat, I cannot let my horses go into a rough country after dark without accompanying them. Also there is the little matter of Nawabzaida Sahib running into trouble. Those hills are known to be full of budmarshs, and worse. So, we come with you, and I myself give thanks to Allah the Compassionate, the Merciful, that he sent us some action. Like the horses, we have been sitting here eating our heads off since August last year. Come, let us go riding together, I grow young again."

Doctor Maclaren, watching and listening, was expecting some expostulation from Sher Ali, but none came. He had strolled over to examine the animal that Wazir Khan had designated for him, and was making much of the big grey horse, murmuring into its ear like a lover speaking to his true love. But of course, thought Robert, this is the heir to Chikor – he would *expect* all this, take it for granted. But he heard the way that Sher Ali thanked Wazir Khan, saw the way the men looked at him, and thought, well, he is a true prince of his people, a leader of men, and remembered the stories that he had heard of Sher Ali's great grandfather, Atlar Khan. This young man was of good blood.

A few minutes later, when the men were saddling up, Robert heard Chunia speaking his name. "Doctor Robert Sahib – will you tell me which horse I will have? I need to know."

Sher Ali had heard her, too, and came back to speak to her. "Chunia, you are not coming. You will stay here, and we will return for you. It is dark, the way is rough, and Arina Begum would be very angry with me if any harm befell you."

"I think more harm will come to me if I walk behind you, Sher Ali. I am coming. Let there be no argument between you and me. I come, either on my feet, or on horseback. Which is it to be?"

Sher Ali flung up his hands. "I am beaten. Wazir Khan, have we enough horses?"

Wazir Khan did a rapid head count, then said, "If necessary, Hasrat, I will take the old one up on my horse. She weighs no more than a handful of feathers." He turned to look down at Chunia. "It is a rough road, oh, ruler of princes, and you are not a young woman."

Chunia looked back at him, her one eye full of fire. "I am able to ride alone, if there be a horse. If not, then I will ride with you. As to the road being rough, I am a woman of the hills, not a southerner. These hills are nothing to me, and the road will be as smooth as glass as I go to care for my beloved child. Let there be no more speech and time wasting. I am ready to go."

There might have been more argument – Chunia looked so frail, but at that moment Kushi came up to say that shooting had been heard earlier that day in the direction of the Galaar Fort. "It is where the road breaks off to go to Mianaghar. One says that this shooting was heard some time before sunset."

Sher Ali muttered a prayer, and in minutes the party was mounted and moving, Chunia sitting behind Wazir Khan, and Kushi, without a backward look at the car, taking over the second grass cutter's hard-mouthed pony. Robert Maclaren rode beside Sher Ali. After one glance at his companion's expression, Robert settled himself down in his saddle, prepared for the kind of riding he had not done since his youth.

The company clattered down the hard road past the empty bungalows of the deserted cantonment, and woke birds that had already gone to roost. The air was full of the voices of disturbed birds, and the beat of their wings. Then the cantonment roads were left behind and the night was silent. Sher Ali and his party made slow progress. The way was so rough, the night was very dark, and there were few stars. They were all tired, and they had to watch the track all the time, worried for the horses on this rocky way. Sher Ali was getting desperate when they arrived at a place where the track forked, and they began to climb. He called to Wazir Khan to ask if they were still going in the right direction, "Is this the turn to Mianaghar? There is a ruined fort, I remember, where the road forks, but I can see no fort."

They had several hurricane lamps, but they were of little help. Robert had a powerful torch but did not want to use it too much. "I must keep it for real emergencies, Tiger. Several times in the past I have had to perform operations by the light of this torch."

"Well, pray to heaven that you do not have to do so this time," said Sher Ali with fervour. He heard Chunia's voice speaking to Wazir Khan and Kushi, and then Kushi spurred his little sure-footed pony up to Sher Ali's side.

"The old one says that this is the road, Hasrat. The ruined

214

fort is on the left somewhere here. Ya Allah! This is a good place for an ambush! The shooting that was spoken about was supposed to have come from this direction."

A good place for an ambush! There was a marked silence from the rest of the party. Robert, peering ahead, said that he could see the ruined fort. "That bulk over there, darker than the sky, that must be the ruin. Tiger, do you think that we gain anything by struggling on like this. Would it not be a good idea to stop and wait for moonrise?"

Sher Ali was loath to agree. Just to keep moving forward, to feel that he was getting nearer to Arina was all that mattered to him, but he knew that it was foolish. He agreed that they should stop. He called out. "Let us get the horses over beside the fort and tether them. Wazir Khan! Set guards. I will take the first watch."

Kushi came running to set up two hurricane lamps, hanging them on the rusty iron hooks set in the walls by the original builder over a hundred years before. Sher Ali went up and tested them, and found them still firmly set. The fort seemed to be full of shadows and voices - the past was still here, and Sher Ali felt part of it. This fort must have always been a place of safety, a place to defend against enemies. The stairs up to the roof of the old tower were crumbling in places but still useable. He went up and looked out on the black darkness of the night, but he knew what he would see once the moon rose, the whole valley would be there before him, perhaps he would be able to see the village of Mianaghar, and beyond it the fort belonging to Chunia's family where Arina would be. He saw her face on the darkness of the sky, saw it as it had been when he had left her standing on the platform in Dera – her lovely eyes had been full of tears. He vowed that he would dry those tears with his kisses one day soon, and walked down from the tower to find more hurricane lamps and see the horses being brought in. He was astonished to see Chunia riding the big animal that had been allotted to Abdel Karim. He went at once

215

to help her dismount, saying, "Chunia, you ride like a *sowar*, but that beast is too big for you. Where is Abdel Karim? Has he deserted us?"

It was Wazir Khan who answered him. "Nay, Hasrat. He remembered his camels and his goats that his son left at the station. He has gone to take them home, then he will return and join us, riding his own horses. You are right, Chunia rides like one of my *sowars* – and better than some."

The night was warm and still. The horses were looked to, fed and watered, and the smell of hot chapattis and curry began to fill the fort. Wazir Khan brought a flask of cold water, and a bottle of Amritsar rum. Everyone had a measure of rum, including Chunia, and Wazir Khan stood up and proposed a toast to the "soon-to-be meeting between his honoured highness and the one who will be his bride". All drank to this, with smacking lips, and Sher Ali looked across at Chunia and saw that her hand had gone up to touch the amulet at her throat. She was supposed to have the sight – what was she seeing in Arina's future that made her clutch for the amulet against the evil eye every time Arina's name was mentioned?

All his feeling of hope left him. What had possessed him to allow Arina to take this crazy journey. He had been a fool, he had allowed Fram and Manika's fears to override his own sense. He could understand that Fram and Manika had been horrified by the massacres that had taken place – they had been left afraid, with good reason. But he should have known better, he should have spoken again to his colonel and taken Arina to safety himself. The thought of the things that could have gone wrong, of Arina being in danger or discomfort because he had been foolish and had allowed himself to be persuaded into a wrong decision was like an itch in his mind.

The food was finished, the others were sitting smoking, relaxing, talking together in low voices. Soon they would fall asleep while he waited for moonrise. He could not sit still.

He got up and walked about restlessly, going round the fort, and once more up into the tower, but could see nothing and went down again, crossed the track and climbed up the scree to the ridge above the road to get a better view of the horizon. Where was the moon? He could have shouted aloud when he saw the silver edge show above the line of the mountains. It came up quickly, a lopsided moon, but there was enough light for him to see the ground around him. He turned to go back to the fort.

The track below was still dark, but here he could see clearly, and as he picked his way along the ridge, he saw a cairn and, beyond it, two others. He caught his breath as he looked at them. They were graves, he knew that at once. He had seen too many such cairns during the time of the frontier skirmishes – graves swiftly dug, covered with soil, and heaped with rocks to mark the spot where men had died, and to keep the grave safe from desecration by hungry jackals. Then he saw the chair, upended, and a stain darker than shadows on the track beside it.

His mind refused what his eyes were telling him. These were old graves, relics of some tribal warfare. He bent, and felt for the soil below the rocks and knew that that hope was doomed. These graves were new. One of the graves was a little apart from the other two. He stood beside this cairn, looking down at it as if he could see through the rocks and the earth to the body that lay beneath.

Grace and beauty, laughter, courage and youth, all that promised happiness gone? If she were the one under these rocks, life would be without value. The night surrounded him, was part of him. He waited, straining his ears for a voice. It was said that a spirit torn untimely from a body would take time to leave the spot where death had come. She would call to him, she would call to him, he was sure. But nothing spoke to him, only a night wind brought the cry of a hunting jackal from the distant hills. He straightened his shoulders and turned away. What sort of a man am I to believe so easily that she is dead? She lives, whoever lies in that grave is not my dear love. I would *know*, he thought, I would know at once if she were dead. Our love is meant to be, to flourish and flower, it is written thus for me and for her. Oh Allah the Compassionate, the All Powerful, the Merciful, let my fears be shameful, let them be false.

He did not know that he had spoken aloud, had no idea how long he had stood there in his own darkness. But he had been heard.

The voice that called him was very faint, but he knew it at once, and for a moment he thought that it had come from the grave behind him. "Sakhi Mohammed!"

"Hasrat, I am here. Come to me, Lord, for I cannot come to you."

"I come, Sakhi, but speak again and again, so that I may find you."

Sakhi's voice was not much louder than a whisper, but the night was so still that Sher Ali was able to follow the thread of sound. It led him further up the scree to where a great rock tilted against the sky. Between the rock and the ground was a cleft, and Sakhi's voice sounded from its depth. Sher Ali hesitated to jump down into the cleft which was hidden from the moon and very dark in case he landed on top of Sakhi. He climbed further up the scree, following the cleft, until he found where it grew wider and it was possible to crawl in. He found Sakhi propped against the rock, wrapped in a horse blanket. Sher Ali kneeled beside him, and before he could speak, Sakhi said, "She lives, Hasrat. But she is in the hands of the accursed one, Yusuf Dyal of Sagpurna, the man you would not let me destroy for you. Yusuf Dyal, the son of darkness."

In a few words he sketched for Sher Ali all the happenings of the day, ending, "Sushi the innocent, is dead and so is Alam Beg, who wished to give his life in your service. One of the porters was also killed. The Begum Sahib was shown Sushi's grave, then she was given a horse to ride and taken away by Dyal and his band. I know not how many men there were, upwards of ten, and there was a boy also."

Sher Ali had asked no questions until the story was told, then he said, "Arina Begum was unhurt, Sakhi? You are sure? She went with them *willingly*?"

"Aye, Hasrat. She was quite unhurt, but she was shocked and frightened. She thought that Dyal was saving her from the dacoits who had shot at her. She thought that he was her saviour." Sakhi paused, and his breath rasped in his throat as he began to speak again. "Who can say what a woman thinks? She thanked him, she spoke quietly with him, but there is something I did not understand – something very strange."

"Sakhi, what do you mean?"

"The dog, Yusuf Dyal, treated her as you would wish her to be treated. He was respectful and gentle. In the shooting, when she ran up the road, she lost her veil – the honoured lady was unveiled before these people, but Dyal took no advantage of it, he looked away from her as one should, and he spoke sharply to his men when they came too close, staring. Dyal questioned her very civilly, asking her if she had any other servants with her, any men servants other than Alam Beg and the carriers. She was slow in answering, and he repeated his question, oh so gently and sweetly, the rat, and she answered and said no that she only had Sushi and Alam Beg, and the men who carried the chair. Then he asked if she had, by chance, seen any of the men who had shot at her, and again she said no, she had seen no one. Her answers are why I am alive tonight, for Gokul only had time to drag me into a shallow ditch beside the track, and lie beside me. If they had searched, they would have found us at once, but the Begum said there had been no other men. It seemed that Dyal believed her, for he called off the search. The Begum saved our lives, but it is strange to me. If she thought him to be her saviour, why should she lie to him? I think that something told her that he was no friend to her, and she was afraid."

My girl, thought Sher Ali, my love, alone with wolves, and afraid, and yet having a care – she must have guessed that Sakhi was about somewhere. What sense, what bravery!

"Sakhi, which way did they go?"

"They continued on the track towards Mianaghar, but I do not think that Dyal intends to go there. He asked the Begum where she was going when she was attacked, and she told him that she was on her way to Mianaghar, to the khan of that place. Be at peace, Hasrat, Gokul followed them and will return as soon as he discovers where they intend to go – they will have to have stopped before sundown, the Begum was exhausted."

Sakhi's voice was fading, and Sher Ali reluctantly realised that the man could tell him no more. He must get help for him before he did anything else. Thanks be to Allah for Robert! He saw disbelief on Sakhi's face when he told him that he was going to bring an English *hakim* to attend to him, and he thought to himself that the shock of seeing and speaking with Robert would go a long way to helping Sakhi feel better. He crawled out of the cleft, and began to go down the scree as quickly as he could.

In fact he did not have to go far because Robert had begun to wonder where he was, had gone to look for him and had woken Wazir Khan and Kushi when he could not find Sher Ali. The three men had walked along the road and up on to the first ridge, as Sher Ali had done. The sight of the overturned carrying chair, and the three cairns had horrified them, and while they were looking at them they heard the tumbling of loose stones and earth as Sher Ali made his way down to them before they could see him. Wazir and Kushi unshipped their guns and Sher Ali heard the low-voiced, "Who goes there? Halt or I fire," and knowing that in these parts there was seldom time to answer before the challenger fired, he dropped to the ground and called, "It is I, Sher Ali, please can you bring the Doctor Sahib quickly, I have Sakhi Mohammed here, badly wounded."

Robert answered at once, "I am here, Tiger, coming up now."

The three men scrambled up the scree to where Sher Ali waited, and he led them to the cleft. Robert went in at once, while Sher Ali told Wazir and Kushi what had happened during the day. When he had told them everything, he said, "Now I must find this man and his band of murderers. I need help. Wazir, where is the nearest army post? There used to be one at Gargallah."

"Not now, Hasrat. There have been many changes. The post has been empty for maybe six months. Why do you want the post? I can bring men, I come from Mianaghar. I can raise you an army, if that is what you want, and no one will question you afterwards. Tell me what you need."

Sher Ali believed him, but was not sure of the lack of questions afterwards. He thought he was very likely to raise a small war. Wazir Khan's eyes were sparkling as he said, "There is no law here now, Hasrat, and who is to forbid me, and my sons and my brothers when we go hunting dacoits who have killed and kidnapped? What say you, Lord?"

"I give you my thanks, and the thanks of my family, and I look forward to meeting your sons and your brothers. It need not be a large army – Sakhi Mohammed thinks that Dyal had upwards of ten men. They come from the Dera streets, I should say. He has no tribal affiliations that I know of!"

Wazir Khan clapped his hands. "Good. We will have a little action. When we have seen Sakhi Mohammed come up from the rocks, I will go quietly to Mianaghar by the upper track and tell my people. They will be ready by dawn."

As he was speaking, Robert came up from the cleft and Sher Ali asked how Sakhi was.

"He has a bullet lodged in his shoulder, which is causing

him great pain, and he has lost much blood. We'll have to get him out of that hole in the ground, and then I will be able to get to work on him."

It was a struggle, and a painful one for Sakhi, who was grey and sweating by the time they had carried him down the scree, and into the one room that still had a roof in the old fort. Sher Ali then had to hold Sakhi steady while Robert, without being able to anaesthetise his patient, probed for the bullet. It was a long, painful and messy business, and Sakhi Mohammed mercifully fainted before Robert was at last able to say, "Oh, thank God," and hold the forceps aloft, with the bullet gripped in its teeth.

Sher Ali was as grey as Sakhi by the time this was done, and had bitten his bottom lip until blood came, suffering with his man. Now as he looked down at Sakhi, he wondered if he would recover from the operation.

"Oh, he will be fine," said Robert. "The wound is clean, and he is a strong man. But he needs better nursing and food than he can get here, even with Chunia's tender care. I should get him down to the mission hospital in Dera as soon as possible, but how? He won't be able to ride for some little time." Sher Ali had been thinking this too, over his thoughts for Arina, which were the undercurrent to all his thoughts now, it seemed. Kushi, who had stayed in the room during the bullet extraction, suggested that he would go back to Dera and bring the car up as far as he could.

"I think it will come as far as the beginning of the first slopes, then if Sakhi could be carried down there, we could be in Dera very quickly."

Robert looked doubtful. "Will the car make it?"

"Allah Kerim – but it is worth trying, I think."

"Right. I am sorry to think that I won't be in at the end of this adventure, Tiger, but one thing I can do is telephone Madore and say that you have been held up, but that you are on your way."

222

"I am very disappointed that you won't be with me. I have begun to look on you as my own personal good-luck charm, and God knows I need one. I am grateful for your offer to telephone my regiment, that will be a help. Also, I wonder if you could contact the District Commissioner, Donald Springer – I think that as he is still there, he is probably still the DC – and tell him what has happened, and what I am going to do. I don't want to end up in a cell in the police *thana* in Dera. But I must get the Begum Arina out of Dyal's hands somehow, and if it means starting a war here, fair enough. I will start it."

Sher Ali sounded depressed and reckless, a bad combination, thought Robert. He knew what was wrong with Tiger. It was fear – not fear for himself, but fear for the girl, in the hands of his enemy. He started to say, "I wish you luck, Tiger," but was interrupted. Chunia had come out and was standing beside Sher Ali.

"What is this, the Doctor Sahib going down with Sakhi to Dera? There is no need. We have already arranged what we will do. Kushi and I will take him down – after two or three days. We have plenty of clean water here, we have food and I myself will look after him. Do not make a big *ghurburr* over unnecessary actions. Doctor Sahib, you are more needed for my Begum, who has had much trouble. Leave Sakhi Mohammed to me and to Kushi. We will look well to him."

Both Sher Ali and Robert stared at her as if she was an apparition.

"Can he ride?" Robert asked.

"Today, no." said Chunia. "Tomorrow, maybe. Then the next day, certainly he will ride, he is not a sick woman, he is a man of the hills. Sher Ali, do you think your honoured father would give you as guardian a man who becomes frail over a bullet in the shoulder? Go you and find Arina Begum, and bring her to safety. We will do very well here."

Sher Ali turned to Robert. "What do you say, Robert? I will

understand if you feel you would prefer to go down with Sakhi. After all, I have no right to ask you to do anything more, and I feel we may be facing a very unpleasant few days. Tell me how you feel about this?"

"Well, of course I am coming with you. Sakhi is in very good hands, and I suspect that if I don't go with you I shall have to deal with Chunia's displeasure, which is something I don't want to face. I will go in and have another look at Sakhi, and then we had better get on."

So there was no argument. Sher Ali was pleased that he would still have his good luck charm, and he saw that Robert really wanted to share what he called "the adventure".

The graves had made Sher Ali realise that what had seemed just the usual malice of a jealous Yusuf Dyal was much more. The old family story of Zeena's elopement came back to him. Could this be Dyal taking vengence for the slur put on his family by Zeena? Both Robert and Sher Ali were deep in different thoughts as they walked back to the old fort.

Robert was amused to think that Sher Ali thought of him as a "good luck charm". If anyone needs a good luck charm it is me, he thought. Please God we don't both end up in the police *thana* for starting a revolt in the tribal territories. Sher Ali's thoughts were with Arina, his thoughts and his prayers. Nothing else mattered.

Nineteen

In Dera, on the day after Sher Ali set off for Mianaghar, Donald Springer, the District Commissioner, was sitting on his veranda opening the day's mail. There was one official letter, stamped and sealed with red wax. As he read this letter, he began to feel the weight of his duties grow very heavy. This letter would cause great trouble for him, and others of his staff. Action would have to be taken at once. He hurried through the rest of the mail, keeping out one letter which was not addressed to him. It was addressed to Major Sher Ali, and he could not understand why it should come to him. It should have gone direct to Madore, where he understood that Sher Ali, the heir to the ruler of Chikor was spending his leave, prior to his marriage. He would have to decide what to do with this letter at the same time as he dealt with the more important news in the official letter. He called for his syce, told him to bring his horse round, and shortly afterwards he rode out to the grass farms, where he hoped to find Rissaldar Major Wazir Khan, who would be able to give him most of the information he needed.

As he rode through the empty cantonments, he wondered how long it would be before the place began to grow shabby after a year's neglect. Surely they, the new army commanders, would garrison this place again soon. It was a pity to let it go into dusty disorder – the desert would soon take over, if the place was left empty much longer. It was a relief to reach the grass farms, which looked, as always, orderly and green.

225

The Rissaldar Major, who was in charge, was a good man, thought the District Commissioner, looking about him with satisfaction. Wazir Khan had absorbed his army training and his discipline, from a long line of serving soldiers, and was a man liked and honoured by his superiors – certainly those who had gone – and no doubt the new commanders would find him as essential as the previous officers had.

The sentry on duty at the gates of the grass farms saluted and opened the gate, and Donald Springer rode in and down the road to the main office. Here two off-duty men saluted him and came to hold his horse as he dismounted. He expected to see Wazir Khan coming out to greet him, but the man who hurried out was Rahman Ali, the Daffadar.

"Rissaldar Major Sahib?" enquired the District Commissioner. He saw, with a sinking heart that the Daffadar was bursting with news, and was anxious and worried. What could have happened to Wazir Khan?

"Collector Sahib," said the Daffadar, using the old title, "Wazir Khan has gone away with four *sowars* and the Nawabzaida Sahib of Azadpur, and the Colonel Doctor Sahib is with him also, and the man Kushi."

The District Commissioner's patience was running out. "Never mind who has gone with him, where has he gone?"

"Sahib, he has gone to Mianaghar. There is also an old woman with him, and another servant, Sahib. This is no small thing, rifle fire has been heard. Also there is a story of a Begum who has perhaps been killed or kidnapped. Wazir Khan has taken arms with him, all four *sowars* were armed. If the Collector Sahib wishes, I myself can leave Lance Daffadar Salih Mohammed here to look after this place, and I can take the Sahib to the Khan of Mianaghar." He paused as he saw the District Commissioner frowning, and then added, "There are few horses here now, Sahib. Wazir Khan took the best for the Nawabzaida Sahib."

Donald Springer, District Commissioner of Dera and the

surrounding *tehsils*, had reason to frown. Kidnapping, murder, a defaulting Rissaldar Major, stolen horses, stolen guns, an unexpected presence of the heir to an important hill state. For a moment he wondered why he had not left he country when he had had the chance. The heir to Chikor state – the Tiger himself, a much decorated young officer in a crack regiment, a charming and popular man, for whom he was holding a letter – surely he could not be mixed up in a kidnapping. The District Commissioner looked narrowly at Rahman Ali, Daffadar.

"Are you telling me that the Nawab has kidnapped a Begum?"

Rahman Ali looked horrified. "Nay Sahib! It is he who has gone to rescue her – the Begum is his future wife! It is Major Yusuf Dyal who has taken a band of men from Peshawar and has taken the Begum, so I have been told."

The District Commissioner groaned to himself. The official letter, with all the red seals was all about the misdeeds of Major Dyal, reported confidentially and under seals – how had this Daffadar got hold of the story? And now it seemed that Dyal had added several more crimes to his name. The various necessary actions that he would have to take loomed up before the District Commissioner. Why did I sign on for another two years? He shook his head at himself, and said, "Very well, Rahman Ali, I would like to have one of your men to come with me. I shall go immediately to Mianaghar to see for myself what is happening."

"You will go yourself, Sahib? Then I will come with you, I will delegate my authority to Salih Mohammed, and I will come with two men. I will also set a guard on your house until you return, then you need have no anxiety about the safety of the memsahib and your son. Indeed, Sahib, these days, with bands of dacoits roaming the hills unchecked, it is wise not to leave one's family and property unguarded. My family I have left in Madore."

He saw the District Commissioner's question coming before

Donald asked it. "There are four mules, Sahib, and two mares in foal."

So there was little to guard, which is why Rahman Ali was so willing to leave his command to a junior, thought the District Commissioner.

"That is well thought of, the guard for my house. Rahman Ali, I will be ready to leave as soon as I have spoken with my wife. Come to my bungalow when you are ready, we will leave from there. I will need one mule for my bearer and my kit."

Just time, thought the District Commissioner, to explain to Joan what was happening, collect a change of clothing and alert the bearer, then I should be well on the road to Mianaghar before dark. We can ride through the night and catch up with Wazir Khan and his Nawab.

In the old fort, Sher Ali was talking to Wazir Khan, who had ridden up to join him with what looked like a dangerous rabble, but turned out to be some members of his family, and several Lance Daffadars who were on leave in the district. There were twenty-five armed men altogether, all well mounted on good strong country horses and, like Wazir Khan, they appeared to be spoiling for a fight. What Yusuf Dyal had with him, Sher Ali could not know but his men were also armed, according to Sakhi Mohammed. No doubt about it, when Wazir's men met up with the men that Yusuf Dyal had with him, it could very easily start a small tribal war. Sher Ali found it impossible to worry about that. All he wanted was to find Arina quickly, rescue her and get her safely home to Chikor. If tribal fighting made that easier, the sooner it started, the better. Please God, make sure nothing has happened to her. In that man's hands, with no one to protect her! Anything that Yusuf Dyal thinks will distress me, thought Sher Ali, he will do. He saw us together, he knows that this girl is more important to me than anything else.

Sher Ali could no longer wait. He raised his hand and called to Wazir Khan, "Rissaldar Sahib, let us go. Keep your hounds in leash if you can, until I give you the word."

"All is well, Hasrat. They will do nothing until you tell me, then I will unleash them and let the fighting begin." His white teeth gleamed in a smile that looked like a snarl, and the men behind him did not look as if they were going to be easy to hold in check.

Sher Ali shrugged. "So be it," he said to himself, and turned to find Robert riding at his side. Sher Ali felt a faint twinge of anxiety.

"Robert, I hope this is not going to make trouble for you. I can see us causing a tribal disturbance, which could be serious. I feel that I should have insisted on your staying away from this – you could certainly lose your job over it. I don't think the government will look kindly on us starting a small tribal war."

"Nonsense," said Robert. "I am far too important to the government to be lightly thrown away. In any case, the risk is worth the excitement to me. I wouldn't miss this for anything. What wonderful rogues these men are, look at their eyes, they are like hunting hawks, hell bent on their prey. With men like these, no enterprise can fail. They are like the highlanders of Scotland – well, come to think of it, that is what they are, highlanders of the north of India. Mix them with some of our Gordons or Seaforths, and you wouldn't know the difference." He looked at Sher Ali, smiling, and saw that his companion was not listening to him.

Sher Ali's mind was far away, with his girl, Robert supposed, and how to get her safely away from this trouble.

It was dawn when they started the last climb. When they came to the top of the steep incline, they could look straight down to a small plateau, still in shadow; though the light was growing.

"We are at the top of the Sarghana Pass that stands above Mianaghar. As I remember it, the way is smoother once we cross the pass and begin to descend. Better for the horses." Sher Ali stopped speaking and stared down as the light broadened, and revealed the plateau clearly. It appeared to be strewn with bodies, like the aftermath of some ambush. Sher Ali forgot his horse's legs, hurled the animal forward, followed by Wazir Khan and his men, and by Robert, who rode more carefully, his heart full of dread at what they might find. Where, on that field of apparent death, could the girl have found safety?

But there was no sign of any woman's body among the men who were lying round the ashes of a fire. Sher Ali found Yusuf Dyal sleeping a little apart from the main group. He called to Robert, who came and bent over the body.

After a very cursory examination, Robert stood up and said, "He has no wounds. He is drugged. Drugged into total unconsciousness. Heaven knows when he will come round, if ever, unless I use some pretty severe treatment, which might harm him."

"Then rouse him," said Sher Ali, "no matter what harm it does him. I need to know where Arina is. Look, over by the other fire, there is a cup that she must have used. She was here, lying among those blankets. Rouse him, I say, I must know what has happened."

But Robert advised caution. "Don't be foolish, Tiger. If I wake him by using methods that could damage his brain, would that help you? If he could not answer your questions? Wait. I will look at some of the others, one of them might be more lightly held by the drug. Let us see."

While they were lifting one after another of the men's sagging heads, Sher Ali suddenly straightened, and stood up to listen. At the same time, Wazir Khan dropped the body he was examining roughly, and said, "I hear a horse coming from the direction of Mianaghar."

Sher Ali turned to look down the track. Wazir's band of men were all alerted at once, and several of them unslung their rifles. Wazir roared at them to hold their fire, and

Sher Ali went forward towards the rider who was now in plain sight.

"Gokul!" said Sher Ali, and ran to meet him as he swerved to a halt and dismounted. Sher Ali shouted to him, "Where is she?"

"She is safe, Hasrat, in the fort of the khan of Mianaghar. She is unharmed, and with the family of the khan. Her maidservant was killed, and also the old man, but she is safe."

Gokul lowered his eyes as he spoke. To see this prince weep was more than he could believe. But surely they were tears of joy! Robert came to Sher Ali. "Your worst imaginations are washed away by those tears, Tiger."

Sher Ali dashed his hand over his eyes. "Yes, thank God. Now let us get on to Mianaghar, and I will see for myself that all is well with her."

"What about these people here?" asked Robert.

"These dogs? Throw them over the *khud* into the ravine, and leave them to regain their senses or not, whichever happens to be the will of Allah. But keep Yusuf Dyal. I want him."

"Tiger, you have just said a prayer of thankfulness to your God. In our bible, there is a verse, 'Vengeance is mine, saith the Lord'. I do not think that you should throw these men over the *khud*. I think you should set a guard on them, including Dyal and, later, take them back to Dera to the police *thana* and let the DC deal with them. I should think quite a few of them are wanted men," said Robert.

As if his words had called them up, the District Commissioner and his little band came riding up the track, as surprised to see the scattered bodies as Robert and Sher Ali were to see these new arrivals.

"What on earth is going on here?" asked Donald Springer, and then seeing Robert, he addressed his question to him. "Robert, I am glad to see you. What is happening?"

Sher Ali went forward at once, before Robert could answer, and introduced himself, and the District Commissioner at once handed him a letter, saying, "I am delighted to see you, Nawab Sahib. I was expecting to have to ride all the way to Mianaghar to discover where you were. I understand that you have been looking for the desperados who molested your future wife. But I was not expecting to find the aftermath of a battle. Please, will someone tell me exactly what has been happening?" Sher Ali, impatient, looked at Robert. "My friend Colonel Maclaren will tell you. I have urgent business in Mianaghar."

"One minute, please," said the District Commissioner. "If I were you, I would read that letter before you go. It is important to you. Meanwhile, Robert, will you oblige me by telling me how all these men died?"

"They are not dead, they are drugged. It will be some time, I think, before they stir."

"Good heavens!" The District Commissioner stared about him. "I must ask you how this came about. Let's have a look at some of them – there is a chap over there who I seem to recognise." He walked with Robert over what he still thought of as a field of battle, but seeing that the men were, in fact, still breathing, stooped over one of them. He stood up again, walked on, stopping to look at the faces of various bodies, bending over one or two to look more closely.

"So far, I would like you to know that you have one of the largest collection of villains that I have ever seen in one place." The DC looked over his shoulder at Wazir Khan. "See, Rissaldar Major Sahib, you have caught the worst of the band that has been ravaging the country from Peshawar to Lachamak Pass. The camel caravans will no doubt call your name blessed. These men have no honour, even among the other dacoits. Bind them for me while they still sleep, and we will take them down to the police *thana* as soon as they can walk. I see there are mules up there, and I also see ammunition boxes, marked with the government seal."

Wazir Khan nodded, and pointed to where Yusuf Dyal still lay. "That is the leader, Sahib. He does a steady run with arms, to sell to those who call themselves defenders. *Mohajiars* who come into the tribal territories to make trouble again." The District Commissioner looked down at the papers he held. "Yes. Yusuf Dyal. Running arms is on the list of his crimes as well. Is that really Yusuf Dyal? He is the heir to the state of Sagpurna, is he not? Was he leading this band of brothers in villainy?"

"Certainly he was," said Robert, as Sher Ali did not reply, deep in his letter. Robert waited a moment, and then continued, "Perhaps you know that he also seems to have kidnapped the young Begum of Chikor, and has caused the death of two of her servants. This is going to cause a great deal of trouble between the two states. Are you looking for him, by any chance?"

"I was looking for one Major Yusuf Dyal. I presume this is he, the same man. I have had a long and interesting letter from Islamabad. So this is the man." He looked at the comatose body in the tumbled blankets. As he looked, he saw the man's eyelids tremble, and said to Robert, "I think this man is waking. I think I should have his hands bound before he wakes properly and tries to get away. What do you think?"

Wazir Khan did not need to be told. At a word from him, one of the men engaged in binding the other villains came over at once, and pulling Yusuf Dyal's arms behind his back, tied his wrists and then his ankles.

The District Commissioner was certain that Dyal was awake, but the man lay still, with his eyes closed. Trying to work out how to get out of this, thought Springer grimly. If he had done nothing else, the guns he had brought into tribal territory would condemn him. The trouble he is in with his regiment is partly about gun-running, and here is the proof. He is finished with the army, anyway.

Donald Springer looked away from the man lying at his feet and said to Robert, "How are the other villains – any of them conscious yet?"

"Yes, they are begining to waken. Heaven knows what they were doped with."

Sher Ali was folding his letter away, and looked up smiling as the District Commissioner and Robert came over to him. He held his letter out to Robert.

"Keep this for me, Robert, and read it when you have time. Such wonderful news! My grandmother has been at work and has charmed my colonel into giving me a month's leave for my marriage, which is to take place in Madore, as arranged. She sent no message by Yusuf Dyal, has not seen him for months. So he lied all along the line. This letter is from my colonel, a very kind letter enclosing that of my grandmother's. You are my good luck charm, Robert."

Robert took the letter held out to him and put it away in his pocket, saying with a smile, "Well, really, you should thank Donald here, who was willing to ride all this way to bring you the good news." He gestured to the District Commissioner.

"I am delighted to have brought good news, Nawab Sahib, you have already done me a good turn. We have been looking for these men for some months. They will now come down to Dera with me and go straight into the police *thana* while their cases are sorted out. Some are already marked for death. As for their leader—"

"Ah yes – their leader," said Sher Ali, his face growing dark with anger. "Where is he? I want him." He looked across to where Yusuf Dyal had been lying and saw him struggling to rise, very hampered by his bonds. Sher Ali's face grew thunderous, he went forward shouting, "By Allah, who ordered this? Let him loose at once!"

Wazir Khan, Robert, and the District Commissioner all looked at him, astonished.

"But this is Yusuf Dyal, Hasrat, your enemy!" said Wazir Khan. "He is the man who kidnapped your Begum, and killed her servants. How can you wish him to be free?"

"Do as I say. Release him. This man bears the king's

234

commission, he is a very brave and decorated officer. Untie that rope! This does not mean that I am freeing *him*, it means that his status as an officer of his country's army is recognised and honoured, even though the man himself is not worthy of any honour. Be very sure that he will stand trial before his peers in due course, but not tied like the criminal he is."

No one spoke as Wazir Khan cut Yusuf Dyal free. Dyal rubbed his arms and wrists, and the tense silence was broken by his loud laughter. Sher Ali looked at him, his face set, saying nothing, and Dyal laughed again.

"Oh what a gentleman you always are, Tiger! A gentlemanly fool. I take it that all this gallantry is to show you in a good light before your little Begum? See, Arina, how noble a man you are about to marry!" He turned as he spoke towards the place where Arina had lain the night before, and his face and bearing changed as he looked for her and did not see her anywhere. He sprang towards Sher Ali, his teeth bared like an animal attacking.

"Where is she, Tiger? What have you done with her? I swear, if you have touched her I will kill you now, with my bare hands."

His sudden rage was matched by Sher Ali's answering fury, which rose as he heard Yusuf Dyal say Arina's name.

"You!" said Sher Ali, "You dare to ask me where she is, and what *I* have done to her? What did *you* do when she was alone and unprotected? You took her prisoner, killed her woman servant, and what else did you do that has made you so suddenly protective of her? If you have touched a hair of her head, I will have you killed. You speak of killing me, you rat's dirt! If you have hurt Arina, your death will come to you in a very unpleasant form, I promise you."

Yusuf Dyal's laugh was more like a snarl. "You promise me death? Ah hah! What do I fear in death? I will meet it when it comes, what else? I promise you something far worse than death. You ask me what I did when she was helpless and alone, up here in this wild country? My foolish Tiger, that is something you will now never know. Not until you come to that moment in your marriage bed – ah, I see you understand me. Not until then will you know if you are holding in your arms another man's leavings, or a virgin. Think on that, Tiger! You will never know."

Before one of the watching men could move, Sher Ali sprang at Dyal, and the two were locked in furious fight. Sher Ali was the stronger, Dyal was weakened by the drug he had been given. But none of the others saw the knife in Dyal's hand until it was too late.

Wazir Khan jumped forward to knock Dyal's arm up but blood was already pouring down Sher Ali's face, blinding him. Wazir Khan was joined by Gokul and Robert, and Dyal was dragged to the ground. Gokul and the District Commissioner bound him securely, while Robert ran to get his bag. His greatest fear was that the knife might have been poisoned, and he began to clean the wound at once. He heard Wazir Khan say, "You, Dyal – take some of your own medicine," and watched him lift the knife to stab at Dyal, holding the knife to the man's eye. "Speak, Dyal – is there poison on this knife? You may choose to answer – if you do not, I will remove your eye and watch for symptoms of poison. Your eye will be gone in any case." His face, his steady hand spoke of a resolution that brought a cry to Dyal's lips.

"I am no serpent! It is clean!" and after a moment Wazir Khan stood back, saying, "I would gladly let my hand slip, except that my prince has forbidden me. Lie there, and think of what you have so far escaped – for the moment. The road to Dera is long and rough – anything can happen. Think on it, Dyal."

Sher Ali was still being tended by Robert. As he began to stitch the wound, Sher Ali winced, and Robert said, "Yes, this is painful, which is no more than you deserve. You lost your temper at a bad time. You are going to have a hideous scar, your smile will never be the same, you chivalrous fool. Why did you set that snake free?"

"A matter of honour," said Sher Ali through clenched teeth, "Arina's honour, which is my own. I should have killed him. I will certainly kill him the first opportunity I get. I swear it."

"Remarkably foolish, that would be," said Robert. "What would happen after that? You must learn to live in the twentieth century, Tiger. These days even princes of ruling houses cannot kill without incurring the penalties of the law. Think of the grief you would cause your family, and Arina would be a widow before she was ever a wife. Come, Tiger, think of Arina, not of what he has or has not done to her. If you want to know what I think, I believe he is captivated by her, and will not have done her any dishonour – any more than you would have done, in similar circumstances."

"You forget – he is my enemy and I am his. He knows what she means to me – think you that he would hold his hand if he had the opportunity of harming me through her?"

Robert pulled the needle through the last stitch, and paid no attention to Sher Ali's groan. "Yes. Stop thinking foolishly, and remember her. That was the last stitch, now you should first speak with Wazir Khan. I must stitch his hand – he was wounded while he attempted to stop our fight. Also Gokul, he may lose a finger if he is left untended. When you have thanked these men, you should make what haste you can to go and find the khan of Mianaghar, and see your Begum. Think of her, alone in a strange place – she needs your strength, Tiger."

Robert spoke gravely. It was enough, thought Sher Ali, I am behaving like a fool. He rose at once, feeling sick and dizzy, and went to speak with Wazir Khan, who turned his thanks aside, saying, "You thank me, Hasrat? Nay, what honour have I won today?" And Gokul, with his hand well bandaged, insisted on riding to Mianaghar with his master.

"Yes," said Robert, "that is a good idea, just in case you find yourself dizzy and fall from your horse. The way you are likely to ride, you could easily come off, so try to take it slowly."

"You are beginning to sound like my grandmother," said Sher Ali, and laughed at Robert's outraged expression.

But it was the last time he felt like laughing on that ride. His head was aching, and his scar was beginning to smart and burn. He rode slowly – he could do nothing else on a track worse than anything he had encountered so far; the surface covered with broken shards of slatey rock.

Gokul, riding behind him was cursing to himself at every step. Sher Ali thought with longing of the cleared paths and carefully prepared tracks that led in and out of the villages of Chikor and Pakodi. He thought of how he would take Arina riding every morning, early, to show her every corner of the state that she remembered with love after so many years away. His heart turned within him when he thought of what she had endured since she had arrived in Pakistan, and his mind turned to what Yusuf Dyal had said.

His head throbbed at every movement the horse made, but that pain was bearable compared to his tormenting thoughts. Every tone of Dyal's voice sounded in his brain, and he promised himself that one day he would kill his rival. He growled the word "kill" without knowing that he had spoken aloud, and Gokul, behind him, looked at him with sympathy. He himself would kill that man, as soon as he had the chance.

At last the walls of Mianaghar came in sight, Sher Ali remembered the path that branched there, and went round the walls to go up the last slope to the Fort of Mianaghar where the khan lived. He pulled his horse up at the high gates, and Gokul dismounted and went to hammer on the gates with his whip. At once they heard running feet, and the gates were unbarred and dragged open, and the khan himself came out to greet them, followed by a slim boy who smiled at Gokul and then came forward to bow very low before Sher Ali and take the reins that he tossed to him as he dismounted.

Twenty

The moon was setting as Rustom and Arina rode up to the Mianaghar fort. Rustom flung himself off his sweating pony and ran to hammer on the gates, shouting his triumphant message.

"She is here, she is safe, and I, Rustom, have brought her!"

At once lamplight began to glow behind the windows and voices called. Yunis Khan came out, shouting his son's name, and when Arina would have dismounted, the khan came to her and lifted her down from the saddle, and carried her over to where Aisin Bibi waited to receive her with open arms and cries of welcome. "Take her, wife, here is our guest at last. Begum Sahiba, you are more welcome than the spring rains! But where is the old one?"

Rustom saved Arina from having to begin the story of events by saying quickly, "Come with me father, I have much to tell you of Dyal, and we must send news down to Dera before those men wake."

His father, avid for news, went with him at once, and Arina turned to smile at the kind-faced woman who said, using the words that Chunia said so often, "Come my bird, you are tired and have been afraid. Come with me, and we will drink tea, and you will rest for a little before you bathe. Come, piyari."

Arina felt the woman's hand on her shoulder, urging her towards the door of the fort. The stairs were steep, and it was still dark. Arina was glad of the woman's firm hand at her waist, helping her up. Her legs had suddenly turned to jelly.

The room she entered was large and dimly lit by a single hurricane lamp, but she saw the red eye of charcoal burning in a stove in the corner. There was a pile of cushions against the wall. The woman led her over to them and said, "Sit, my child. I am Aisin Bibi, the mother of Rustom, and here is also my daughter Hamida. We bid you welcome to our hearts, and to our home." This speech of welcome said, the two women set about rousing the stove and making tea.

"Drink, my child and then lie down and sleep," said Aisin, bringing the tea. "I will wake you when your bath is prepared."

Arina drank the tea while the woman asked questions that Arina could not answer. What could she say when all she wanted to do was forget the events of the day before? She told Aisin that Chunia was waiting in Dera for transport to come for her. "We will send for her, maybe today or tomorrow." How would they get her here past the barrier of those men, wondered Arina, but before she could ask, she fell asleep, and Aisin covered her with a light shawl and went out, taking the lamp with her.

Outside the door, Aisin found her son sitting at the top of the stairs.

"Ho, Rustom Bahadur, chief among men! What do you here? She will sleep for a while. Is there news? I heard some noise and talk below. What is it?"

"Yes, there is news. One of the villagers went to Dera yesterday, and when he returned he came upon much activity on the plateau. It must have happened just after I left with the Begum. He said there was an English Sahib there, and a Nawab, and the Commissioner Sahib, he who stays in Dera. They have old Wazir Khan with them, and some *sepoys*. They were waking the drugged men. My mother, I do not know if he speaks the truth, but he says the Nawab is from Chikor.

Gokul, the Begum's servant who came with me, has gone to see if this is indeed his Nawab, Sher Ali. If it is, he will bring him here at once."

"*Ya illa!*" said his mother, "The Nawab from Chikor, and the Choti Begum sleeps unbathed, undressed, and her hair like a wig of rope with dust. Go and see what is happening, and come back and tell me when he is coming. I will let her sleep as long as possible."

It was daylight, streaming in through four large windows, that finally woke Arina. For a few minutes she had no idea where she was. She sat up and looked about her. A large room with windows wide open on to a balcony, where doves were strutting and fluffing out their feathers in the early morning sunlight. In the room she saw that piled against the walls were many cushions, the floor was covered with carpets, the whole room spoke of comfort and care. Then she saw a tin bath and that told her where she was. She was in the home of Chunia's relatives, she remembered the woman Aisin telling her she would be wakened for a bath. She stood up, and someone must have been watching her for at once Aisin came in, followed by her daughter Hamida, carrying two steaming buckets of water. Both Aisin and her daughter seemed flurried, apart from greeting her briefly they did not talk to her until another bucket of water was brought in by an older woman, obviously a servant, for she was spoken to very sharply when she started to talk. But Arina had heard the beginning of what she had said, and her heart began to beat very fast.

The woman had said, "They have been seen," and was immediately told to be quiet. "Now is not the time for speech. Go and prepare more hot water."

The woman left at once, one hand over her mouth and her eyes turning to Arina with a guilty look. She has been told not to say something in front of me, guessed Arina. There must be news, but what news that I must not hear? If it was good they would surely tell me. Supposing that man

Dyal has been seen on his way here, looking for me – with his band of dacoits. Those wolf-faced men, and their leader. She shuddered, standing naked in the tub, and Aisin said at once, "Is the water too cold?"

"No, I thank you. But there has been news, I think? Is it bad news?"

Aisin did not answer, she poured two full dippers of water all over Arina, from her head to her heels, dipper after dipper, so that Arina could ask nothing more, then when she started to shampoo her hair Aisin said, "No, piyari, no real news. Lalla, whose mouth is too big and tongue too loose, was repeating village rumours. There is a cloud of dust on the road, a bird had flown up with a clap of wings, *so* of course there is an army approaching, and there has been gun fire. Village gossip! All lies, all imaginings. Come now, let us dry your hair quickly, and dress you in festive garments. I will give you the clothes that Hamida will wear for her marriage. She is greatly honoured that a bride of a prince will wear her dress!"

But why do I wear festive dress? wondered Arina. My marriage is weeks away – and miles away too. Oh Tiger, where are you now? How will I get news in this place? There has been some news, I know there has – but good or bad, it seems I am not to hear it. She submitted to being rubbed and patted, her hair was combed out so roughly that she winced. Why such a hurry? Oh for Chunia, who used to take her time. I found it tiresome then, but how happy I would be to see her now. There must be a reason for this haste.

Now her hair, still damp, was being plaited. It would never dry if they did this. But plaited it was, and the end was tied with a red cord with tiny silver bells on it, as Sher Ali had used to decorate his falcon's feet. The little hooded bird – why did she think of that bird now?

Aisin and Hamida were now dressing her, in great haste. She had no shoes, and no veil. She asked for a veil, and Aisin said,

"I have no veil to give you, piyari. We of the tribes do not go veiled. Modesty is in your eyes and in your actions and in your bearing. So we think." As Aisin finished speaking, Arina heard voices from below.

Aisin turned on Hamida and the servant Lalla who were gathering up discarded clothing and hissed at them, "Take out the bath and those buckets, Lalla. Hamida, pull back the curtains and shake the cushions. Must I do everything? Now, let me put your earrings on, piyari – such beautiful earrings! You are lucky that those men did not pull them from your ears." She began to put them on Arina's ears, her hands were shaking, and her excitement was obvious. All this haste. Who was coming? Arina had a sudden, utterly ridiculous thought. Suppose that it was Sher Ali himself! Then there would be a reason to be excited. But she told herself not to be foolish. This was just a mad, wild dream, born of her longing to see him. Sher Ali was miles away, up in the hill station of Abottabad, how could he be here? Yet dreams did come true. After all, the long dream of the prince and the bird with bells on its feet and the wonderful horse, that dream had come true.

She had heard voices downstairs – one of them could have been Sher Ali's voice. The dream was taking her over, as it had done once before – in Manika's house in Karachi. That clear voice . . .

There was no mirror into which she could look to see the shadows of the past. But the crystal voice she had heard once before sounded loud in her mind. "There is no bridge which love cannot cross. Love is more powerful than time or space. Remember, and believe."

Clear, sweet the words sounded, ringing to echo and die into silence. Arina still half in a dream, found she was alone in the room. Where had the women gone? They knew that someone was coming, but they had not told her who it was. Why? The empty room was frightening, there was something she did not know. What news was coming? She could not stay in the room.

She hurried out to the balcony, where the doves still crooned, preening each other.

The sun was so bright that it seemed to make dreams impossible. How could she have imagined that Tiger would be here? Dreams and voices from the past. She dreamed too much. Jessie in far away Scotland had often told her that. But grandmother had never chided her for dreaming. Beautiful Zeena had had her dreams. Arina turned away from the sun and went to the curtained door, pulled the curtain back, and walked in.

Down in the courtyard, Sher Ali had thanked Rustom and praised him for his bravery in delivering Arina safely to his mother. Rustom then led off his horse, and Sher Ali was left to endure a long speech of welcome from the khan when all he wanted was to know where Arina was. The speech seemed endless. Not every day did Yunis Khan receive a prince. Finally, Sher Ali's longing to see Arina overcame his good manners.

"Where is Arina Begum, Khan Sahib?"

Yunis Khan, stopped in mid-flow of his oration, was offended. "Why, where should she be but upstairs in the care of my wife, Aisin Bibi. When you have bathed and eaten I will show you."

But Sher Ali had left him, he was already going up the stairs. This staircase was all that lay between him and Arina. He wondered how she would greet him after all that had happened to her, would she turn away from him in anger, blaming him for not being with her when she needed him? Would she be afraid to stay in a country where such things happened?

Sher Ali was by this time afraid of what crisis he would meet, but he went up the stairs quickly in spite of his fears, longing to see her. There was a screened door at the top of the stairs – this must be the entry to the women's quarter, the harem. He pushed the screen aside and went in.

The room was large, light and airy. Through four high

windows he saw the sky and felt a breeze that brought a faint, pleasant smell of sandalwood and jasmine. It was a woman's room, he thought. Thick carpets covered the wooden floor, many big cushions were piled against the wall. There was a stove in one corner, with a copper samovar steaming over glowing charcoal. A low arched door led out to a balcony.

There was no sound, the room was empty, but the heavy curtain over the door was moving. It was too heavy to be moved by this slight breeze, he thought and went to pull it back just as a girl walked in. She did not see him, and turned at once to pull the curtain closed again, and all he saw was her back. She was dressed in green and her dark hair was plaited and hung straight down her slender back to below her waist. He thought it was a very attractive back. He saw that her feet were bare, they looked as if they had been carved in ivory, delicate, high arched feet. In a minute, when she turned he would ask her where he might find Arina. She turned, and his question died on his lips. It was her eyes, wide with shock, that told him who she was. Those eyes that had first attracted him, smiling at him out of a child's face all those years ago. They were not smiling now. Had his scar frightened her? Revolted her? He dared not ask, could only gaze at her, here so close to him, more enchanting than he remembered, still a person unknown. He longed to begin to learn everything about her, and here he stood, unable to speak, afraid to ask her anything.

Arina, after the first shock, saw him with so much joy and relief that she too was for the moment dumb.

He had been wounded, she could see part of a long ugly puffed scar, curving down from one corner of his left eye. It looked very inflamed, but he was alive and, here, staring at her in silence. She remembered that all embracing stare. How quiet he was, he had not said a word when she came in, just stared at her as if he had never seen her before. Perhaps he truly did not know her in these strange clothes – and no veil! The silence grew, and the only sound was the voice of the doves on the balcony. The last time they had been together had been on Dera station. She must break this silence, they were alone, but it would not be for long – Aisin Bibi would come.

"Do you remember Dera station?"

If he thought this a strange question at such a time, he did not say so. "Yes. I remember it well. You asked me a question – do you remember? I could not answer as I wished. Will you ask me again?"

Her answer was so soft that the words were almost lost in the crooning of the doves.

"Tiger, we are alone. Is it suitable that we kiss?"

"It is most suitable, Begum Sahiba."

His arms enfolded her as he bent to kiss at last the lips that were so willingly raised to his.

The doves, disturbed, flew up with a clap and flutter of wings, but no one heard them, no one saw them go.

140,